PIRANHAS IN THE BIDET

A snappy guide to better partnerships with your customers, your people and yourself!

Phil Jesson

Indepenpress

First published in Great Britain by
Indepenpress Publishing Ltd
25 Eastern Place
Brighton
BN2 1GJ

ISBN 9781906710262

Printed and bound in the UK

A catalogue record of this book is available from
the British Library

Cover design Jacqueline Abromeit

This book is dedicated to the memory of Simon Milne

He was a Leader who had it all

Thank you, Simon.

Acknowledgements
and
Apologies

Where do I start with my acknowledgements? Firstly, a big "thank you" to every single member of 4 Platoon. When we met, I thought my role was to train you to become effective soldiers. When I left, I knew that you had trained me to become an effective officer.

I would like to thank some great leaders I have worked for – Simon Milne, Geoff Straw, Derek Cripps and Lars Sjogren. You trusted, supported, challenged (too frequently, sometimes!) and gave me the opportunity to develop under your caring wings.

I would like to thank everyone who has worked for me during my commercial career – including the people who may not have valued my contribution. I learned a lot through your feedback and the reflection, analysis and personal development in the years that followed.

The "F" word appears four times in this book, as part of the dialogue between the book's two main characters… sorry Mum! Thanks also to my long-suffering Dad. We had our moments but we got there in the end.

I would like to thank the many clients I have worked with during the training and consultancy phases of my life. Thank you for some great times – I enjoyed helping you convert your dreams into a profitable, sustainable reality. A special "thank you" to Alan Buckle, Colin Stanley, David Padbury, Christine Adames, Ian Thomas, Mandy Nickerson, Steve Richardson, Jon Lowe, Jim Dickens, and Tracey Bovingdon. (There are quite a few quotes and one-liners in the book and, where possible, I have tried to acknowledge the source. If I have used one of yours, and have failed to acknowledge it, then I apologise.)

Thanks to the many friends and business associates I have worked with on client assignments over the years. Special thanks to Martin Dunkerley, Geoff Thomas, Ken Minor, Tony Bray, Ken Allison, Ray Gudge, Richard Ellison-Smith, Simon Kelly, Norman Carter, Nigel Randall, Holly Nix, Dale Robinson and Fred Robson.

Thanks to Stuart McCullough, at Bentley, for the loan of the car (all in the interests of detail and accuracy… of course!).

Thanks to Brian Chernett and all my colleagues at The Academy for Chief Executives (www.chiefexecutive.com). Thank you being the most caring, supportive and whacky group of people I have ever worked with.

I would also like to thank the professional speakers, friends and consultants who have been "with me" whilst I have written *Piranhas In The Bidet*. Special thanks to Simon Hazeldine, Sue Hughes, Prof. Philip Hesketh, Prof. Justin Davis-Smith, David Thomas and many others for their guidance and support.

To my children, Becky and Michael, I hope that this book gives you an insight into what I have been doing all these years and inspires you, in some way, to live your lives to the full. I love you dearly although I now have your pictures in my wallet where my money used to be. If this book only sells three copies, don't forget your wallets when I'm old and wrinkly!

To Joanna, my wife, you are the true love of my life. A few lines at the bottom of a page could never be enough… which is why the rest of this book is for you. "Life" rather than "living" truly began when I met you. You are my coach, my guide, my inspiration, my soul mate and my partner in every sense of the word. Let's carry on *"making sparks underwater"*… forever!

Thanks also to you, the reader, for buying this book. I hope that *Piranhas In The Bidet* and the supporting material on www.piranhasinthebidet.com inspires you, in some small way, to improve your organisation's heart-count and helps to create a generation of leaders who will do a better job than we did. I hope that the book's many ideas, tools, techniques and occasional wit and wisdom will help you to create a better partnership with your customers, a better partnership with your people and a better partnership with yourself.

Regards and best wishes for the challenges that lie ahead.

Phil Jesson

www.piranhasinthebidet.com
www.philjesson.com
phil@philjesson.com

About the Author

Phil Jesson is a professional speaker, coach and consultant who has worked with a range of companies from SMEs to blue-chips including Pirelli, Tarmac, Exel Logistics, Fedex and Grant Thornton.

He passionately believes that business leaders should stop measuring key performance indicators and start measuring "heart-count" i.e. the number of hearts and minds emotionally aligned with organisational objectives. As Phil puts it, *"Heart-count should match head-count".* With his wife Joanna, he runs a consultancy based in Leicestershire which helps clients create the strategies, leaders, teams and skills needed to form effective partnerships with their customers and their people.

He has two photographs of his grown-up children in his wallet *"where the money once used to be."* He actively supports Aston Villa on Saturdays and *"often seeks counselling on Mondays!"*

Contents

PIRANHAS IN THE BIDET

A snappy guide to better partnerships with your customers, your people and yourself!

Chapter 1
The "U" is You!

Simon Gray sipped a glass of orange juice whilst glancing at his FT. The front page featured the story of another terrorist outrage in the Middle East and a proposal to rebuild the infrastructure of two of its warring nations. Simon shrugged his shoulders whilst loudly straining the orange juice through his teeth. He leaned back, stretched and combed his hair with his fingers. It was 6am – far too early in the morning to be solving long-running, global conflicts.

He turned the page, briefly scanned the markets section then moved on to the sports features. He avoided a titillating article on a sporting hero's affair with his attractive agent and settled for the calm serenity of the summer cricket. It was 21 June and the team was struggling again, with an innings defeat looking highly likely. Simon was planning to watch the cricket highlights on TV later in the day but, according to the journalist, there was little point as it would *all be over by lunchtime*. He turned the page again, looking for a more optimistic story. All of the home nations were also doing badly in the "friendly" football championships. There was an article written by the England manager about his team's lack of defence, but he was under pressure and clearly doing his best to defend and keep his own job. His two star strikers had disgraced themselves in a club the night before and his captain was now calling for *'major changes in team strategy and direction'*. Simon smiled and chuckled to himself – the last time that he personally had called for "major changes in strategy and direction" had resulted in a vote of no confidence and the messy and very public departure of the Chairman at his previous company.

He turned to the back page. The newspaper was enjoying the annual ritual of vilifying the country's leading tennis player who was close to retirement, having *'let the country down again'*. A poignant photograph featured the player packing his kit bag and looking at his watch. His time, it would appear, had 'run out'.

Simon noisily sipped his orange juice once again. Manners were not important in a sleeping household. He was struggling to find any good news so put the newspaper down. He stretched again and as his arm dangled over the side of the armchair it touched a plastic box containing yards of tangled, black electrical spaghetti connected to years of defunct household essentials and toys. He eventually found the TV remote control and flicked it three times before realising that it had been "robbed" – the girls had borrowed the batteries again for one of their computer games.

He muttered under his breath, leaned towards the TV and prodded the on-off switch with an aggressive finger. As he sat down again, he was quickly joined by two immaculately dressed, smiling TV presenters. They laughed and joked their way through a feature on the Prime Minister's dress sense then, as the main news slot approached, they became noticeably more serious and businesslike. The programme's familiar signature tune played in the background and images of the Middle East casualties appeared in graphic detail on the screen. The male presenter repeated the world headlines that Simon had scanned in the newspaper earlier, whilst his female colleague waited to interview an Israeli politician whose tired face was displayed on a TV monitor in front of her.

Simon was restless. He flicked the TV remote control again then, remembering that it was useless, threw it across the kitchen. It bounced off the wall and landed in a wastepaper bin. He retrieved it on his way to the toaster, where he cut himself two slices of his favourite organic bread. The smell of fresh toast was always a joy to Simon.

It reminded him of his childhood in Somerset, for some reason. Perhaps it was his parents' good home cooking. He shut his eyes and breathed deeply. As he opened his eyes he reached across the immaculate worktop of the newly fitted designer kitchen to locate the low-cholesterol spread and a knife. The noise of the knife-on-toast scraping signalled to the Irish Setter that his long wait was over. Rory had been patiently waiting for a glimpse of Simon's breakfast for the last hour and leaped in the air as the first piece of "healthy" toast was tossed his way. "Well held. Rory!" muttered Simon quietly, mindful of the cricket result. "Carry on like that and you'll be in great demand for the next Test." The dog cocked his head to one side, looking puzzled but remaining vigilant. Another slow minute went by, but this time the dog was ready. The second piece of toast was a fast full toss, which required a jump to the right but, with all four legs off the ground and his neck straining, he just managed to catch it. "Well held again, Rory – you're now definitely in the team!"

Outside, the rain fell slowly to provide some short-term relief to the Grays' desert-like back garden. It had been a very dry Spring and the Summer rain was a pleasant and welcome surprise. A stray rabbit had activated the external security lights and Simon could see glistening raindrops on the leaves of the apple trees in the extensive orchard. They had over fifty fruit trees in total. Thirty came with the property, "Thatcher's Grove", and twenty had been added by the Grays during the previous year. The trees were spaced and distributed evenly across their three acres and now drooped like cold, wet soldiers on an early morning parade. Simon picked up the kitchen binoculars, which were normally reserved for watching the visiting heron as it clattered in through the trees on its way for lunch at the pond. He slowly surveyed the well-kept shrubs next to the orchard and eventually located the trespassing rabbit. It was munching a dandelion whilst taking cover under a sodden deck chair. "Bugger," muttered Simon, "the kids must have left the chair out yesterday."

Rory looked up, thinking that Simon was talking to him. "As you were, Rory," said Simon as he tossed another piece of his breakfast in the dog's direction. The dog was surprised by this last instalment and missed the toast, which landed upside down on the gleaming and expensive Italian-tiled kitchen floor. "OK, so I was wrong about your catching skills," said Simon quietly, as the dog nudged the toast across the floor with his nose. Simon ignored the oily smear that quickly appeared on the tiles. Stella would be furious. He turned the TV off and switched the kitchen radio on. The last chorus of *Lovely Day* was fading in the background. "Lovely Day – I don't think so!" muttered Simon, as he glanced again at the summer rain outside.

He headed for the hall, shuffled through a mountain of anoraks, ski jackets, school hats and scarves and eventually found his favourite old green Barbour jacket and a new golf umbrella. One was a battered remnant from his university years and the other a gift from a client following a "brainstorming session" in a corporate hospitality box at Ascot. The umbrella was jammed in the hat-stand which swayed alarmingly as Simon became more and more frustrated with it. Rory decided to offer his assistance but was soon buried beneath the cascading clothes. He barked his displeasure and was immediately reprimanded by Simon.

"For goodness sake Rory – be quiet, be quiet!" He ushered the dog away with a gentle sweep from his right foot and waited for a reaction from the rest of the family. Upstairs, Simon's wife, Stella, stirred slowly in their four-poster bed. She thumped the floor with a shoe, which was her polite way of saying "Shut up!" At the other end of the house, their six-year old twin daughters, Claire and Lucy, were already starting round two of a ferocious pillow fight. Claire had lost the previous day and was seeking her revenge in the eagerly awaited re-match.

Simon retreated along the long hallway, but something caught his eye. He flicked through a calendar on the wall and moved the pages to June. He noticed that it was the longest day of the year and smiled as he was up and ready for one of the longest days of his year. It was the second week of his new job as Chief Executive of Alderton's. His first week, which had been based at the company's head office in north London, featured the usual series of handshakes from enthusiastic go-getters and some anxious looks from others who were wondering if they would keep their jobs under Simon's new reign. He was finding his feet and was learning about the company's glorious past but not so glorious present. He was also beginning to form a picture about the quality of the product range and the effectiveness of his efficient but comfortable sales team. During the first week, he brought home mountains of paperwork and computer printouts that he read after supper with Stella, whilst they watched *Desperate Housewives*. Simon paid little attention to the TV murders, affairs and rumours. He was deeply immersed in his own new drama and was burning considerable amounts of midnight oil as part of a ninety-hour, weekly commitment to his new employers.

Simon's managers had provided him with some "helpful information" to read. In some cases the information had been very useful. In others, it was nothing more than a departmental manager's hastily constructed justification for hanging on to his job – or an unconvincing case for minimum change and maintenance of the status quo.

Simon had also been given a list of twenty names by his HR

Manager – the "NTG List" as she called it. The names were the "next to go" in the event of more redundancies. These were nervous times. Some of Alderton's people were successfully embracing change, some were resisting it and others were walking away from it, hoping that tomorrow would be rather like yesterday used to be.

Simon smiled as he quietly read aloud the quote underneath the June calendar picture in the hallway. It featured a wise, Greek-looking character from 480BC dressed in the long, white gown of the day. *'All is flux, nothing stays still.'* Simon tore it from its wire ring-binding and put it in his shirt pocket. "Very apt," he thought, "this sums up my new role and job description in one sentence!" "Week Two", as it was referred to on the induction programme, would be Simon's first opportunity to get out and about in the field. Today, he was going to visit one of Alderton's two factories and was looking forward to his first visit to the "sharp end".

Three miles away George Willis steered the Bentley into a silent, still garage forecourt and switched off the windscreen wipers. Apart from the inadequate glow from an overhead security light, the garage was in complete darkness and was awaiting the arrival of the first mechanic. It was the perfect place to park. He checked his watch – it was 6.15am.

As the rain fell steadily, he located his flask and poured himself a cup of steaming coffee – "Brazil's Best", his favourite. It was always worth the lengthy early morning ritual of preparing it. A flick of the finger activated a cup holder that emerged from a panel on the dashboard and unfolded gracefully. "Just like *Thunderbirds*," he thought, "whatever will they think of next!" He located the news channel on the radio and tuned in to the serious events of the day that were shaping the Middle East. There was a strange and uncomfortable contrast between the Bentley's luxurious, leather-upholstered world and the tragic, bloody events that were unfolding a few thousand miles away. He looked at his watch. He was now in range of Simon Gray's house and in plenty of time for their first meeting. He reclined his seat, leaned back, shut his eyes and savoured the smell, and the memories, of Brazil. The windscreen soon became misted but it did not matter. George was back in Rio where he had once worked as a waiter between jobs in the merchant navy. Ever since, he had always treated himself to "proper coffee", as he called it. It was the best way he knew to start the day and, today, it was also the best way to forget about a troubled world.

Simon returned to the kitchen with his Barbour jacket over his arm and pretended not to hear the friendly screams from his fighting daughters, or the sound of Stella calling optimistically for her first cup of tea. He quickly retreated to the quiet sanity of the study and shut the door, leaving his forlorn Irish Setter outside. He checked his briefcase, located his diary, flicked a few pages and awaited the arrival of his new driver.

Jean Scrivenor, Alderton's Chairman for the last four years, had arranged for Simon to have one chauffeur-driven trip each month, for six consecutive months, to take him to visit the company's factories, major suppliers and customers. Being chauffeured, according to the Chairman, would allow Simon to indulge in the *quality thinking time that was needed to help rescue the company and drive it forward'*. It was Simon's *'welcome present'*. Jean Scrivenor wanted her new Chief Executive (the fourth in six years) to have a motivational start to his new role. *'I would rather see you driven around than driven!'* she had quipped at Simon's second interview, laughing loudly at her own joke. At first, Simon thought that this luxury was a little unnecessary and ostentatious. However, he soon became comfortable with the Chairman's idea and, privately, was enjoying the thought of the status of it all. Stella was immediately comfortable with the idea. As far as she was concerned the monthly chauffeur-driven treat was all very much deserved. Simon needed the car to meet the mental challenges and physical demands of the new job. What a shame it was that the neighbours would not be able see the car at such an early time in the morning.

Simon fiddled with his blue and pink striped silk tie in front of the full-length mirror in the study. He turned his head and flicked his hair into place. He brushed his hand across his face, looking for any blemishes on his skin, which was still lightly tanned as a result of the family's skiing holiday in Morzine earlier in the year, topped up by the occasional session at the local health club and spa. The scar from his black run adventures was healing nicely. In fact, Simon quite liked it as he thought it looked like a duelling scar from an earlier century. He adjusted his trousers and was pleased to find that his belt felt looser than the previous week – the exercise routines at the gym were working well.

But something was not quite right. Simon adjusted and fiddled with the tie but decided to discard it – a token gesture to the more relaxed, open-neck business world that he expected to find at his Midland's factory. He located his A-Z map, which was neatly folded on a shelf devoted entirely to his global travel exploits. On the left was Adelaide and Austria and, four feet to the right, was Zacatan and Zanzibar. He dug deep into his new Armani briefcase, a recent thirty-fifth birthday present from Stella, found a highlighter pen and put a circle of luminous yellow on the top of page 45 of the A-Z, around Dudley.

There were two factories in Simon's new business empire. One was "down south" in Lightwater and one was in Dudley, the heart of the Black Country. Within Alderton's there was a friendly but sometimes tribal rivalry between the two sites, which were affectionately known by staff as "the light side" and "the dark side". Lightwater had always been part of the company's proud 100-year history and heritage, but Dudley was a recent acquisition that had not yet adopted or fully accepted the established Alderton's culture and the need for change. The following week Simon was planning to visit "the light side", which had all the trimmings of the Home Counties and was famous for its efficiency, customer service and dedicated workforce. Today, however, it was "the dark side". Located just outside Dudley, the old factory had seen better days when it was part of the war effort. Gleaming new fighter aircraft were once towed out to fight for their country but the tired, old building was now ready for retirement. The factory had four production lines, six supervisors, three managers, one highly stressed site director and a workforce of 235 people recruited mostly from the surrounding towns of Wolverhampton and Stourbridge. The site also had dozens of problems and a morale problem that even Churchill would have found daunting.

The noise of an approaching car crunching its way across the pea gravel prompted Simon to put the map in his briefcase. He caught a glimpse of a man walking past the study and ten seconds later there was a gentle knock on the kitchen door. It was George Willis, the driver. Noticing the drawn curtains at the front of the house, he had decided to knock quietly on the kitchen door in an attempt not to disturb the sleeping Gray household. He need not have bothered – the house was now alive with racing, noisy footsteps, a sleepy stumbling Stella and a slightly mad, re-awaked barking dog with an oily yellow smudge on his nose.

Two hugs for the girls, a kiss for Stella and a pat for the barking dog later and Simon Gray found himself face to face with his new driver who was standing in his kitchen doorway. The early morning chaos of the Gray household ejected Simon so quickly from the kitchen that the driver had to take two steps back to avoid being trampled. Simon Gray was six feet three inches tall and an ex county-standard rugby player who weighed 16 stones – not the sort of person to argue with at any time of the day. For a couple of seconds George Willis resembled Simon's dancing partner as he delicately stepped backwards to avoid a rapidly expanding puddle in the drive. Somehow, he had managed to preserve the immaculate shine on his expensive black shoes. They sat like mirrors at the end of his blue, uniformed legs. His trousers had razor-like creases, his jacket looked brand new and his distinguished, well-groomed grey hair was neatly tucked into his matching blue cap, which had been dampened by the early morning rain. The droplets caught the light from the kitchen and glistened like a sprinkling of silver dust. He was in his late fifties and had a heavily lined face that had obviously seen some "action" over the years. He also had an affable smile and penetrating but friendly eyes.

Simon would later tell Stella that the new driver reminded him of "someone I couldn't quite put my finger on" – a familiar newsreader perhaps, or the presenter of a TV antiques programme. As the door shut behind the men, two small faces could be seen jostling for position. They bobbed up and down to compete for the small glass pane in the kitchen door.

"Who's that man with Daddy?" asked Claire.

"Daddy's new driver," said their exhausted mother as she located the much-needed teapot.

"But the man is wearing a uniform with a soldier's hat!" added Lucy. Stella looked out of the window.

"No, that'll be his chauffeur's hat," said Stella.

"Why does he want to show us his fur hat?" said Lucy, trying to steal the attention from her sister.

Stella sighed but then smiled. "I didn't say he was showing us a fur hat, darling…I said that the chauffeur had a hat…you know…on his head." Stella's taste buds received their early-morning call as she sipped her tea. She smiled. "The joys of parenthood," she thought, although her smile slowly disappeared with each sip. With one girl on each knee, she settled down to explain the "fur hat", hoping that she would soon be saved by the pips of the 7am news. They always signalled the start of Stella's weekday ritual of a frantic breakfast, 30 minutes of chaos in the bathroom, a dash for the school bus and a drive to her office on the outskirts of Royston, accompanied by George Michael, Bob the Builder or whoever else had managed to find their way into the car's CD player.

Meanwhile, her husband was settling down in the top-of-the-range Bentley driven by his new driver. Paperwork was quickly spread across the spacious leather upholstery and Simon's new Cross pen, a gift from his previous management team, was poised for some early-morning action. They were now five miles down the road from the sleepy village of Mapleford, without a word being said. The timely arrival of a road junction prompted Simon's first question.

"I forgot to ask you if you know where you're going?" he asked, without realising that it was a clumsy and rather inappropriate first question to be asking a professional driver.

"Always," said the driver.

"Always what?" queried Simon nervously.

"I always know where I'm going," added the driver. "The agency gave me a full briefing – they have all your plans logged for today."

"How have they been able to do that?" asked Simon.

"From some sort of timetable they were given, I suppose, sir."

"Maybe they've been given a copy of my induction programme," mused Simon.

"Maybe they have, sir…maybe they have," muttered the driver, turning his head as he waited for two cars to pass. He turned onto the "A" road that signalled the official start of their journey out of the county. The car sensed freedom and quickly gained momentum.

"What's your name?" asked Simon, painfully aware that he had forgotten some of the social niceties that should be displayed, in particular by a Chief Executive, to one's new chauffeur.

"Willis, sir," replied the driver.

"That's a bit formal, isn't it? What's your Christian name?"

"Everyone calls me Willis – including Mrs. Willis. Mind you, she's also been known to call me George Nelson Willis from time to time…sir."

"That's an interesting name," replied Simon, trying to develop the conversation.

"Yes, my father was a great fan of Admiral Nelson, who apparently once said that he owed all of his success in life to being a quarter of an hour early. My father liked being on time, sir…and so do I."

"I'll try not to be late then…err…Willis. But can we drop the 'sir' thing please, if you don't mind," said Simon. "It makes me feel uncomfortable."

"It's a mark of respect, sir. I've always called my bosses 'sir'…err… sir."

"Well, as I said, it makes me feel uncomfortable and I'd rather find an alternative…is that's OK with you, George…I mean Willis."

"Very good, sir," added Willis, choosing to completely ignore Simon's request. His eyes were now firmly on the dual carriageway ahead.

"What dreadful weather," said Simon, trying to change the subject.

"No such thing, sir."

"I beg your pardon?" replied Simon.

"No such thing as dreadful weather – just inappropriate clothing!" said Willis. "Like most things in life, it's all down to preparation and planning!"

Simon Gray withdrew from his first clumsy discussion, reluctantly accepted, for the moment, that he had been 'knighted' by Willis and reached for his diary and phone to continue the important, early work of his day. His mobile lit up and flickered into action – a selection of Alderton's managers were about to receive an early morning pep talk on their way to work. The Bentley was travelling in a westerly direction, the road was drying steadily, conditions were improving and their side of the carriageway was moving freely. Willis flicked the cruise control and the countryside passed effortlessly by, at a steady 80mph. He adjusted the temperature and settled back in his soft leather seat. The chrome instruments and dials had a traditional look which appealed to Willis. "I bet these haven't changed for fifty years" he thought.

Ten quiet minutes passed by. "What's on the agenda in Dudley today, sir?" asked Willis, glancing up at the rear-view mirror. "If you don't mind me asking."

Simon looked surprised. "You sound like my Chairman," he muttered, without making eye contact.

"It was a serious question, sir," continued Willis, "I would genuinely be interested to learn why we're going there…if that's OK with you, of course?"

"Not now, Willis, please, I'm trying to think. Ask me again in an hour," said Simon. "I've got a business to rescue."

Willis glanced up at the rear-view mirror but could only see the side of Simon's head. He was sitting on the back seat wrestling with the demands of his executive workload. Meanwhile, signs to Graffham Water were soon replaced by signs for Kettering then Market Harborough. They were making good progress and there was plenty to keep Willis occupied. The rolling green landscape was an example of middle-England at its best. Pretty villages, grazing animals and old market towns with prosperous new industrial estates on their perimeters were all appreciated by Willis, who loved the English countryside. Simon also loved the countryside, but didn't seem to notice much of it that morning.

The road was now dry, the Bentley's headlights had been switched off and the traffic was flowing. Simon Gray was deep in thought on the sumptuous back seat whilst George Willis eagerly awaited the opportunity to return to his unanswered question. He shuffled and straightened himself in his seat and looked up at the rear-view mirror once again. Just under 40 minutes of the requested hour had gone by.

"So what's on the agenda in Dudley, sir?" said Willis, bracing himself for another frosty reply.

"Not yet, Willis, I'm still very busy."

"Oh dear, I'm sorry to hear that," replied Willis.

"What do you mean by 'oh dear', Willis?"

"Well, I've always believed that 'busyness' is a sign of mediocrity, sir. The busier people are, the more average they're likely to be."

"I'll ignore that remark if you don't mind," said a surprised Simon, who was beginning to feel a little flustered.

A further ten minutes went by. "So where are we off to, sir?"

"You really don't need to know," said Simon, tapping away on his calculator. He was irritated because he could not get a long column of numbers to add up correctly. He looked up. "Correct me if I'm wrong, Willis, but I thought you were supposed to be my driver… not my boss…or my coach."

"I can be many things, sir," said Willis, with a steady calmness that Simon found just as irritating as his uncooperative calculator.

Simon leaned forward so that he was a few inches away from Willis's left ear.

"Listen, Willis, I don't want you to be many things today – just one. You may have caught me on a bad day but just drive this car and let me manage the business side of things. This business has been running successfully for many decades and I've been running successful businesses for some time too. I think that Alderton's and I can manage without your input today. Can we just get to Dudley… if that is OK with you?" Simon leaned back and settled down, looking flushed after his unexpected skirmish with Willis.

Three more miles passed by quietly.

Willis glanced at the rear-view mirror once again. "Ah, but that's the point, isn't it?" he said, flicking the indicator to overtake an eastern-European truck that had just swerved out into the middle of the road.

"What's the point, exactly?" said Simon, leaning forward once again.

"Well, the point is that your business is *not* successful today, is it, sir? It needs all the help it can get at the moment! That's why you've been appointed, presumably. I've read the business sections in the newspapers and I've seen your company's website. I'm sure your business needs help from you, as the new man at the helm, but perhaps it needs help from others who might be able to help…like the people inside your business …and outsiders…even people like me!"

Simon breathed deeply, counted to ten and lowered his voice. "Willis, I apologise for jumping down your throat a few minutes ago but tell me exactly why you think that any of your front-seat-driver comments are likely to help me today?"

"I'm not sure I was going to make a comment, sir, I was simply going to ask a number of questions."

"You mean dumb questions," said Simon, before realising that his remark was more than a little hurtful and insensitive.

"But I've never been frightened of asking dumb questions either," said Willis. "Much better than making dumb mistakes!"

"That's your thought for the day, I suppose?" said Simon sarcastically.

"If you want it to be, sir…if you want it to be."

An uneasy mile followed.

"Anyway, I'm famous for my questions," continued Willis. "I've always believed that in life, and in business, it's not just about knowing the right answers, it's also about knowing the right questions. Take your new job, for example, sir. You won't be learning anything today in Dudley if your mouth is moving. When you talk, you'll say something that you already know, but when you ask a question, and someone else does all the talking, *you* might learn something new. Don't you also think that if people listened to themselves more often they would talk less?"

"Thanks for the lecture Willis…and *who*, exactly, thinks you're famous for your questions?" demanded Simon, whose cheeks were steadily reddening by the mile.

"Says Mrs. Willis, says my kids, the tennis club committee, the people at the Hospice, my colleagues in the Merchant Navy Association and the customers in the shop. They all like my questions."

"What bloody shop?" snapped Simon.

"My newsagent's shop. Mrs.Willis is the mainstay of the business now but I help out from time to time."

Simon sat in silence. Not only was he being steadily driven around the bend by an insubordinate chauffeur – he was also being driven by a moonlighting newsagent! With the M6 now in sight, he leaned forward again. Although Willis's left ear was becoming remarkably familiar, Simon decided that it was time for some different tactics. "Willis," he said in a quieter, calmer voice, "all I want from you today is your skills as a driver. I don't want your constant chatter from the front. On another day I would love to hear about your lovely, interesting life…but not now. OK?"

"Of course, sir…you're the boss…but remember that during our short trips together during the next six months, you have a choice."

"And what choice might that be, Willis?" enquired Simon, with very little interest.

"You can either permanently look at the back of my head or occasionally listen to what's in the front of my mind," said Willis. "If you want to know the business road ahead you could try asking those who are coming back…old sweats like me!" Willis waited until he caught Simon's glance in the rear-view mirror. "You never know, sir, but my hindsight could become your foresight!"

"Thank you…I'll give all of that some thought, Willis, but in the meantime, perhaps you could turn the radio on," added Simon, trying to find an alternative to replace the unwelcome and provocative remarks.

Willis turned the radio on and the scanner located some suitable middle-of-the-road tunes. The second song was interrupted by a local traffic announcement although the queue of stationary traffic was already visible on the brow of a hill one mile ahead of them. Willis could see three lanes of red brake lights and the blue flashing lights of the emergency services. The car slowed to negotiate the accident then found its cruising speed again for the next stage of the journey. For twenty minutes, three lanes of the motorway struggled to cope with the delayed north-bound traffic. As the Bentley approached Coventry, Willis glanced at the rear-view mirror again and noticed that Simon was looking thoughtful. Something he had said had registered. Simon was devising a few extra questions for his first meeting in Dudley but said nothing, however, to Willis.

The music resumed to accompany the next stage of their journey. "I don't like Mondays," said Willis.

"What?"

"It's on the radio now, sir," replied Willis. "You know, the Bob Geldof song."

"Really?" said a disinterested Simon. "Absolutely bloody fascinating!"

The DJ interrupted their conversation. *"That was The Boomtown Rats, this is WMFM and here is another song to make you smile on a damp, depressing Monday morning."* The opening bars of the song certainly made Willis smile and he discreetly turned up the volume. As the car headed north along the M6 to Birmingham, the unlikely new team of Simon Gray and George Willis were accompanied by one of Tony

Blair's 1997 election anthems *Things can only get better!* Simon shook his head in disbelief. "They can't get much bloody worse!" he muttered under his breath. Willis thought the timely arrival of the music was very amusing and had to look away from the rear-view mirror in case Simon caught sight of his smile. He was going to enjoy working with his new boss. He was sure of it.

Thirty minutes later they stopped for a toilet break at the Services. It was a strange experience for both men. Having travelled as "un-equals" for over 100 miles, with one man sat in front of the other, there was something very levelling about standing next to each other in the gents' toilet. They stood side by side, both feeling awkward, but said nothing to each other. They returned to the Bentley as "un-equals" once again, with Simon striding ahead, mobile phone attached to his ear. He reached the Bentley first and impatiently tapped the roof with his fingers whilst he waited for Willis to unlock the car. There was a short delay while Willis took the necessary time to fold his jacket with military-like precision. He started the car when he was ready, checked the traffic situation on the range of satellite-linked gadgetry on the dashboard and guided the car to rejoin the north-bound traffic.

"I needed that stop…and don't you think that, in life too, wisdom doesn't just come from the miles we travel but also from the stops we choose to make?" said Willis.

There was no reply. In the back of the car, Simon was deep in thought and feeling a little guilty. He hadn't handled Willis very well that morning and he knew it. He had been abrasive and rude. Maybe it was tiredness, or nerves, or adrenaline. Maybe it was Willis' constantly-probing questions and unwelcome, unnecessary chatter. With the Coventry skyline in sight, Simon decided to try again.

"Willis, if you really want to know what's on the agenda today… one of the things I'll be doing in Dudley is getting to know the people in my business – you know, trying to build a few key relationships in the factory, here and there. '*Pressing the flesh*', as my American Finance Director would say." Simon's conciliatory nature was very noticeable. There was a warm tone and relaxed manner that accompanied his words.

Willis looked up at the rear-view mirror. "Thank you for telling me, sir, but do you really think that will help you?"

"I certainly do, Willis. Why are you questioning it? People like to see senior directors getting to know them and their business. It's a no-brainer!"

"Sounds like a questionable use of time to me," replied Willis. "I'm not sure how that will help *them*."

"It's not supposed to help them – it's supposed to help *me*!"

"Well, there you have it in one, sir. Some CEOs would go for the approach that would help *their people*...to help them."

"But surely, Willis, you must agree that any time invested by me in understanding the people in the organisation has got to be a good use of time?"

Willis said nothing. He was overtaking a long convoy of camouflaged vehicles that was occupying the inside lane. "Poor bastards," he muttered. "Off to the Middle East, maybe."

Simon waited until they came alongside the lead vehicle which had a long, menacing barrel and a red and yellow flag on its front wing.

"That was a question, Willis, in case you hadn't noticed," he said.

"Sorry, sir," said Willis. "I'm with you now...I think understanding half a dozen people would be OK but there's a choice here, isn't there? One man, i.e. you, can attempt to understand half a dozen people or 240 people can attempt to understand one man – I know which one I would go for."

"But I need to understand the Dudley set up and the type of people within it!" protested Simon.

"Of course you do, but at the end of the day, sir, people in all organisations are more or less the same, aren't they?" replied Willis.

"No doubt you're now going to tell me why," said a disinterested Simon, staring out of the window.

"Well," continued Willis, "let me put it this way. In any business there's a man or woman at the top – you, in the case of Alderton's."

"Well spotted!" said Simon sarcastically.

Willis continued, unperturbed. "Underneath you, there will be senior managers responsible for some things and senior managers responsible for other things. There will be an extremely important, mysterious person somewhere in your business and a senior manager looking after things that nobody else wants to manage. There will also be a PA who works with these senior people who is actually running the business.

"All organisations I've worked for have a good looking manager with no talent at all, plus an office bookie, a barrack-room lawyer, a cheerleader, a yes-man, a group of managers designing new reporting processes that make it difficult for other people to get their proper work done, a scapegoat, a trainee scapegoat and a supervisor for things beginning with 'H'. In an office somewhere you will find an out-of-touch director carefully tailoring a mission statement that looks like everyone else's and drafting 'shared core values' that nobody else either shares or values!

"Further down the typical organisation there will be a bean counter, an office Romeo who has sown some wild oats and is now hoping for a crop failure, a disillusioned new recruit, a creep, an informer and a back-stabber. There will be a director who barely knows what's going on planning the departure of those that do, someone who thinks they're the top dog and someone else who thinks they're the underdog. There will be someone who has the negatives from last year's Christmas party and a large lad buying doughnuts in the canteen stood next to a director responsible for cost cutting and corporate anorexia.

"There will also be an empty office from which strange sounds emerge, a bright, under-used graduate doing the filing and old what's-his-name in the end office. Somewhere else in an open-plan office there will be some lively brainstorming going on and behind closed doors, in another part of the business, there will be some blame-storming going on. At the start of each month, the training department will be trying to plant and develop some good new shoots and, at the end of the month, some irritating line manager will want to pull the plants up to see if their roots are growing!"

Willis was smirking and clearly enjoying the mischief of the moment. His left hand resembled an animated signpost as it waved and pointed to the locations of his imaginary departments and divisions. "Many organisations have a sales-prevention department manned by people who claim to be customer-driven, a dodgy looking cleaner who makes inappropriate remarks about what they've heard in other offices, a director responsible for moving the goalposts, a receptionist who will be on the phone talking to her boyfriend, a bitter and twisted ex-manager happy to share plenty of unresolved 'baggage' with new impressionable recruits, an office flirt who is famous for appalling near-the-mark innuendo and a security man who will probably be asleep…"

"Cynical and very amusing, Willis. Have you done?" said Simon. "Is that it?"

Willis shook his head. "Certainly not, sir. Somewhere else in the typical business there will be a passed-over manager waiting for retirement, a head-case in the warehouse, a sexist in HR, a delivery driver with maximum points on his licence, a relative of the chairman struggling to make it on their own merit, a post-room gossip who leaks your best-kept secrets, a young geek in IT, a keeper of good jokes, a keeper of some rather bad jokes, a top salesman who is so good he could sell an egg-beater to Humpty Dumpty's widow, a lad in Finance who always knows the day's sports results because he's constantly monitoring them on the web and a smarmy new manager who has probably already slept with six people in the sales office!"

Simon leaned forward again. "Willis, what's your point – or perhaps there isn't one?"

"My point is, sir, that all organisations are much the same and that the CEO is the *only* difference. Next time someone invites you to comment on your organisation's USP – your unique service proposition – remember that the 'U' is *you*! You are the uniqueness – you are the difference. So returning to my point about your objectives today, there's little point in trying to get to know a lot of people during your first visit. It might look good but the workforce will probably see it as nothing more than fairly obvious PR gloss. They will, however, be very interested in something else, sir."

"What might that be?" enquired Simon, who had managed to relocate his sarcastic tone of voice once again.

"They'll want to know about *you*, sir."

"That's the same thing, surely," replied Simon.

"No sir. As I said earlier, I'm not talking about you getting to know half a dozen people, at best, during the course of the day. I'm talking about over 240 people getting to know more about *your* plans for the future – so they can be reassured, so they can focus on the future, so they can look forward to coming to work tomorrow. They will see you as a dealer in hope and need to know what to hope for. They'll want to know what makes you tick – the things you believe in. You might see your job as 'running something' but they'll want to know that you also 'stand for something'! Your words today will create their worlds tomorrow!"

"Willis, I've got plans to do all that softer stuff later – team briefings and so on," said Simon dismissively. "We've recently launched a 'People First' campaign but I've got some other priorities for this first visit. I've got a business to rescue."

Willis caught Simon's eye in the rear view mirror. "No, I'm not talking about team briefings, sir...and by the way...a slogan is not a strategy. I'm talking about your first 'state of the nation' update in the canteen or conference room or warehouse – anywhere where you can get them all together.

Simon sighed. "We're back to where we were earlier this morning, Willis. You do the driving and I'll do the managing. But if you really must know, I've always believed that the best way of making money is to stop losing it! I want to talk to my managers about the numbers. I want to look at the stock we're holding, the trade debtors, weekly material usage, capital employed less fixed assets, our current liabilities, all the ratios, our borrowing, our margins, how hard the assets are working and the return on capital...you know, the stuff that business is really about!"

"I'm sure they'll find that very interesting, sir. They'll certainly be able to sleep well tonight."

Suddenly there was an awkward silence in the car as Simon slumped back into his seat, shaking his head in disbelief at Willis' remarks. Willis also knew that he was pushing his luck. He was trying to make a point but knew that he had probably overdone it.

Simon wasn't sure what Willis was actually saying, or why, so he chose the easy and safe option and withdrew from the conversation. "Fine, Willis, let's leave it there then, shall we? I'll look forward to telling you how well it went later on today. Meanwhile, why don't you turn off that background radio rubbish and tell me about yourself rather than interrogating me all the time."

"What would you like to know, sir?" said Willis, who also welcomed the opportunity to move the conversation on.

"You decide," replied Simon, disengaging from the moment.

Willis straightened himself in the seat. He could feel excitement and pride as he contemplated a conducted tour of his family tree and its root and branch achievements over the years.

"Well, I'll tell you a little about my family. As I said earlier, there's a Mrs. Willis – my lovely Anne. She's semi-retired now, following a very successful business career, and runs the shop. We're very close – the sort of people who always hold hands when they go out. Mind you, if I let go of her hand, she goes shopping! We've been married for just under 35 years. We have four children and seven grandchildren. One of my children, my eldest son Trevor, lives in America now. He works in the Diplomatic Service. My eldest daughter Lorraine lives in Sydney with her Australian husband. She's recently gone back to work as a teacher. He's a farmer, by the way. Then there's Richard, my other son, and Debbie, my youngest. They're both running their own businesses. Debbie has just been nominated for a major customer service award for running the best construction company in the region. We're going to the awards dinner next week, with all of our fingers crossed."

"And Mrs. Willis?"

Willis felt angry and deflated. He realised that Simon had not been listening to him at all – he was just going through the motions. "Probably best if I concentrate on the road now, sir," said Willis, quietly. "Lots of traffic – I wouldn't want to get distracted." His sarcasm was lost on Simon.

"Whatever, Willis, I could do with a bit of peace, actually – I need to get my head around these numbers."

"Ah, yes," said Willis. "The numbers! I've worked for plenty of bad leaders who have hidden behind good numbers."

"Meaning what, exactly?" demanded Simon. "These numbers are important, Willis!"

"Fine, but after you've looked down at the bottom line, sir, remember to look up at the horizon once in a while," muttered Willis.

"Just shut up Willis, for God's sake! Your comments are both unwelcome and painful – they're like piranhas in the bidet! Stop snapping around my private parts and just drive. Please just bloody drive!"

Willis obliged, concentrating on the motorway network and the labyrinth around Birmingham and the Black Country.

At 8.55 precisely the Bentley arrived at the security barrier of the Dudley factory. A nervous security man recognised the car as a result of his comprehensive briefing during the previous week and abandoned his normal, thorough security routine. He emerged from his hut whilst straightening his tie, quickly noted the Bentley's registration number, nodded to Willis and pointed to the reserved parking space next to a tired flowerbed that had seen better days.

Simon Gray had arrived at the Dark Side!

He collected his things from the car and walked purposefully towards the factory's reception area. He disappeared for a minute then returned to the parking space where Willis was busy caressing the Bentley's headlights with a chamois leather cloth.

"Willis, I forgot to mention that we're leaving at 4pm. Sort yourself out with a coffee and lunch later – the day is yours. Reception will find you an office and a phone if you need a change of scenery." Then Simon headed for the reception area and disappeared once again.

Fifteen minutes later, Willis sat in the Dudley canteen with a ketchup-stained daily newspaper spread out in front of him. He collected a cup of weak machine coffee (certainly not Brazil's Best) and managed to force down half of it during the 30 minutes that followed. He was on his own now – apart from a nervous job applicant rehearsing answers to interview questions whilst sipping a cup of water in the corner of the room.

The Dark Side workforce was busy in the sprawling factory that occupied four acres. The wartime airfield site was now a cramped industrial estate and showed no outward signs of "victory" or the material wealth that was created in the decades that followed. Willis could still see the motorway traffic on an elevated section in the distance although he could no longer hear it. The noise from the factory was all he could hear now – machines, forklifts, and the occasional laughs and shouts from a colony of smokers who met outside in a small area at the back of the despatch area known, since the smoking ban, as "lepers' corner".

Willis gathered his things. "Where shall we go today, George? I think we'll go to the National Exhibition Centre," he muttered quietly to himself. He knew that his boss would be busy until 4pm so he had plenty of time on his hands. He walked past the goods inwards area, then the training department and made his way back to the car.

At 10am he left the factory and headed off towards the exhibition centre for the rest of the day. In one of the halls there was a Human Resources exhibition and, in another, an exhibition on angling. He had time to visit both and decided to start with HR so he could sound knowledgeable and useful if Simon asked him any questions later. "Mind you," he thought, "not much chance of that!"

Willis collected Simon at 4pm, as requested. He looked tired and a little pale. He tossed his briefcase in the back of the car but did not reach for his paperwork or mobile phone. He looked very thoughtful and said little. Willis could sense that Simon needed a little space and obliged by remaining silent but attentive as the Bentley found its way back to the motorway and headed southwards. After a further 15 minutes, Simon looked less stressed and appeared to have come to terms with his difficult day.

He leaned forward. "So, what sort of day have you had, Willis?"

"A good one, sir. And yours?"

"Not bad…but not too good either."

"Really?" replied Willis looking up at the rear-view mirror, trying to sound surprised. "In what way, sir?"

"It doesn't really matter, Willis. Let's just say that I told them how it is on the numbers and they just sat there, saying nothing. I was hoping for some ideas or at least a reaction of some sort but it wasn't to be. They just went through the motions. I'll have to revisit the numbers issue on another day. The surprising thing was that when I asked them for feedback, they said it was a good meeting."

"Ah yes," nodded Willis like a wise old sage, "that'll be dissonance theory then."

"What the hell is that?" said Simon. "Sounds painful."

"Well," continued Willis, "students and new army recruits often have to endure humiliating initiation ceremonies when they join a new institution or community. It's often a public, institutionalised bullying that no-one in their right mind would want to undergo."

"So what?"

"The so what, sir, is that after it's over, the great majority say that it's a *good* thing!"

"Why on earth would they say that?"

"Simply because if it was a really bad thing, they should have refused to do it. Since they didn't, the only way for them to maintain their self-respect is to find good reasons for thinking it a sensible thing to have done. Therefore, in turn they'll probably do it to their successors. This is why 90 per cent of people who attend training programmes or meetings say it was a good thing. Well, they would, wouldn't they? Otherwise they would have got up and left…but nobody can bring themselves to say that it was a complete bloody waste of time!"

"That's made me feel really great, Willis! Thanks for that," said Simon sarcastically. "Anyway – where did *you* end up today?"

"Well, the most interesting part of my day was the angling exhibition in Birmingham – you know, seeing all the new rods and equipment and so on."

"Hmmm, angling," muttered Simon, "very interesting. Isn't that the sport where you have a worm on one end of the line and a fucking idiot on the other?" Simon smiled at the speed and quality of his hostile remark.

Willis remained calm. "Well, angling works for me, sir. It helps me to relax and think things through. Apart from the angling, I also stuck my head in the door of the HR Exhibition – very interesting."

"And where did you go, Willis – the National Exhibition Centre?"

"Yes, sir, I've always enjoyed the NEC – plenty to see, plenty to learn."

"Excuse me for asking this, Willis, but how will the HR exhibition help you in your job as my new driver?"

"It won't, sir, but it may help me to help the significant others in my life. I like to keep in touch with current business thinking and people-management, even though I'm not in the front line of business life anymore."

"If you're all fired up to play at being Alderton's Chief Executive again perhaps you can take me off your significant others list, Willis."

"You weren't on it, sir, but you could be on it if you'd like to be."

Simon sat awkwardly for a moment. "Well let's imagine that I would like to be on it for the next few minutes...but only a few minutes! How would you have handled my job today – as the new CEO?" Simon leaned back and smiled, rather cruelly, thinking that Willis would be overwhelmed by the size and complexity of the question.

Willis glanced up again at the rear-view mirror, caught Simon's attention and said, "How long have you got, sir?"

"About 140 miles, I think, Willis, plenty of time for you to give me the benefit of your vast boardroom experience." Willis did not react to Simon's sneering remark. "And another thing, Willis, whatever experience you've got is, if you don't mind me saying, from another era...to be blunt...from yesterday's generation."

"There's certainly a generation issue, sir, but not the one you're focusing on," replied Willis. "I'm a Baby Boomer and you're from Generation X but the generation you should be worried about is neither mine nor yours! You should be worried about the one that was born after 1980 – Generation Y. After all, the future belongs to these 'millenials', doesn't it? Some of them are working for you now and more will be working for you tomorrow."

"So what, Willis? What's your point?"

"My point is, sir, that if Alderton's is to recover its former glory it needs to recognise just how different and important these people are – they have different needs and expectations and all CEOs will need to win them over."

"Go on, Willis," said Simon, looking confused.

The car slowed as Willis prepared to make his point. "Well, as far as their expectations are concerned, they'll want employers like you to offer a lot more than money. They'll demand flexibility and expect companies to move them around, and upwards too, in a portfolio career. They won't have a lot of time for rigid structures and by-the-book procedures. They'll want more choice, better work-life balance, more learning opportunities, quicker international experience, sabbaticals and projects that have high levels of social responsibility."

"What exactly do you mean when you say 'flexibility', Willis?"

"These people will want a blurred lifestyle – they'll want to put the kids to bed, then do some work from home. They'll also want the flexibility to accelerate and decelerate their careers, depending on their circumstances."

"OK. I see what you mean," said Simon.

"They're going to want shorter career horizons, maybe two to three years, not eight to ten, and believe that *they* own their career, not the company they happen to be working for. They won't trust corporations as much as NGOs and will expect companies to have a low impact on the environment. They'll actively seek out leaders who share the same values and reject those that don't.

"Leaders without values will quickly become leaders without followers. This new generation will evaluate their employers more than their predecessors ever did. To put it another way – *they* will choose *you* – if you're lucky enough to get them! There's going to be a serious shortage of talent and good people will be able to take their pick. Maybe your role is to ensure that they pick Alderton's!"

Simon was deep in thought. "Thanks for the lecture, Willis…and where will I find these Generation Y people then?"

"Through blogs and podcasts and social networking sites like Facebook and MySpace," said Willis. "That's how they work, that's how they've always lived. Did you hear the feature on the radio this morning about the trends that will affect us in the future?"

"No, I was listening to the stuff on the Middle East," said Simon.

"The journalist, Sue McGillivray, said that only five per cent of the new jobs in the next ten years will come from the EU and the USA. According to her, 30 per cent will come from India and 65 per cent from China. Alderton's will have to face up to the fact that somebody, somewhere, will be able to make the same products cheaper and that somebody, somewhere, will also be able to make the same products quicker. Many companies in this country will be forced to go up the value-chain and that will require more talented, creative people. These sort of people…"

"…are to be found in Generation Y, presumably," said Simon, completing Willis' sentence.

"Absolutely right, sir. Talent can be found in all generations, of course, but CEOs will need to spend most of their time investing in people who have the greatest stake in the future."

"OK, Willis, I think I owe you an apology. Forget my comments about you being from a different generation – you clearly know more than I do on this one. Your awareness and insight is impressive. How come you're so knowledgeable on this stuff, by the way?"

"My family is very important to me, sir. My grandchildren are all Generation Y and I try to keep up with the way that their future will differ from my past. Al Gore hit the nail on the head at that Live Earth concert, didn't he – Generation Y will be a generation that will be asking you and I one key question: 'Why?'"

"Hmmmm," replied Simon. "Fair enough and, as I just said, please accept my apology. I was out of order. I'm very sorry."

"No offence taken, sir. None at all."

Simon settled back into his seat. "So can I return to my original question, Willis – I asked you how you would have handled my situation today?"

"Well, sir, as I said earlier, I think other Chief Executives I've known or worked for would have gone for a different objective today – you know, we were talking about it this morning, if you remember."

"How could I forget it, Willis!"

Willis braked suddenly and tooted the car horn to alert a young motorcyclist in front of him. He tutted a fatherly reprimand at the youngster, then continued. "I genuinely believe that the best CEOs I have worked for explained their vision for the future at the earliest opportunity. They understood that their job was to get people from where they were to where they'd never been. If I was an Alderton's employee meeting you for the first time today, I would want you to show me a future."

Willis looked up and noticed Simon nodding. He continued. "Chief Executives don't advance very far unless they can work through others. Although strategy may be formulated in the boardroom, it's implemented on the ground – in the deep, rain-soaked trenches of each and every department. A lot of CEOs I've worked for would accept, years later, that they spent too much time on management – working on the physical resources within their business – you know, the stock, the property, the money, the factory and so on. If they were here now, they would tell you that they should have spent more time on leadership – the *emotional* resources within their business. They should have spent more time winning the hearts and minds of their people. They should have spent more time building a *passion centre* rather than a profit centre!"

Simon interrupted. "This is all good stuff but you're not telling me anything new here, are you, Willis? With respect, your comments are a BFO – a blinding flash of the obvious!"

"Maybe they are sir…so let me put it another way," continued Willis. "What is the head-count within Alderton's?"

"You know the answer to that already, Willis. You've looked at our website and we've already talked about it today. We have about 240 people – give or take a couple of new trainees."

"Right…but what's the heart-count within Alderton's?"

"The what-count?" said Simon.

"How many of your 240 people have got their hearts and minds emotionally caught up with Alderton's objectives? How many are aligned with what you're trying to achieve? How many are playing the same game as you and the other directors?"

Willis was pleased with the quality of his questions and the passion in his delivery. He paused for a reaction and noticed that his CEO passenger was looking very thoughtful.

Simon withdrew into the comfort of his leather seat and was silent for a further five minutes. He rubbed his face, slowly, then rubbed his fingertips on his forehead.

His eyes were closed. "That heart-count question is very fair, Willis," replied Simon, "but, there again, you are famous for your questions, aren't you, Willis!"

"Apparently, sir."

Willis smiled and Simon took out his pen once again. He flipped the top off, scribbled a few notes then continued. "I've got no idea what the heart-count is Willis. If I had to guess I imagine it would be no more than 40-50 people, bearing in mind recent events…i.e. some rather clumsy redundancies managed by our HR Department."

"Perhaps they should be renamed the Human Remains Department then?" said Willis.

Simon smiled but said nothing as he knew that Willis' observation was both fair and accurate. Willis could see that Simon was still writing, but continued. "You see, sir, the way that I look at it is that you've been appointed as their CEO but you've not yet been appointed as their leader. *They* will decide if you're their leader, not you. That honour has to be earned – and one of the best ways of earning it is to give Alderton's a meaningful vision for the future. The best CEOs I've worked for knew that the numbers were important but they also knew that the numbers were a downstream consequence of developing exceptional service and exceptional people. These CEOs also gave their people a map of the corporate dream – the 'promised land', if you like. They knew that if they were able to identify and show people where the organisation was going, they were already halfway there! Were you listening to 'Business Breakfast' on the local radio channel this morning? Did you hear the results of that survey?"

"No, as I said, I've been tuned in to the Middle East stuff all morning. What were the results of the survey?" said Simon.

"Well, apparently only 35 per cent of people in the organisations researched knew what their organisation was trying to do, only 25 per cent of people were able to muster any enthusiasm for it and only 15 per cent felt that they were able to execute their goals! So take your situation now. A clear vision for Alderton's will provide a sense of purpose, keep tiers of people focused on larger issues and unite Lightwater and Dudley through common goals. It will also act as a vehicle for change…"

"And how, exactly, will it do that?" said Simon.

"…because any change will take you closer to the vision," explained Willis. "You won't be accused of having change for change's sake. Another benefit is that a strong vision will allow you and your managers to parade your colours in front of the troops. It will help sort out priorities, provide day-to-day challenge and excitement and it will stay in place long after you've decided to move on. When my son Richard recently sat down and did some work on the vision for his business, he made sure that it was within reach but just out of sight. He also made sure that it included simple, inspiring and action-orientated language – mental images, if you like. Richard is the CEO now and I think he's got there by asking the right questions, not by knowing the right answers. When he started his printing business a few years ago he built a 'pentathlon' of key issues – five things, in the right order, that would take him from nowhere to somewhere…or *from nobody to somebody*, as he said at the time."

"And what were his five key areas, exactly?" enquired Simon.

"The five were Situation, Strategy, Structure, Systems and Staff," said Willis.

Simon looked a little frustrated. "That doesn't tell me a lot, does it?" he barked. Why don't you stop telling me your son's autobiography, Willis, and start relating all of this stuff to my real world at Alderton's?"

This time it was Willis who quietly counted to ten. He stayed calm, resisted the temptation to retaliate, and continued. "OK, sir. Let's take 'Situation' first.

"Well, it's not going to be last, is it?" said Simon, the frustration still showing in the tone of his voice.

Willis slowly counted to 20, pretending to be absorbed in a minor traffic incident on the other side of the road, then continued again.

"Situation, in an Alderton's context, means that the company needs to get its head around the things that are happening inside the business and also the things that are happening outside the business."

"No doubt you have some more of your famous questions for me, Willis?"

"Well, they're Richard's actually but, related to your world, they would be things like:

Where are you in your marketplace today?
Where are your competitors?
Where are you similar to them and where are you different?
Where does the profit come from?
Where does the profit get lost?
How is the business performing compared to its objectives?
How do Alderton's customers feel about you – particularly the key accounts?
What is known about the future marketplace?
How will the future differ from the past?
What future needs will your customers have?"

Willis was deliberately talking very quickly so that Simon struggled to keep up.

"Hang on, Willis, hang on!"

The traffic slowed to accommodate a traffic management crew who were tossing orange cones from their vehicle to cordon off the inside lane of the motorway.

Willis continued. "I can't remember all of Richard's thinking but I know there were questions like:

What do your customers want you to do that you are not currently doing?

What are the business-critical issues being discussed in customer board-rooms across the country and how much of this is Alderton's aware of?

What would a SWOT analysis look like?
What would a STEEP analysis look like?"

"I know all about strengths, weaknesses, opportunities and threats but what is a STEEP analysis?" said Simon. "I've not heard of it before."

"You probably have, sir. It helps you look at external factors that may impact upon your business – Social, Technological, Economic, Environmental and Political."

"OK," said Simon, "I understand that."

"Would you like some more 'Situation' questions?" asked Willis, warming to his new position as consultant to his boss.

"Keep them coming – but not too fast, man!"

Willis continued with his 'Situation' questions for a further two minutes. "…then once you and your colleagues have got your heads around the Situation, you would move on to address Alderton's Strategic issues," he finished.

"Yes, I can imagine what they would be," said Simon, "I did some work on these last week. I've got them here." Simon shuffled some paperwork on his lap and eventually found what he was looking for. "You mean questions like:

What does Alderton's want to become?
What is our vision for the future?

…that's all the stuff you've just been talking about, Willis, isn't it?

What do we want our uniqueness to be – our bit of magic?
How will we know if we're on course?
Which products and services should we be selling?
Which markets should we be selling them to?
What should our pricing be?
What should the numbers look like?
How could we achieve differentiation?
What values and beliefs do we want Alderton's people to promote and defend?
What should our objectives be?
What would the benefits be of achieving these objectives?
What would the consequences be if we don't achieve these objectives?

I'm happy with those, Willis. What are the next questions…on 'Structure'?"

"Let me give you one more question on Strategy, sir. It's about the vision again – if you had to draw Alderton's vision for the future, what would it look like?"

"Bloody hell, Willis!" said Simon. "That's a bit whacky, isn't it? Ninety per cent of my people couldn't cope with a question like that!"

"But ten per cent of them will be able to do it, sir, and they will do it well – remember that a good vision is visual as well as visionary. Now, back to your question about 'structure'…"

"…no real surprises here," said Willis. "They include questions like:

What does the current structure encourage and what does it discourage?

If the business was starting today would it have the same structure?
How should Alderton's be structured to deliver its future strategy?

"Is that it?" said Simon. "That's a bit obvious, isn't it?"

"It might be, sir, but I think the problem with 'structure' is often that companies decide too early in the process what their structure should be, then decide what strategies the structure is capable of delivering. I'm sure that you've been to some very important meetings in the past where item one on the agenda was *How should we re-structure the business?* It's a fair question but it should follow the questions about strategy. The structure should be built to deliver the strategies or, as my son Richard would say, *'Form should follow function'*."

"Or what?" said Simon. "What will happen?"

Willis continued. "If organisations don't develop the structure to deliver the strategy then they end up with all sorts of dead wood occupying quiet sleepy jobs in back offices, waiting for retirement. These people have got to find a place in today's world, be redeployed in another role or they have to go."

Simon nodded. "I suppose your fourth area, Systems, would include questions like:

What systems will be needed to link the whole organisation together?
What are the key processes that run throughout the business?

I like effective processes," added Simon. "I think that good processes run across an organisation in the same way that rivers run across international borders. Rivers don't see border crossings – they are simply focused on getting to the objective – the sea! Within Alderton's, our processes should run across departments and divisions to get to the customer." Simon paused for a few seconds.

"Nice picture, sir," said Willis. "You must remember to include that in your first state-of-the-nation briefing. It's both visual and visionary."

Simon smiled. "Thanks Willis. So…what's your last 'S'?"

"The last 'S' is Staff, sir…people, basically. There are dozens of questions here."

Simon interrupted as he flicked the pages on his lap. "Hang on Willis – here they are – you mean questions like:

What words would accurately describe Alderton's culture today?
What words would accurately describe the culture that we need in the future?

What management style is best suited to deliver the objectives?
How should the communication process work?
How will Alderton's create a motivational working environment?"

"So that it's not work," said Willis, interrupting.

"Pardon?" replied Simon. "I'm not with you."

"Well…if you get it right, sir, your people will want to come to work because they won't see it as *work* – will they?"

"Very good, Willis. You're obviously famous for your one-liners as well as your questions," said Simon.

"I try to be, sir, I try to be."

"What else, Willis?"

Willis continued. "Questions like:
All organisations have an 'us and them' – who are Alderton's?
What will Alderton's people have to do more of?
What will they have to do less of?
What will they have to be better at?
How are people coping with change and what help will they need?
What is the process within Alderton's for identifying training needs?
How much of the development needed can be handled by line managers?
How much should be handled by external resources? – training companies, personal coaches and so on.

"Willis, right now I need a comfort break – where the hell are we?"

"Near Rugby, sir…south-bound this time."

"I was right about Hell, then. Pull over at the next Services please. I need a break."

Simon Gray emerged from the Services 15 minutes later clutching a newspaper, an "Ideal Home" magazine, two comics and a packet of milk chocolate buttons for Rory. Within another minute they were heading south once again. The evening traffic was beginning to build up although they managed to stay just ahead of the main rush. They were making good progress and Simon was soon deep in thought again on the back seat of the Bentley. He sucked on the end of his pen and shuffled his sheets of paper. Willis felt happier. It had been an interesting day for both men although at times it had felt like a battle of wills and wits.

Suddenly, Simon resumed the conversation as if there had been no interruption at all.

"Well, that's been very helpful, Willis. I'm impressed…and have you remembered all these killer questions from your previous jobs?"

"Err…yes, sir…and as a result of the help I've given to my kids and friends in their businesses."

"One day you must tell me what your previous jobs were – but maybe not now. There's a lot of stuff here for me to think about and discuss with the Board tomorrow," concluded Simon.

"Why the Board, sir?"

"Because that's where this stuff sits, Willis. Strategy starts at the top and all that…"

"I have a slightly different view," said Willis.

"You don't say! I shouldn't really be surprised, should I, Willis? And what is your slightly different view?" enquired Simon.

"I think many companies approach the development of strategy in completely the wrong way," offered Willis. "Shame really – it's far too important to be left solely with the Board!"

"Steady, Willis – I'm starting to listen to you. Don't rock my boat… again!"

Willis didn't apologise. He felt he was on safer ground than before. "Don't you think that most board meetings are a little like panda matings?" he continued, with a cheeky grin on his face.

"What on earth do you mean, Willis?"

"You know…where expectations are always very high but the results are often very disappointing!"

"Very funny…I don't think. Get back to your point please, Willis," replied Simon, shaking his head.

"When I said that strategy was too important to be left to the board what I meant, sir, is that in many companies I have worked for, strategy was nothing more than a set of actions developed in a country house hotel in a vain attempt to justify expenses. These strategies were inevitably created by safe, loyal, senior company men. The main at-tribute these senior people had was experience…but just how relevant is *'experience'* in a world where the future looks nothing like the past? In times of rapid change, maybe experience is your own worst enemy. Besides, don't you think that 'experience' is the name that directors often give to their mistakes? Senior people often defend the past as it helps them retain their corporate privileges. Think of it, sir. Where are you likely to find people with the least diversity of experience, the largest investment in the past and the greatest reverence for corporate dogma? At the top! And where do you find people responsible for creating strategy? At the top! So maybe 'experience' is potentially dangerous for Alderton's. Has a decade or two made your top people more willing or less willing to challenge the industry's conventions? Has their experience made them more curious or less curious about life outside their industry?" Willis checked his rear-view mirror and couldn't detect any signs of displeasure from Simon. "Many boards of directors and the ancient Pyramids have a lot in common – they are old, they don't move and nobody is certain how they came to be in that position! There are normally two parties at work within organisations – the party of the past and the party of the future. The Board is often the party of the past, although it will always claim to be the party of the future."

"Thank you Willis – I assume that was a party political broadcast on behalf of the Workers Revolutionary Party!" said Simon.

"It wasn't meant to be, sir. What I'm saying is that the best strategies are not necessarily developed by your most senior people. As the old Chinese proverb says, 'a fish rots from the head'. Maybe you need a few young wild ducks involved – you know, people who refuse to fly in formation. Although these people may appear to be disloyal, they often passionately pursue improvements through an approach that could best be described as 'disruptive loyalty'."

"OK," said Simon, "I suppose I could form some sort of strategic working party – a group of people from different levels and parts of the business, each with a different view of Alderton's world. I could create a group of people that would include some 'new managers' and some of your 'difficult people'. It could also include head office people from Hendon and people from the Lightwater and Dudley factories."

"Don't forget the 'younger people', sir. When I think of the organisations my kids have worked for, they were the ones with the biggest stake in the future but they were often remote from the process of strategy creation."

"Surely, Willis, you're not suggesting that I put a young secretary or someone from the factory floor into a strategic working party? That's bloody ridiculous!"

"Why not! Your two factories are not communist organisations built to precipitate the fall of capitalism, sir! They probably house mountains of human potential. All I'm saying, sir, is that strategy is best built by a number of people – including those who have a new, refreshing, different or objective view of it. You could explain the strategic planning process you want Alderton's to follow, then invite applications from people who think they have something to contribute. How about that?"

Simon looked thoughtful. "And you think that this approach will work do you, Willis?"

"It will work for a very simple reason, sir. If Alderton's people help plan the battle they won't battle the plan! People do not resist their own ideas."

"Well, it's certainly different to how I've done it before, Willis – no doubt about that."

"It's also effective, sir. Think of the heart-count. You're going to need a lot more that 40-50 willing hearts and minds. You're probably going to need over 180 people on board to stand any chance of success. Alderton's won't change if you're the only person who wants it to! If you don't get the heart-count up we probably won't be making our six trips together – it could all be over in three or four!"

Simon sank back in his chair again, remained silent and made some discreet notes once again. The only sound was the traffic outside and the occasional piece of rush-hour traffic news on the car radio inside. Willis turned the volume up a little but Simon didn't notice. He was deep in thought.

The security forces were making progress in the Middle East and a number of men were *helping the authorities with their enquiries*. In the UK, the leader of the Opposition was threatening to resign unless he received more support from his colleagues and, on the other side of the House, the Minister for Health was predicting the collapse of the National Health Service. On a lighter note, the Prime Minister had just won the prize for best-dressed man, according to the readers of a popular lifestyle magazine.

"A bit like my day," thought Willis. "I've been helping my boss with his enquiries, I've come close to resigning and I've been talking to someone who needs urgent help to improve the health of his organisation. Not sure about his dress sense, though!" he thought, catching a glimpse of Simon's shirt in the rear view mirror. Willis smiled as he flicked the car indicator to signal their return eastwards, back along the A14. He relaxed and quietly observed the countryside once again for an hour. Both men appeared to be enjoying the silence and the break from their earlier creative tension.

As the car crossed the county boundary Simon leaned forward. "Despite our occasional differences I've enjoyed our trip today, you know," he said. "You got off to an appalling start, Willis, we nearly had a major breakdown, but you finished well!"

Willis looked in the rear-view mirror hoping to detect a smile from Simon, but realised his remark was deadly serious. "Thank you, sir. I enjoyed it too…and I'm not bothered by your breakdown comment, by the way. It's at the point of breakdown that we often have breakthrough."

"Fair point, Willis," replied Simon. "And, despite your earlier dismissal of the word 'experience', I hope that I'm learning to value yours. I think that your experience could be a great asset."

"Did you hear about the old lady who decided to go on a safari in Africa with her faithful, elderly poodle?" said Willis, ignoring Simon's compliment.

Simon leaned forward. "No, Willis, it doesn't ring a bell."

"Well, one day the poodle started to chase some exotic butterflies through the bush but soon realised that he was lost. Wandering about, he noticed a young leopard heading rapidly in his direction with the clear intention of having lunch. The poodle thought to himself, 'I'm in deep doo-doo now!' Noticing some old bones on the ground, he settled down to chew them with his back towards the approaching leopard. Just as the big cat was about to leap, the wise old poodle said, 'Boy that was one delicious leopard! I wonder if there are any more around here?' Hearing this, the leopard halted his attack in mid-air with a look of terror on his face. He turned and ran off into the trees. 'Whew,' said the leopard, 'that was close – that old poodle nearly had me!'

"Meanwhile, a monkey who had been watching the scene from a nearby tree figured that he could put this knowledge to good use and trade it for protection from the leopard. So off he went to find the leopard, but the wise old poodle saw him drop from the tree and realised that something must be up. The monkey soon caught up with the leopard, spilled the beans and struck a deal.

"The young leopard was furious at being made a fool of and said, 'Here, monkey, hop on my back and come and see what I'm now going to do to that conniving poodle.' The old poodle saw the leopard coming through the bush with the monkey on his back and thought: 'What am I going to do now?' Instead of running off, the poodle sat down with his back to the attackers, pretending he hadn't seen them, and just when they got close enough to hear, he said impatiently: 'Where's that damn monkey? I sent him off an hour ago to bring me another juicy leopard!'"

Simon laughed loudly from the back seat of the Bentley. "That's very funny, Willis, and I assume there has to be a moral in there somewhere?"

"There is a moral, sir…don't mess with the oldies as their age and skill will always overcome youth and treachery. Brilliance often comes with age and experience…as it does with me, of course!"

"Very good, Willis," said Simon, who was still chuckling and smiling. "I like that one!"

A minute later Willis added, "And by the way, you said earlier that we'd had the occasional difference but there's nothing wrong with that, sir. They say that, in business and in life, you should always find a partner who doesn't agree with you. All good teams are a collection of differences, aren't they?"

"I suppose that's another one-liner from the Willis School of Management, is it?"

"I prefer to think of it as the Willis School of Leadership, sir."

"Ah yes…of course!"

"Hopefully, today has been a better experience for you than a day at the Christopher Columbus School of Management," said Willis.

"What exactly is that?" said Simon, tidying his papers as the car re-entered the sleepy village of Mapleford.

Willis smiled and turned to face Simon to catch his attention. "Well, when he left he didn't know where he was going, when he got there he didn't know where he was and when he got back home he didn't know where he'd been!"

"Very good, Willis, see you next month – the 24th I think it is. I've got your mobile number, haven't I?"

"I'm sure you have, sir. Have a good month! By the way – here's a present for you." Willis located his wallet, took out a first class stamp and handed it over.

Simon looked confused. "Err…thanks, Willis. Err…very nice!"

Willis smiled. "I know you have dozens of things to do and dozens of things on your mind, sir. But consider this humble postage stamp. Its usefulness lies in its simple ability to stick to one thing until it gets there! Whatever we've learned today, I hope that we both stick to it until we get there. See you next month."

Simon smiled back and shook Willis' hand. "Goodbye Willis."

The front door of the Gray's house opened to the noisy accompaniment of a barking dog and jumping, giggling girls both trying to throw their arms around their father's neck. The newly purchased presents were offered and gratefully received and Stella shouted a distant but warm welcome from the kitchen. Simon shut his eyes, breathed deeply and savoured the smell of roasted chicken accompanied by a lemon and herb aroma. Rory caught a fleeting glimpse of his chocolate buttons but never got to see them as they were quickly intercepted by Claire and Lucy. Simon put his briefcase in the study then went to find Stella. It was good to be home.

Willis completed his paperwork while the Bentley still sat in the Gray's drive. Through the windows he could see the Gray family re-connecting with each other and catching up on the day's news. The dog barked loudly as it competed, unsuccessfully, for their attention.

Willis tidied the front seat of the car and unbuttoned the top button of his shirt. He started the engine for the last time that day, released the Bentley's foot brake and headed for the end of the lane once again.

"You've had a good day today, George Nelson Willis…a very good day." He smiled. "George – your first objective has been achieved!"

Wit and Wisdom
Chapter 1 Summary

1. Organisations are the same – you are the difference! Your words will create their worlds – Leaders are dealers in hope and need to create powerful visions for the future so that people know what to hope for. If you are running something, your people will also want to know that you stand for something – your values and beliefs will be important to them.

2. Business is not just about looking down on the bottom line – it is about looking up at the horizon and the future.

3. You can be appointed as CEO but you can't be appointed as a Leader. The employees control that honour – it has to be earned.

4. "Busyness" is a sign of mediocrity. The busier you are, the more average you are likely to be. Stand back from it all and indulge in some quality thinking time.

5. If you know where you are going you are already half-way there. Try the five stage business model – Situation, Strategies, Structure, Systems and Staff.

6. Board meetings are a little like pandas mating – expectations are always high but the results are often disappointing. Strategy is far too important to be left solely to the board – try forming a strategic working party and involve a few wild ducks – people who refuse to fly in formation.

7. Many boards and the Pyramids have a lot in common – they are old, they don't move and nobody is certain how they came to be in that position!

8. There is a difference between "disloyalty" and disruptive loyalty. Don't fear people who are "not like you". All good teams are a collection of differences.

9. Involve people – if they help plan the battle they won't battle the plan! People do not resist their own ideas.

10. Measure your organisation's heart-count as a percentage of your organisation's headcount. Become a passion centre as well as a profit centre. If you get it right, people will come to work because they won't see it as "work".

So, is anybody looking after your customers better than you?

Look forward to seeing you on 13th

Richard

Richard White, Academy Chairman - Leeds, Bradford & Halifax | 29 Ashwood Gardens, Gildersome, Leeds LS27 7AS | **Mobile:** +44 (0)7985 874 252 | **Email:** richard.white@chiefexecutive.com

Chapter 2
Look After Your Customers Before Someone Else Does

"Good morning, Willis – did you see the cricket?"

"I did, sir, it was very exciting, wasn't it?"

"I knew it was going to be tense, but not that tense!"

"I know. I was on the edge of my seat. It was a great turnaround, wasn't it? The impressive thing about the team is that they seem to have developed a belief and confidence that we haven't seen for a long time."

"…and wasn't it great to see them all being so supportive towards each other at the end of each over?"

"…and the captain has done such a fantastic job, hasn't he? It's a completely different team culture from the past."

The two men chatted about the weekend's cricket like two seasoned TV commentators. One provided the ball-by-ball commentary and the other interjected with timely observations, match statistics and conclusions. Somehow, the surrounding countryside seemed to be aligned with their conversation. They drove through a picturesque, timeless village with a hilltop church as its landmark and a cricket pitch as its heart. One side of the pitch was surrounded by a dozen old oak trees that had witnessed hundreds of games over the years. The scoreboard from the weekend was still visible and showed that one of the teams had scored an impressive 287 runs.

"That's more than just a respectable score, Willis. I wonder which young men of the future were playing on that pitch yesterday? Perhaps they will make the England team one day? Who knows…? Anyway, how was your weekend?"

"Fine, sir, how was yours?" Willis was concentrating on a learner driver in front of him and was happy to quickly pass the conversation back to Simon.

"A bit tiring, actually," replied Simon. "Sometimes I think parenting is a mixture of part joy and part guerrilla warfare! I love them really, though. Mind you, when the girls start playing their bloody instruments it can be painful. They've been at it all weekend."

"What do they play?" enquired Willis. Having overtaken the learner driver, he was now looking at the back-end of a milk float going about its early-morning deliveries.

"Claire's learning to play the piano and Lucy has just acquired one of the school's violins. They've been practising for the village fête later in the month. Their school is providing the afternoon entertainment… if you can call it that!"

"I know what you mean. I had a similar experience with my eldest, Trevor. He played the violin for three years. I think it's an instrument of pure torture that must have been invented by someone with cotton wool in their ears."

"Exactly!" said Simon, nodding in agreement. "But did you know, Willis, that there are two instruments that are actually worse than a violin?"

"Really…and what exactly are they?" enquired Willis.

"Two violins!" quipped Simon.

The two men laughed loudly together – it was a first. On previous occasions they had laughed at different things, or at each other. It was a promising start to the day.

"So you had a bit of a musical weekend, then?" continued Willis, glancing at Simon in the rear-view mirror.

"Yes, but we also had a cocktail party on Saturday evening. Some of Stella's friends from Mapleford and their other halves. Usual sort of thing – a bit tedious, predictable gossip, usual keeping up with the Joneses stories. Personally, I can't see the benefit in buying things I don't need with money I don't have just to impress people I don't like! Our guests weren't the most interesting people I know, or the brightest…but don't tell my wife I said that, Willis."

"Fine, sir. I'm not a party animal either. I'd rather have a nice meal at home with my wife, Anne. I've always thought that a cocktail party is an event when you invite everyone you know to come over to your house at six o'clock to put beer stains on your best rug prior to them buggering off at eight o'clock."

"And then the bastards decide to go somewhere else more interesting…" added Simon "…without inviting you!"

They laughed together again. It was a very pleasant start to the day.

"So, who are we going to see, today, sir?" As the laughter subsided, Willis was keen to build on the warmth of their conversation. He was also hoping for a more positive response from Simon Gray than the opening remarks he had received the previous month.

"I thought you might ask me that, Willis. I'm going to meet the Chief Executive of Durkin and Timperley, our biggest customer."

"Have you asked to see him or has he or she asked to see you?" enquired Willis.

"A bit of both," said Simon, "my PA arranged the appointment but there've been a few issues lately which prompted their CEO, Colin Durkin, to phone my office."

Willis raised an eyebrow and glanced in the rear-view mirror. "Issues, sir?"

"Yes, Willis…issues in the form of a few serious problems, if you really want to know." In the rear-view mirror Simon could see Willis still raising his eyebrow, so he continued: "Yes, we lost one of our account managers three months ago and things have slipped since then. All sorts of problems, so I'm told."

"And the customer is now unhappy about the situation?" asked Willis.

"Yes…to put it mildly," said Simon. "I'm not sure exactly what he wants to cover today but I think he'll be doing all of the talking and I'll be doing all of the listening."

"Probably a good thing then," said Willis.

"What is?"

"…that you'll be doing all the listening, sir. It will give your Mr. Durkin an opportunity to let off steam. A wise old bird and all that…"

"You've lost me, Willis," said Simon.

Willis continued, slowly shaking his head from side to side as if he had connected with some strange spiritual source of ancient wisdom. In a sing-song voice he said:

"A wise old bird sat on an oak, the more he heard the less he spoke. The less he spoke the more he heard, why aren't we like that wise old bird?"

"Where did you get that one from?" asked Simon.

"My father, sir. It was one of his many sayings."

"Was your whole family blessed with one-liners and smart-arsed quotes, Willis?"

"I've no idea, sir, I don't think so. Mind you, I've always enjoyed messing around with words and studying the English language. Did you know that when you re-arrange the letters in 'mother in law' you can end up with 'woman Hitler' and if you re-arrange the letters in 'snooze alarms' you end up with 'alas, no more Zs!'"

Simon laughed. "Really, Willis? I think I need to write those down to see if you're pulling a fast one. Where's my pen?"

Willis smiled. "But seriously though, sir, this customer service issue with Durkin and Timperley might be a blessing for you as you're bound to learn a great deal. They say that the beginning of wisdom is silence and the second stage is listening. There's clearly an opportunity for both today."

Simon continued, unimpressed with Willis' words of reassurance. "Anyway, I can't say I'm looking forward to this meeting with Colin Durkin. He's bound to be highly critical."

"But in business, sometimes our worst critics are more useful to us than our best yes-men," said Willis. "Don't you think that honest differences, discussed openly, are often a sign of healthy progress? Things get said and are out in the open. Anyway, in your relationship with Mr. Durkin you're going to find it difficult to make any sort of improvements unless you know where you're starting from."

"Alright, alright, those are fair points, Willis," said Simon, "but I still think we are about to take a step backwards with this account"

"But there is a school of thought that says that if you're on the edge of a cliff, progress is actually a step backwards...a time to re-think, a time to re-group and all that."

"Another fair point, Willis. I see that you're on good form today."

"Thank you, sir. I'm just trying to be positive."

"And does that mean that you think I'm being negative?"

Willis looked up at the rear-view mirror. "Well, I know that when I'm being negative and think that there's a problem, the problem is often my negative *thought,* not the problem itself."

Simon reflected on Willis' remark as the car continued to speed along the northbound A1. It was 7.30am and Mapleford was well behind them. The countryside was already wide-awake and hard at work. Harvesters were poised for action on the edge of the fields and were waiting for the late July sun to dry the early morning dew that was glistening on the crops. The fields reminded Willis of a painter's palette. Yellows, greens, golds and numerous shades of brown – they were all there, laid out in squares and rectangles on the rolling hills, for miles around. In a field to his left, Willis could see a green tractor with two working dogs desperately clinging to the trailer whilst the vehicle negotiated a deep rut in the field. The dogs were obviously used to it and, with tongues out and tails wagging, they managed to stay balanced and united with their master, ready for their sheep-herding duties still to come.

Simon saw them too. "My lazy dog could do with a good, hard day's work," he muttered as he imagined Rory making a nuisance of himself around his stylish kitchen back in Mapleford. He smiled as he thought of Claire and Lucy giving Rory a few of their Shreddies whilst Stella's back was turned.

This was one of Willis' favourite times of the year as it reminded him of childhood summer holidays at Mr. Selsey's farm when he used to assist with the grain harvest and harrowing but, with the Monday traffic gaining momentum, he re-focused on the road ahead. He liked the A1 as there was always plenty to see, but it was notorious for accidents, particularly when slow-moving lorries and tractors attempted to dart cross the dual carriageway. He was enjoying life and this was no time to end it. They were heading for Nottingham – the home of lace, bicycles, Robin Hood's medieval exploits and a once-famous and successful football club.

The road was clear and the traffic was moving freely. Simon's head was buried deep in the sports section of his newspaper and he was happily reading anything and everything about the tactics behind England's memorable weekend cricket win. From time to time, he would chuckle and offer another interesting view or match statistic.

By now they had been travelling for one hour and a bored Willis thought it was time for another of his probing questions. He coughed quietly to attract Simon's attention. Simon did not look up and appeared to deliberately lift his newspaper so that the prospect, or threat, of any potential eye contact was removed. Willis noticed the raised newspaper but was unperturbed. He coughed again.

"So, have you had a good business month, sir?"

"Hmmm…" said Simon, without looking up. "Yes, I have actually. I've made good progress with that strategic working party idea we talked about last time."

"Good progress?" enquired Willis. "In what way?"

"I mean good progress, Willis!"

"Ah…but there's a difference between good motion and good progress, sir. A rocking horse moves a lot but makes no progress! So do you mean progress or do you mean motion?"

"OK, Willis, I mean I'm making real progress." Simon dropped his newspaper and leaned forward. "I've got 12 people on the strategic working party and we're lined up for a session next week to look at our future direction. I've also started three project teams from across the business to look at a number of implications arising from these sessions. I'm also planning to run a another strategic session when we come back from our family holiday."

"Where are you off to…somewhere nice?" asked Willis. It wasn't his best question of the day but he sensed that he needed to respond to the obvious change of topic.

"We're going to Florida, Willis. Have you been?"

"No, sir, I haven't. They say it's a great place…if you happen to be an orange!"

"Very amusing, Willis," said Simon. "We're going to Orlando in a fortnight. Stella booked it on the web months ago – long before I knew about my new job at Alderton's. We got a very good deal – that always appeals to me! It'll be the first time for the girls, of course. They can't wait to see America."

"It's a great country," said Willis, "I love the place. I was lucky enough to see a lot of both Americas on my travels some years ago. I've got some great memories."

"I've not been to South America but the USA is a great place, isn't it?" continued Simon. "But someone once said that it's the only nation in history that has gone from barbarism to degeneration without the usual interval of civilisation! Mind you, I mustn't let my Finance Director hear me saying anything like that – he's from Boston, and I don't mean Lincolnshire – well, not to my knowledge anyway. I'm looking forward to the break."

"I have a very simple way of knowing if I need a holiday," said Willis, smiling.

"Go on then, Willis…you're obviously dying to tell me."

"I've always believed that if I ever look like my passport picture… then I probably need a holiday!"

Simon smiled. "Very funny, Willis. I must remember to tell Stella that one."

Another 20 miles sped by and Willis decided it was time to return to the business agenda. "And what about your trip to Lightwater last month, sir?" he said. "Did that go ahead as planned?"

"It did and it was fine, actually, Willis…well remembered, by the way. It all went well. They're really on the ball down there. The Light Side are a really good team. I've got some of them on the working party, of course. Hopefully they'll be able to show the Dark Side and head office a few tricks."

The Bentley slowed and negotiated a roundabout near a large country estate where Georgian houses and farms nestled amongst trees that overlooked the dual carriageway. A recently constructed by-pass had restored the village, its pub, butcher's shop and smithy to its former quiet and secluded glory. In the distance, Willis could see a field where over a dozen chestnut-coloured horses were grazing contentedly.

"They're hunters, I think," said Simon, whose attention had also been caught by the delights of the countryside. "And do we approve of fox hunting, Willis?" he enquired, although he half-knew what Willis' answer would be.

"No, we don't, sir, as a matter of interest. I do have a little sympathy though."

"Really? You surprise me…and why's that?"

"Well," continued Willis, "youngsters who spend their childhood years being beaten up by fierce nannies at home, then by bullies in the dormitory, are more likely to want to murder wildlife in their later years, aren't they?"

"I had a nanny and I went to school at Stowe…" said Simon, frowning. "…so what exactly is your point?"

"I'm saying no more, sir," said Willis as he quickly fiddled with the car's gadgetry on the dashboard.

Simon picked up his newspaper, crinkling it noisily as if to make a point, and returned to something he considered more interesting than Willis' provocative remarks. Thirty minutes passed and Simon's

47

business agenda of the day was rapidly becoming the focus of his attention. He glanced at his watch. They were making good time.

"So what do you know about key account management and customer service then, Willis?" Simon asked.

Willis was surprised by the question, which clearly marked the end of their tense but friendly morning banter and monthly update. He visibly rose a little in his seat, ready to give an insightful answer to Simon's question.

"Why does key account management feature in your thinking today?" asked Willis, trying to gain a little extra thinking time before answering the question.

"Well," said Simon, "it features for a number of reasons. Firstly, the company we're going to see today, Durkin and Timperley, represents 12 per cent of Alderton's business. That's a huge amount and, although their business is very welcome, it also makes me feel very uncomfortable.

"Secondly, I know that key account management is becoming more important to us as time goes by. From the reports I've been reading it would appear that 55 per cent of our business came from 20 per cent of our customers in 1995. Today, 78 per cent of our business is coming from 20 per cent of our customers. We're a living example of the Pareto Principle – presumably you've heard of the 80-20 principle, Willis?"

"I certainly have, sir. I know that for 80 per cent of the time my wife wears only 20 per cent of her shoes – but wants to keep all the others, of course! For 80 per cent of our time we walk on 20 per cent of our carpets, 80 per cent of the time I play 20 per cent of my CDs and records..."

"Willis...I'm talking about the business aspects of the Pareto Principle, not your wife's shoes or your bloody carpets!" Simon shook his head, quietly counted to ten and continued. "I'm talking about the 80 per cent of business coming from 20 per cent of my *customers*," he said, leaning forward to emphasise the point. "This KAM stuff is going to be key to our survival. I've already identified that we have 16 key accounts and a similar number of key prospects – you know, dream companies that would change the fortunes of the business...if only we had them on board."

"So what makes an Alderton's customer a 'key account' as opposed to an ordinary customer?" said Willis.

"A number of things, Willis. I've developed some criteria and I think that I've got them written down here somewhere. I did some work on this last Friday. Hang on a minute – here they are. Yes, there are five criteria, listen:

1. Are they, or could they become, a £500k per annum customer giving us 25 per cent margin?

2. Are there good relationships in place already?

3. Is there a good culture fit – you know, do we believe in the same things?

4. Is the customer looking for more than just a good price?

5. Do they have prestige or strategic value to us?"

"What does strategic value mean for Alderton's?" enquired Willis.

"For example, when the customer is able to open doors and introduce us to larger companies within their group… 'open-sesame accounts', as I sometimes call them," said Simon.

"And what about competitor activity, sir? Is that another one for your list?"

"It depends what you mean," said Simon.

"Where a competitor of yours is experiencing major problems and a short-term opportunity exists for you to attack their most important customers. Would that be a key account?" said Willis.

"Good one, Willis," said Simon, "and I suppose the reverse situation is true – where a competitor is becoming increasing active on one of our accounts. Maybe we've got seven criteria then." Simon sucked the end of his pen, paused for a further minute then looked up. "Come to think of it, some are probably more important than others, so I think I might split them into 'essential criteria' and 'desirable criteria'."

"Sounds a good idea to me," added Willis from the front seat with the confident air of an expert on the subject.

Simon continued. "I'm doing all the talking again, Willis. As I said, what do you know about key account management? You seem to be avoiding the subject."

"Not at all. I know a little about it," replied Willis

"And where did you acquire this knowledge?"

"Well most of what I know I've learned from the CEOs I've worked for," said Willis.

"Carry on then, I'm all ears," said Simon, intrigued by the prospect of Willis' answer.

"Well, I once worked for a Swiss engineering company, and the first thing I can remember my Chief Executive saying was that a key account was *'a lot more than a normal customer with a few more noughts on the end of it'.*"

"Obviously…" muttered Simon.

"I can remember him saying that the purpose of KAM was to stand out from competitors, not to stand up to them."

"You mean differentiation, Willis."

"I think I know what I mean, sir," said Willis.

"Quite…and the third thing?" said Simon, attempting to quickly move the conversation on from his rather pompous remark.

"The third thing I can remember is that if you get KAM right, you'll be seen as an exceptional business partner, not an ordinary supplier, and the fourth thing he used to have a bee in his bonnet about was that key account management should add value, not cost. In theory, a company's products and services should not cost customers anything."

"We don't give the bloody products away, Willis. All of our products have to cost something!"

"Well, maybe they shouldn't," said Willis, a smile on his face as he awaited Simon's response.

Simon breathed deeply for a few seconds. "Well, I suppose it was inevitable that we'd cross swords again sometime today, Willis. Clearly the piranhas are still circling around in the bidet!" Simon's cheeks were beginning to turn pink. "Come on then, tell me why Alderton's products shouldn't cost anything!"

Willis smiled but remained calm. Noticing the empty, clear road ahead, he turned his head slightly and said, "Because, sir, the return on the customer's investment should outweigh the price…so, therefore, there would be no cost. As my old boss used to say: *'Good companies are never expensive, even if they charge a lot!'* Willis turned again to face the road, feeling very pleased with himself. He felt like an England cricketer who had just hit a boundary with some calm footwork and a casual flick of the wrist. There was silence from the back seat and another country mile sped by.

"You have a point, Willis, but your point is a very theoretical one," conceded Simon eventually.

"Not at all, sir. If Alderton's does a good job why should your customers feel any pain? Why should they feel that the transaction has *cost* them anything? They should feel that the transaction has created some *value* for them. When they are out and about in the field, selling, I assume that your account managers, or whatever you call them, are able to show your customers and prospects the likely return for every £1000 spent with Alderton's? I assume that they're also able to produce testimonials from happy customers able to comment on what Alderton's has done to their bottom line?"

Simon shook his head slowly, looking thoughtful. Out of Willis' sight, he scribbled a few points on his pad. "So what's your smart-arsed killer question on this issue, Willis? I need a question that I can add to the list I'm going to raise with the strategic working party. No doubt you've got one?"

Willis continued. "How about this question then…if Alderton's was arrested and charged with adding value to its customers, would there be enough evidence to convict it? That'll do, won't it?"

"That'll do nicely, Willis. Where did you get that one from?"

"From another ex-Chief Executive of mine, sir. It was a chemicals company near Nottingham, strangely enough. It was some time ago, of course. He believed that his account managers shouldn't fight over a slice of the customer's cake – he believed that they should help the customer to make a bigger cake – you know, help customers to grow in *their* world. He believed that all organisations were in the financial services business – i.e. providing customers with improved profitability. He saw the account manager's job in very black and white terms – i.e. to put some 'black and white' on to the customer's bottom line. He once told the account managers at a sales conference that their job was to have the solutions to problems that customers didn't yet have. He also said that the only way they would sell more products and services was not to keep talking about their products and services."

"What exactly did he mean by that?" enquired Simon.

"He meant that they should stop boring the customer with lectures on products and services and concentrate on things that mattered to the customer," explained Willis. "He also used to say that whenever they looked at a price they were about to quote they should remember that VAT meant *'value added tomorrow'*. I can remember talking to my daughter about this bottom line value concept when she took over the construction business. She put a lot of good KAM ideas into place, actually."

"Was she successful, Willis? Eh…sorry, I've forgotten her name. Which daughter are we talking about?"

"Debbie, sir. Yes, she was very successful, as a matter of fact. I can remember some of the slides that she used during her early meetings and team briefings. I can't remember them word for word but they said things like:

We will only improve our profitability if we improve theirs!

The first rule of business is to look after our key accounts before someone else does!

Customers don't care how much we know as long as they know how much we care!"

"You've got a good memory, Willis," said Simon.

"I wrote some of the slides with her, sir."

"But I thought you only knew a little about key account management, Willis?" continued Simon.

"I do, sir. Fortunately, it's not rocket science, is it? Despite attempts to complicate it, I think it's just about selling products and services that don't come back to customers that do…and the ones that you particularly want back are the key accounts. It's an example of one of the business basics, isn't it?" said Willis.

"And no doubt you are going to tell me what this business basic is, Willis?"

"Of course." Willis took his time as he overtook another full grain lorry heading north. A steady flow of grain trickled down from the tailgate, reminding Willis of his favourite waterfall in the Dales. The silence caused by the short delay in the conversation acted like a drum roll for his grand-finale, still to come. "The business basic is very simple, sir. If you're an expert in the customer's world you will probably never have to sell again!" said Willis. "Would you like a quick test to see how good Alderton's is at that, sir? I know that Debbie used this test with her people."

"Well it's got to be better than looking at this awful industrial area on the left, Willis," said Simon. "What an eyesore! What is that place?"

"I think it's a cement factory, sir. Dreadful, isn't it? Not very green either." Willis returned to his challenge. "So would you like my quick test to see if you're an expert in the customer's world, sir?"

"Have I got a choice? You're obviously keen to share it with me… so go on then."

"Let's take your meeting with Mr. Durkin this morning," said Willis. "Imagine that his PA shows you into an office where Mr. Durkin greets you in a friendly manner, pours you a coffee, then announces that he has asked one of his new managers to join the meeting as he/she will have an involvement with Alderton's in the months to come. OK so far?"

"Yes, Willis, but when are you going to get to the point?" said Simon in a bored voice as he reached across the back seat to locate something in his briefcase.

"Now, sir," said Willis. "Imagine that Mr. Durkin then says that he would like to start the meeting with a short presentation from you… for the benefit of his new manager."

"That wouldn't be a problem, Willis. I've acquired a fair knowledge of our business already. I could do that and I've also got a few slides on my laptop," said Simon.

"Ahhh…but I don't mean doing a presentation on Alderton's," said Willis. "Imagine that your Mr. Durkin asks you to do a short presentation on *his* company to show his new manager that you really understand *them* and *their* business and to demonstrate that you're working with them in a spirit of *partnership*. Imagine that he asks you to include in your presentation your understanding of *their* products and services, *their* market position, *their* competitors, *their* short-term, medium-term and long-term objectives, all *their* numbers…"

"You mean turnover, market share, profitability and so on?" asked Simon.

"Exactly that," agreed Willis, "and imagine that he tells you that page three of *their* updated website is worth you commenting on in your presentation as well as including a reference to some of *their* recent press coverage…"

"Stop there, Willis, you've made your point. I couldn't do that, and you know it! I don't quite know how to say this, but you can be a depressing bastard at times. I'm sure, if I wait long enough, I might find some of your piranha comments motivational!" said Simon, tossing his pen into his open briefcase.

"Perhaps you're not meant to find my comments motivational, sir...yet! Maybe I can help you today by asking the right questions and being a pain in the arse – no, let me rephrase that more politely. Maybe I can be the sand in your bed, making life a little uncomfortable from time to time," smiled Willis.

"How about uncomfortable all of the time!" said Simon.

"Thank you, sir," said Willis, with a contented smile on his face. "I'll take that as a compliment. If I could change my metaphors, remember that the more I can make you sweat in practice, the less you'll bleed in battle."

"Who came out with that smart-arsed remark?" demanded Simon.

"Nobody really famous," replied Willis, "an old, obscure Chinese general, I think."

A further ten minutes went by. The industrial area was replaced by rolling countryside once again. Simon abandoned his attempts to repair his expensive but broken pen and was now quietly taking notes with one of the girls' bright pink pencils. He leaned forward to attract Willis' attention in the rear-view mirror.

"Earlier, you mentioned the words 'working in a spirit of partnership', Willis, but I'm not sure exactly what you meant by that," he said.

"Well let me put it this way, sir. In my lifetime I've witnessed the evolution of the account manager. 'Sales' has changed quite a lot and I've been around while it has gone through a number of evolutionary stages. In the seventies, sales reps left their caves and set off to hunt their commercial prey with little more than a bag full of stories and rather bad jokes. They entertained their customers over a mug of coffee, made them laugh with their amusing stories, compared sports results, swapped scandal and office gossip and left clutching a last-minute order before moving on to the next unsuspecting customer where the same, well-rehearsed routine was performed all over again. By the eighties, things had progressed a little..."

"Were you ever in sales, Willis, or is this all theory?" asked Simon.

"I was in sales," said Willis, "firstly for a French pharmaceuticals company, then a publishing company in Reading."

"Bloody hell, Willis, your CV must be 30 pages long. You've worked for everybody! So back to the eighties then…"

"Yes, as I was saying…things progressed a little and sales reps evolved and developed some good presentation skills to explain the features, advantages and benefits of their products and services. However, many had become walking technical handbooks and were doing far too much talking. Sadly, their ears had not developed as well as their tongues. They didn't listen – they just waited to speak, whilst taking a breath in between sentences. Their language was often combative. Customer objections were perceived as obstacles that needed to be overcome using a number of slick, foolproof techniques. They didn't understand that objections were often genuine concerns that needed to be understood and handled sensitively…that they were often the first signs of genuine interest indicating the position of the customer…that they were often an attempt to change or improve a proposal, not to destroy it. But the sales reps just carried on talking to an audience of one and a…"

"…a market of none?" enquired Simon.

"Yes, that's right," said a puzzled looking Willis, "have I said that before?"

"No," replied Simon, "I'm just beginning to learn how your strange mind works. Carry on, Willis. Let's have the nineties then…?"

"Err…oh yes…the nineties," said Willis, who felt that he had temporarily lost his momentum. "The nineties saw the arrival of a much softer, more skilful approach, I think. At last, account managers started to show a genuine interest in the customer's business and it was no longer seen as a hit-and-run process with a win-lose outcome.

"Fortunately for my two daughters, the role and contribution of women in the nineties was also truly recognised. Up until then, women in business had to be twice as good as men to go half as far. But their empathy, listening skills, intuition, relationship building and natural conflict management skills left many men behind."

Simon interrupted. "For God's sake don't let my wife hear you say that! So let me get this clear in my mind, Willis. The gossiping sales rep *entertainers* of the seventies evolved into boring *informers* in the eighties, then into consultative *problem solvers* in the nineties. I assume that there's a final stage in this evolutionary shaggy-dog story? To be honest, it *is* going on a bit!" added Simon, impatiently.

"The last stage," said Willis quickly, "is where we are now. Trying to stand out from competitors, or differentiation, as you kindly reminded me it was called, is very difficult these days. In Debbie's business, many of the traditional competitive weapons like product development, pricing, distribution, advertising and so on can be copied very quickly by her competitors and, in the eyes of her customers, everyone is selling the same sort of thing these days. So the best way of standing out today is to develop people who are capable of operating as *business partners*, not as suppliers, and this needs high relationship management skills and high levels of understanding of the customer's business."

Simon was deep in thought. "So if, in the future, Alderton's is to be perceived as an effective partner by its key accounts, how would we actually measure that, Willis? How would we know we were perceived as partners?" But before Willis could say anything, Simon had answered his own question: "I suppose we need some sort of partnership indicators, don't we? If a key account customer gave us the occasional piece of confidential information that would qualify, wouldn't it?"

Willis looked up. "You mean if the customer said something like *'Keep this under your hat, I shouldn't really be telling you this...'*?"

"Exactly," said Simon, "because that statement would be based on trust...and that would say a lot about the state of the relationship. It would confirm that we were going in the right direction, wouldn't it? That would be a good partnership indicator."

"It would. Another indicator would be contact at different levels within the customer's business, presumably?" added Willis.

"Yes, you're right...clear evidence of multi-level contact..." said Simon "...and another indicator would be if a customer agreed to a rolling contract rather than the usual fixed term contract."

"What about hospitality?" added Willis.

"You mean if the customer comes out to play and always attends our corporate hospitality events?" said Simon

"No. I mean if the customer invites you to attend *their* events and picks up the bill!" said Willis.

"Nice one, Willis," said Simon, turning the page of his notebook. "I'm going to call that reverse-hospitality."

Willis continued: "And what about the issue of price sensitivity? Would that be another?"

"It would," said Simon. "This is the stuff that you were talking about earlier. Price will always be an important consideration but if price sensitivity drops, over time, that has got to be a good indicator, Willis. I'm on a roll here – can we pull over for a coffee at the next opportunity? What about that big hotel overlooking the reservoir on the Old Coach Road that runs parallel with this motorway – do you know the one I mean?"

"Do you mean The Highwayman Hotel? It's incredibly expensive, sir. I've been to a wedding reception there. It's very pricey – they're the sort of people who'll steal your eyeballs and then come back for the sockets!"

"I'll treat you, Willis. We've got plenty of time. This is good stuff and I need to keep going with my list of…what did I call them?… partnership indicators."

"How many indicators have you got on your list at the moment?"

"Five I think, but we need ten. I like nice round numbers. Is that the hotel? It looks beautiful, doesn't it? Bloody hell, there's a man in period costume on the door. Do we have to pay to go in? Good grief – he's dressed up as a highwayman! But you did say that they were a bunch of robbing ba—"

"—bar stewards can be found in the lounge, sir," said Willis, stealing and finishing Simon's sentence. "Where would you like your coffee? I'll go and order it for you, then leave you in peace."

"No – I'd like you to join me, Willis. At the moment I'm enjoying listening to what's in the front of your mind rather than just looking at the back of your head!"

Willis smiled, enjoying the special moment. Simon had remembered something he had said the month before. "Shall we park here, sir?…then we could walk through the grounds."

"Good idea. Park over there…next to that green Aston."

They gathered their things and slowly walked through the grounds of the famous Highwayman Hotel. They admired the pines and old oaks overlooking the gravelled pathways that meandered between the rhododendrons, bamboo and bright green acers. The grounds were silent, apart from the sound of a woodpecker to their right and a gardener's spluttering old lawnmower away to their left on the slopes of the hotel's famous golf course in the distance. As they passed an ornamental pond, Simon smiled and touched Willis' arm to alert him to some large fish basking on the surface. "Not exactly like your piranhas, Willis?" They moved closer and counted at least a dozen fish moving in clear water between the oxygenating weeds and lily pads.

They entered the hotel and nodded to the doorman. He raised his hat then brought it down with a flurry, pointing to the spacious lounge area overlooking the reservoir, with one long sweep of his arm. The two men smiled at him, then at each other, and continued onto the patio. What seemed like acres of old flagstones provided a beautiful vantage point to admire the wildlife in the foreground and the flotilla of small boats on a man-made lake. Willis noticed that the boats appeared to be going around in circles.

"Probably school kids on holiday, Willis," added Simon, "they're learning the ropes – literally."

They sat down in the lounge. Simon opted for a chair with an adjacent table whilst Willis selected a sumptuous sofa that was so soft and accommodating that he almost disappeared into it. The coffee arrived, together with a pile of ginger biscuits that smelled divine. Willis thought of Mrs. Selsey's cooking and the biscuits he used to enjoy all those years ago on the farm during his school holidays.

The two men emerged half an hour later and slowly returned to the car. Willis checked his map, as they had taken a slight detour to get to the hotel, and Simon continued to scribble on his pad from the back seat. He frequently turned the pages to retrace his thinking and, at times, the pages fluttered so quickly that Willis thought that the pad resembled a Mississippi paddle steamer. They left the hotel car park at a dignified and respectful speed, passing some frustrated golfers near the exit drive that took them along the western side of the lake.

"I've got a great list now. Thanks for your input, Willis. You came up with some great ideas."

"How many did we end up with, sir?" enquired Willis as he slowed to avoid two squirrels. "By the way, if you eat one of those squirrels, sir, it comes with a health and safety warning – it may contain nuts!"

"What are you on about, Willis?" said a puzzled Simon. "I was about to answer your question and now you're talking about bloody squirrels!"

"Sorry, sir."

"Back to planet Earth then, Willis. We went into the hotel with five partnership indicators. Would you like to hear a summary of the others that we came up with over coffee?"

"Yes…and sorry…I forgot to say thank you for the coffee and biscuits," said Willis.

"No problem – glad you enjoyed them. Here we go then," continued Simon. "As we've already covered five, I'll start with indicator number six, then.:

6. Is there any evidence of joint activity between the customer and Alderton's?

Do you remember that one, Willis? Joint product development, joint meetings, joint action plans – that sort of thing. I'll run down the rest of the list:

7. Does the customer willingly accept our new products and services?

8. Are we involved in their strategic planning process?

9. Does the customer give us referrals?

10. Does the customer provide written testimonials or act as a reference site?

11. Does the customer treat us as a dotted-line member of their team?

12. Does the customer give us last-minute opportunities to change our proposal?

13. Do changes in personnel (theirs or ours) effect the relationship?

14. Does the customer copy us in on their emails?

15. Are timings aligned?"

"I've forgotten what that one means," said Willis. "That must be one of yours, sir."

"It's about working with the customer using the same timings? Basically, Alderton's plans need to be aligned with the *customer's* business year, not ours."

"Ah yes," said Willis, "I remember now – are there any more?"

"We're getting a bit thin on the ground now, Willis. Hang on… yes, there are a couple more:

16. Do our customer contacts fight our corner in front of their colleagues?

17. Does the customer treat us as the industry expert?

18. Do we get tipped off by our allies in the account, rather than having to deal with any nasty surprises?"

"That's it, Willis…for today," concluded Simon.

"What about this one," added Willis. "Can Alderton's account managers produce a one-page summary of the customer's business showing what the customer's future plans are?"

"I like that one, Willis. Remember your uncomfortable story earlier this morning when I had to imagine that I had to deliver a short presentation to the customer on the state of *their* business? Well, if we had some sort of one-page summary of where the customer's business is today, where they are going and how they intend to get there, a presentation like that would be a relatively easy task, wouldn't it?"

"So that makes 19 indicators then," said Willis.

"Yes. We need one more for a full house of 20…and I thought we would be struggling to get to ten!" said Simon, looking very pleased with himself.

Willis continued. "Do you remember my earlier comment that it's impossible to make improvements in business unless you know where you're starting from, sir?"

"Well, I suppose that would be true in business and life generally, wouldn't it?" said Simon.

"Right," said Willis. "So maybe indicator number 20 could have something to do with customer feedback and how they feel about the service that you're currently providing."

"Good point, Willis…are we meeting, exceeding or falling short of our customer's expectations? Come to think of it, did you hear that item on 'Business Breakfast' the other day on how customer expectations have changed?"

"No I didn't, actually. What did they say?"

"Well, they said that ten years ago, customer loyalty was determined by suppliers meeting and exceeding expectations. That's an obvious point, but the interesting thing today is that the world of customer service has changed and customer loyalty is driven by *exceeding* expectations – just meeting them is no longer good enough."

"That makes sense to me," said Willis. "Customers, when given a choice of where to spend their money, are going to go back to the place where someone exceeded their expectations and made them feel special. Alderton's customers will forget what you say and do but they're not going to forget how you made them feel, are they? As a matter of interest, how would Colin Durkin, your biggest customer, answer that question – the one about expectations?" said Willis.

"That's what worries me," replied Simon.

"We've just gone through Melton Mowbray, sir," said Willis. "We've still got time to build a list of questions you could ask him. Then, if you listen closely enough, he'll probably explain exactly what he thinks your business is all about."

"You're right, Willis. That's a fair point. I'll create the right environment then ask him some questions to establish his perceptions. I'll jot some down now."

The road twisted and turned for ten miles passing by busy farms and several new housing developments on the edge of pretty villages. The Bentley slowed to allow some racehorses to cross the road. The lead rider waved his approval but Willis didn't notice as he was busy making a mental note of a small, independent Stilton cheese factory on the other side of the road. His whole family loved the stuff.

Simon looked up, unaware of the reason for the delay. "Right, Willis, have a listen to these questions. Imagine that you're Colin Durkin on the receiving end of this lot! What do you think? Be honest…

Colin – where is Alderton's meeting your expectations?
Where are we exceeding your expectations?
Where are we falling short of your expectations?
What has happened since our account manager left?
What unresolved issues are there?
How do we compare to other suppliers in our industry?
How do we compare to suppliers in other industries?
How would you sum up Alderton's in a sentence?
If we could put the clocks back, what could we have done differently?
Do you see us as a supplier or a partner?"

"Those sound like excellent questions, sir…I can imagine your Mr. Durkin responding very well to those," said Willis. "I can think of a couple more, though."

"Go on then, Willis. By the way, we've just passed that famous rose grower on the outskirts of Nottingham – we must be nearly there," said Simon, with a hint of tension in his voice.

Willis continued. "How about:

If Alderton's was an animal or a bird, what would it be?

If you had to give Alderton's marks out of ten, how many marks would you give the company?"

"I'm not sure I like your animal question, Willis," said Simon.

"Give it a go, sir. It worked for me when I took over the tennis committee."

"What do you mean, Willis? This is a serious meeting I'm about to attend – I'm not sure I what your tennis club has to do with it?" protested Simon.

Willis continued. "When I took over the tennis club committee I asked all 150 members that question, as part of a survey we did, and they told us that we were like a Labrador"

"So woofing what?" said Simon, provocatively.

"It wasn't a compliment," said Willis. "As a club they thought we were soft, friendly, loyal, and so on, but not dynamic, aggressive or competitive enough to win any of the local leagues. I won't bore you with the details, but the animal question told us a lot!"

The car left the elevated section of the Nottingham ring road and dropped down onto an industrial estate between a power station and the railway station. They quickly found the entrance to the Durkin and Timperley site and drove slowly past a long line of executive saloons before eventually finding the visitors' spaces.

"See you later, Willis. I'll be about two hours…or two minutes if it goes badly! If I don't emerge from Durkin's office by 12, you'd better call for an ambulance!"

Willis leaned out of the window as Simon started to sprint to the reception area in an attempt to avoid a sudden downpour. "Think positively, sir. Sometimes, when customers are being negative the odds are that you're not the target – you just happen to be within range. Every problem is an opportunity in disguise."

"Not now, Willis, I'm out of here!"

Simon Gray straightened his tie as he took shelter under the canopy entrance to the building. He looked up and admired the acres of reflective glass on the side of Durkin and Timperley's head office. He would later tell Stella that the building reminded him of the opening title sequence from "Dallas", the seventies TV programme. There was black glass everywhere.

Willis stayed on site and busied himself in Durkin and Timperley's showroom and staff shop. Although he didn't have a pass for the shop he came to the conclusion that the young man behind the counter probably thought that he was Colin Durkin's new driver. With his chauffeur's hat under his arm, Willis had entered the staff shop with an air of natural authority and left an hour or so later with discounted purchases under his other arm, in a similar manner. He was back at the Bentley by midday, but Simon didn't emerge until 2pm.

Fortunately, the scan button on the Bentley's radio managed to locate Johann Sebastian Bach who, along with the Berlin Philharmonic Orchestra, orchestra, very kindly managed to fill the time with their Brandenburg Concerto. Willis missed part of their performance due to the call of nature and a return trip via the staff canteen, where he bought a sandwich and an apple.

His musical afternoon ended when Simon opened the door and tossed his things across the back seat as he folded his jacket. "Home please, Willis. That's it for today. I thought we might have time to call in to see another customer on the way back but they phoned my mobile to re-arrange the meeting. It's probably a good job, really, I'm done-in!"

The Bentley slid quietly and effortlessly out of the car park and headed south. Major road works near West Bridgford soon halted their progress but provided an opportunity for the inevitable post-meeting interrogation from Willis.

"So how was your Mr. Durkin then?" enquired Willis.

"Firm but fair," replied Simon. "The opening minutes were a little tense. He said that he believed business was a lot like tennis and that those who don't serve well, lose!"

"And presumably, he thinks that Alderton's isn't serving well at the moment?" enquired Willis.

"Right," said Simon, "he thinks that we're 'two sets down, about to start the third set...and likely to lose the match'."

"Still something to play for, then!" said Willis, encouragingly.

"Right again," said Simon. "I can't complain, really. As I said, he was very fair. By the way, the questions we prepared worked well, Willis...very well, in fact."

"Really, sir. Any surprises?"

"Well, he thinks that we're falling short of expectations in five areas, meeting expectations in two areas and exceeding expectations in only one area. He thinks that we're a six out of ten company that's industry average. He sees us as a supplier not a partner and thinks that we're worse than suppliers in other industry sectors who come to see him. He thinks that the last account manager was 'a bore' and the one before that an 'indiscreet gossip'. Apart from that…he thinks we're wonderful!"

"Hmmmm…not to worry." Willis was desperately trying to think of something positive and uplifting to say. "Well, sometimes you can be drowned by too much praise but saved by a little constructive criticism! No such thing as bad feedback, I always say – all feedback is good feedback."

Simon was looking out of the window and said nothing.

"So it was a much longer meeting than you were expecting, wasn't it?" continued Willis.

"Yes it was," replied Simon. "After he'd beaten me up he did take me for lunch so I can't think too harshly of him. I also got an opportunity to ask a few more questions about their future."

"What sort of questions do you mean?" said Willis, as he pulled up at a zebra crossing by the university. Hundreds of students appeared to be heading home for pizza and chips.

"I asked him how his business was changing, what pressures they were under from outside the business, what pressures they were under from inside the business, what his objectives for next year were, where he would be happy to see us have more of his business providing we sorted out the current problems, what we would have to do to move from six out of ten marks to ten out of ten marks…oh, and another thing…he thinks that we're an elephant!"

"So you asked him the animal or bird question, then?" said Willis.

"Clearly," replied Simon. "He thinks we're an elephant because we're *'intelligent, but slow'*, we're *'lumbering, unable to change direction quickly'*…and because we *'occasionally crap on people from a height'*!"

"Hmmm," replied Willis. "Well at least you now know where you're starting from! But getting it wrong is also part of getting it right, of course. As Henry Ford once said: *'It's an opportunity for you to begin, more intelligently, once again'*."

"Maybe," replied Simon, as he gazed out of the window at the slowly moving traffic building up on the ring road. "One thing's certain – Colin Durkin's perceptions have now become Alderton's rather dismal reality!"

Willis tried again to motivate his tired boss. "You can't have a rainbow without an occasional storm and a few clouds," he said, as he turned on the windscreen wipers to deal with a sudden downpour.

"Good timing with the rain, Willis. You must have a direct line to God – your talents are endless!"

"Thank you, sir," said Willis, unperturbed by the gloomy sarcasm.

"And can we cut down on the number of one-liners please, Willis!" Simon returned to his pad and flipped a couple of pages.

"Certainly, sir. I was only trying to offer a few words of encouragement."

Ten minutes passed and Willis was ready with another idea. "He was born in 1947."

"Who was?" said a surprised Simon.

"Try and guess who I'm talking about," said Willis. "Here's another clue – he always enjoyed his sport but struggled with the standard technique. Do you know who it is yet?"

"Of course I don't," said an irritated Simon. "If we must play your stupid game, I need some more clues please."

Willis responded. "He went to the Olympics and represented the USA. He was in the same Games as his fellow countrymen Tommy Smith and John Carlos."

"Do you mean the black power salute guys?" enquired Simon.

"The very same," replied Willis. "My mystery man won the gold medal and his magical number was 88.5." Willis looked up at the rear-view mirror. "Have you got him yet?"

"Is it the high jumper, Dick Fosbury?" said Simon.

"It certainly is – well done! He was the guy who developed the high jump technique that's now widely regarded as standard."

"He was before my time, Willis, but I've seen the film footage. He went over the bar backwards, didn't he?"

"He did, sir. He got as far as he could get with the standard technique and realised that something had to change. He developed a new technique that meant he could only move forwards in his sport by going over the bar backwards! To put it another way, he changed the rules of the game and stood out from his competitors rather than standing up to them. Differentiation, I think you called it!" Willis paused and smiled.

"Willis, are we going home the same way?

"We are, sir…unless you want me to take another route?"

"No, let's go back to the hotel. We can have another cup of coffee or tea. I want to get this whole customer service and key account management thing sorted. I've got some good ideas in my head and probably a lot of bad ones. Your Fosbury story has got me thinking too. Perhaps an Earl Grey will help clear my mind."

"Fine, sir, we're about 45 minutes away – would you like me to keep quiet?"

"How does that work then, Willis? I'm not sure that you *can* keep quiet, can you?" said Simon, smiling at his own joke.

Willis, noticing Simon's smile in the rear-view mirror, did not take offence. He obliged with silence and guided the Bentley through the early- afternoon traffic back to the Highwayman Hotel. Little had changed, he thought, apart from the rain that had reduced the ranks of the golfers. There were fewer cars, so he managed to park the car in a bay close to the hotel entrance. .

Simon walked ahead, deep in thought, and soon found some damp golfers settling down to their refreshments in the lounge. He continued to walk through the long corridors and annexes. Willis eventually found him in the library and sat down within range, but just out of sight.

They were soon joined by an enthusiastic young waiter who took their order, then reappeared ten minutes later. Willis stood up, leaned over, poured the Earl Grey and awaited further instructions.

"It's quieter in here," observed Simon, "none of those noisy bloody golfers!"

"I see that they've abandoned their green tees and opted for cream teas," said Willis with a smile on his face.

"Very good, Willis, very good! So you can make them up yourself then? I thought all your one-liners were always borrowed from somebody else – you know, all these ex-CEOs that you've seen off over the years!"

"I should have asked you if you wanted the milk in first," said Willis, choosing to ignore Simon's remark.

The two men sat sipping their Earl Grey teas but Simon looked impatient and restless. This time, he barely noticed the fixtures and fittings of one of Olde England's finest hotels. He scribbled furiously on his pad whilst Willis surveyed the rows of dusty brown books recalling old colonial battles and famous polar expeditions from the past. Sensing Simon's needs, he buried his nose in a book on William Wilberforce and the abolition of slavery.

Simon eventually looked up. "Right then, Willis. I need your thoughts on this. I think I've come to a number of conclusions about Alderton's future and how all of this key account management stuff affects us," said Simon, looking down at his notes. "There are some things in here that I need to share with the strategic working party."

"And what are these things, sir?" said Willis, obligingly.

"A number of things, actually," continued Simon. "Firstly, I've come to the conclusion that, at the moment, we're in a nightmare situation because Alderton's is putting in lots of activity but there's no clear vision for the future. I want us to become experts in the customer's world! This will help to improve our profitability as a direct result of improving the customer's profitability first. We need to help them grow or, as you said earlier, help them make a bigger cake rather than fighting over a slice of the cake.

"Secondly, our account managers have got to stop being gossips and bores and become brilliant at talking to customers about *themselves*!"

Willis put his cup down. He was impressed with Simon's passion and commitment which, in their short time together, he had not seen before.

Simon continued. "Thirdly, I'm going to make key account management a major strategy – a strategic bridge, if you like, to help us deliver our vision for the future."

"Nice language, sir. Strategic Bridge…that's very visual…very evocative."

"Fourthly, I'm going to make sure that all the right KAM foundation stones are in place. You've probably noticed that I've been making notes, Willis. Let me read you some of the stuff I've written since my meeting with Colin Durkin. At the moment, Alderton's believes that it's the customer's job to remember us. This action plan will make sure that customers don't have the opportunity to forget us:

1. I am going to introduce regular key account audits – there will be a process for proactively auditing the perceptions of Alderton's most important customers. We need to establish our customers' perceptions and also find out more about our competitors."

"Good idea, sir. The more you know about your competitors, the fewer you have."

Simon looked up, said nothing but glared. Willis remembered Simon's comment about the one-liners and took the hint.

Simon continued:

"2. I am going to make sure that we resolve all outstanding problems and issues before we attempt to sell additional services to these key accounts.

3. Key account management will become part of the Board's daily life – I realise now that KAM needs to start at the top or it will not start at all.

4. We will no longer neglect our key accounts until it is time for us to renegotiate the contract. From now on, contract renewal will start on day one.

5. I am going to have a word with our FD who has been putting pressure on the sales team. He needs to understand that key account management is a medium-long term strategy and that it is not a quick fix to produce a short-term result. Alderton's needs to understand that we will sometimes have to spend this year's budget in pursuit of next year's results.

6. I am going to restructure the sales office and support teams. We've had a lot of tribal warfare, so I'm told, between the various factions and departments – and between the departments and head office in Hendon. I am going to restructure the business so that the sites become responsible for providing a service to customers and head office becomes responsible for providing an internal service to them. We need to understand that the quality of service we give the customer is influenced by the quality of service we give each other! Alderton's needs to understand that there are only two roles in this company – customers and suppliers. Sometimes we are the customer and sometimes we are the supplier.

7. I am going to make sure that key account management is something that we do with customers, not to customers. I'm going to set up a series of best practice and networking meetings with customers from the same market sector and I'm also going to invite some of them to talk to us at conferences.

8. I am going to draw up a KASH Profile for an Alderton's account manager showing the knowledge, attitudes, skills and habits needed to perform effectively in the role. In the event of an account manager leaving the company, the KASH Profile would drive the recruitment process as it would show the profile of the ideal candidate.

9. I am going to introduce a 'red tape' prize for Alderton's people who have ideas on how to reduce the amount of red tape and bureaucracy – the bullshit that gets in the way of effective key account management

10. I'm going to run quarterly 'Lost Account Review Days' to understand why we lost the account and what is needed to win the customer back – these sessions will be attended by all departmental managers

11. I am going to put pallets of returned product in the staff canteen so that we are all confronted by the implications of any shoddy, poor quality work

12. I am going to charge my time back to departments that cause key account grief – if I have to get involved to sort things out, the department will have to pay normal consultancy rates for my time.

13. I am going to make sure that the right people are managing the right accounts."

"Is that not the case at the moment, sir?" enquired Willis.

"No, sadly it isn't. At the moment the customer gets the account manager who happens to live closest to them! Fate and circumstance haven't worked well for us, Willis. From now on we need to make sure that the best account manager for the job is handling each key account."

"But what does that actually mean, sir?"

"It means, Willis, that each key account will be managed by the person who is best qualified to help the customer achieve *their* objectives and the person who is best qualified to help Alderton's achieve its objectives. 'Situational' account management, if you like. Where was I? Yes, thank you, I will have another cup of tea but no more of those delicious biscuits. I'll need to spend another week in the gym. So, let me carry on:

14. I'm going to introduce, via the strategic workshops, the issue of measuring progress with our key accounts.

I'm not sure how this one will work, Willis, I need to revisit it. However, I do know that what gets measured gets done. Make a note of that one-liner, by the way, Willis – mind you, you probably invented it! Anyway:

15. I want people to understand that, from now on, key account management within Alderton's is going to be a team sport. Although I've heard my account managers use the phrase 'my customer', for some of their smaller accounts I want them to use the phrase 'our customer' when referring to our key accounts. I'm going to make sure that time is set aside for director activity in the field and I am also going to introduce the idea of a skills matrix so that we know which account managers have expertise in each of our market sectors."

"How would that help, sir? I'm not sure I understand that one," said Willis, looking a little puzzled.

"It would mean that when an account manager has a major meeting or presentation to make in a market sector that he or she isn't familiar with, they would know which colleague to phone for advice or to involve in the meeting," replied Simon.

"Will their busy diaries allow for that?" said Willis.

"Not at the moment, Willis…but they will do! I'm going to insist that, for one day each month, time is allocated for these team days. I'm also going to introduce quarterly key account team reviews where representatives from sales, operations, IT, finance and customer service get together to review progress within each account."

"And how will these teams keep up with developments in between these quarterly sessions?" said Willis.

"Another good point, Willis. I'm going to suggest that we build highly visible account plans. There will be some sort of file on our system that bolts together the various pieces of intelligence we need for each key account, our intentions for the future and the tactics and implementation plan needed to achieve them."

"Don't you have that sort of thing at the moment, sir?" said Willis, a hint of surprise in his voice.

"No we don't, Willis. At the moment, we have an over-complicated data-capture system that apparently loses things alphabetically!"

Willis laughed but, sensing the seriousness of the moment, settled down again quickly and raised the ornate silver teapot once more. "I've got an idea," he said. "Why don't you call this team account plan 'The Partner Plan'? Isn't that a more positive phrase than referring to it as a "'file'? A plan looks forward, not backwards."

"Great idea, Willis, let me make a note of that. I like that…The Partner Plan! I'll raise that at the workshop and see if we can decide what it should contain."

"Have you heard the story about the two men on the canal, sir?"

"No," said Simon, "but I think I'm about to!"

"Well, the two men were on a canal – one in a rowing boat and the other in a canoe. After ten minutes, the man in the rowing boat asked the canoeist to pull into the side and swap over. The canoeist, who was a little confused, resisted and pointed out to his friend that they were travelling at the same speed and that there would be no point in swapping over. They continued for another ten minutes then the man in the rowing boat pulled into the side, insisting once again that they swap over. 'What exactly is your problem?' said the confused canoeist. The man with the rowing boat smiled. 'Well, I've been thinking about this since we set off. I've been looking backwards – at where I've come from. You're looking forwards – where you are going to'!"

"Nice story," said Simon. "The partner plan would certainly be a canoe, wouldn't it? It would look to the future, not just report on the past. I might use your canoe story when I'm with the strategic working party, if that's OK with you, Willis?"

"Fine, sir, absolutely fine. Glad I can help."

The two men left the hotel at 5.30pm and headed south-east to join the A1. After a few miles Willis held up and waved a magazine to attract Simon's attention.

"I came across this in their reception, sir. If you're looking for a good read, it has some interesting statistics in it about customer service. Apparently a five per cent increase in customer retention leads to an increase in profits of between 25 per cent and 125 per cent. Also, 70 per cent of customers who have a complaint resolved to their compete satisfaction are more loyal after the complaint than they were before it."

"Really? I'd better have a look at it then, Willis."

Simon said nothing for the next hour. Willis could see that his passenger was deep in thought. Simon would remain motionless for five minutes, looking very thoughtful, then enthusiastically move his pink pencil across his pad, noting more gems and questions that would be raised with the strategic working party.

With Mapleford church steeple on the horizon, Simon finally put down his paperwork and began packing his briefcase.

"I liked Nottingham, Willis…or the little we saw of it. No sign of Robin Hood though."

"He lives on Maid Marion Way now," said Willis. "His statue and the castle still get a huge number of visitors."

"I thought I saw the football ground, Willis. Is it on the same side of the river as the county cricket ground?"

"It's on the same side of the river but on the opposite side of the road, sir. By the way, did you ever hear the Clough story about his conversation with the lad in the boot room?" enquired Willis.

"Clough?" asked Simon.

"You know, sir…Brian Clough, the Nottingham Forest football club manager."

"Of course. I imagine that there are lots of stories about him" said Simon. "He was a legendary figure in the city, wasn't he?"

"He certainly was, sir. Anyway, 'Cloughie', as he was called, phoned one of the lads in the boot room and said, 'Go and get me a coffee, young man'."

Simon chuckled. "That's a very good impression of him, Willis."

Willis acknowledged the compliment and continued. "The lad on the other end of the phone said, 'I'm busy'. Clough repeated his request, with a few choice words added no doubt, and said, 'Listen son, if you know what's good for you, go and get me a bloody coffee – now!' The lad stood his ground and said, 'No, I'm busy at the moment but I'll fetch it in half an hour…when I've finished polishing these boots.'

"Clough, who was apparently incandescent with rage, said, 'Do you know who you're talking to?' and the lad said, 'Yes, you're Mr. Clough, the manager'. 'Absolutely right son,' replied Cloughie. 'And do you know who *you're* talking to, Mr. Clough?' asked the lad. 'No son, I don't,' said Clough. 'Good,' said the lad, 'so bugger off and get your own bloody coffee!'"

Simon and Willis laughed loudly together. It was a great way to end their day.

The Bentley slowed as the Gray household came into view. Simon could see Claire and Lucy playing in the front garden with a friend. Stella was in the front garden, still wearing her stylish work outfit, with a trowel in one hand and an ornamental conifer in the other. Simon gathered his things, climbed out of the Bentley and leaned into the open window. "No doubt you're going to tell me the moral of the Clough story, Willis?"

"Maybe the moral is that we should all end the day with some laughter. I think that laughter is good exercise – it's a bit like jogging on the inside!"

"You're right, Willis. I like that one! See you next month. I'll phone you if there are any changes to the plan."

"Fine, sir, have a good month then," said Willis, watching as Simon walked across the lawn, abandoned his briefcase and kicked a football past Lucy into her makeshift goal. He then proceeded to run behind the goal, waving to an imaginary crowd of adoring fans. "Another goal for Forest!" he shouted. "The Cup is theirs once again! Gray has secured his place in Forest's long history!"

"What Forest, Daddy? asked a puzzled Lucy.

"Doesn't matter, darling," said Stella, smiling. "It's just your dad being a complete...dad!"

Simon put his arm around Lucy's shoulder to console her for letting in his match-winning goal. He beckoned to Claire and her friend, collected the briefcase, grabbed Stella with his other arm and ran towards the front door. "And there goes the team, through the tunnel, heading for the showers!" he shouted. The girls squealed and wriggled free, narrowly avoiding the threat of an early bath. They returned to the garden and Simon hugged Stella as they stood together in the doorway. He brushed Stella's hair from her face and gave her a long kiss before squeezing her backside. She pretended to be offended, smiled and kissed him on his forehead.

"Right then, Mrs. Gray, I think it's time for me to pour you a glass of wine while you relax in a nice warm bath," said Simon.

"Where are you going, Mummy? Come back and play!"

"I'm just going to run a bath for Daddy," said Stella, as she shut the door behind her.

Meanwhile, George Willis smiled. He was pleased to see that all was well with the Gray family.

He started the Bentley and made his way out of Mapleford, back to the main road. He paused for a minute at the junction to allow a harvester and a long queue of traffic to pass by. As he waited, he stretched his arms and legs and smiled once again. Simon Gray was a good student, appeared to be learning a lot and was learning very quickly.

"Willis, old chap, your plan is coming together nicely…very nicely in fact!"

Wit and Wisdom
Chapter 2 Summary

1. It is difficult to make improvements in business, or in life, unless you know where you are starting from!

2. Unhappy customers are your greatest source of learning (Bill Gates).

3. Good companies are never expensive even if they charge a lot – it is about value, not cost. Remember that VAT means Value Added Tomorrow.

4. The first rule of business is to look after your key accounts before someone else does. Customers will forget what you say and do but they will never forget how you made them feel.

5. The only safe customer is one where you are exceeding their expectations, not just meeting them.

6. If you become an expert in the customer's world you will probably never have to sell again.

7. The role of a key account manager is to improve profitability as a result of improving the customers' profitability – it is not about fighting over a slice of the cake – it is about creating a bigger cake for the customer.

8. Key account management is a team sport – it is not about solo performances.

9. Honest differences, expressed openly, are often a sign of healthy progress.

10. Stand out from your competitors – don't stand up to them. Sometimes, you have to 'do a Fosbury' and go over the bar backwards to move forwards.

Chapter 3
They Decide If You Are A Leader, Not You!

It was 29 August and the golden-tanned Grays were re-discovering their house in the English countryside, having returned from Orlando the day before. Whilst the children were still asleep, Stella dealt with her 253 emails, then made a start on the girls' washing. However, she was still in holiday mood and, accompanied by Mick Hucknall and the Scissor Sisters, tossed the clothes into several piles and danced her way across the landing and around the bedrooms.

Claire and Lucy had been up for hours. They were playing in their bedroom with the collection of toys and souvenirs from Disney and MGM Studios that now littered the floor. Still high on a heady mixture of jet lag and adrenaline, they picked up each toy and played with it before the attraction of the next became irresistible. Stella threatened to put the toys in the dustbin unless they were neatly stored by the time she got to their room. The girls knew that their mother was only joking – or was she? By 9am they had responded to Stella's "threats" and were munching their way through Coco-Pops and toast in the kitchen. Simon was busy putting the dishes away and wiping the worktop surfaces.

"What time are you fetching Rory, dad?" shouted Clair, noticing the empty dog basket.

"I'm not, darling, your mother is fetching him later today," replied Simon.

"Can we give Rory his present today?" asked Lucy.

"And what present is that, Lucy, my darling?"

"The red bone shaped like the Death Ray Blaster at that steam park," said Lucy.

"I think you mean 'theme park'," grinned Simon. "Yes, of course you can give him your present today – will he know what to do with your Death Ray whatever-it-was bone?"

"He'll be able to shoot the squirrels with it," said Lucy enthusiastically. "He'll shoot their heads off and all the blood will squirt out!"

"Urrrrgh!" shrieked Claire, who proceeded to spread a dollop of red jam on her toast, as if to make some gory point. Simon smiled and headed for his study, shaking his head. Two weeks of adventures in Florida had given his daughters a new, tom-boy dimension.

Their surprise house-guest, Gerry Manning, joined Simon in the study. He had arrived the night before to share some figures and statistics with Simon. The Grays had known that he would be coming sometime that week but, as his arrival had been only two hours after their return from Florida, it had put the household under considerable pressure and caused some friction between Simon and Stella. As Finance Director, Gerry Manning had been instructed to hold the fort during Simon's absence but overall company performance was still poor, the numbers were worrying, but slowly improving, and Gerry had decided that Simon needed to see them at the earliest possible opportunity.

For the third time in as many months, the Bentley slowly crunched its way through the pea gravel of the Gray's drive in Mapleford. George Willis sat behind the wheel looking as smart and presentable as ever. His crisply-ironed white shirt was finished off with an untypical peach and lime coloured tie that would have looked at home in a Carnaby Street boutique in 1967. It was an anniversary present from his wife, Anne.

Parking the car, he decided to stretch his legs as he was a little early. He walked around the Gray's front garden but, as he felt he was trespassing, he stayed on the slate path that meandered through a beautiful Lakeland landscaped garden, complete with an impressive waterfall and fish pond.

He walked slowly past a row of proud lupins and inspected them for signs of greenfly. He bent over, touched the leaves and petals and, from a distance, must have looked like an ageing member of the Royal Family inspecting the front rank of soldiers on parade. A family of squirrels darted through the trees behind the orchard. Autumn was on the way and Mapleford was changing from greens, pinks and blues to a rich tapestry of reds, yellows and browns. After a further five minutes of sniffing the scent on the roses, re-arranging the tangled sweet peas and admiring the fish, Willis' attention was caught by the sound of a closing car door. He quickly turned to see that Simon was in the back seat of the Bentley with another man by his side.

"Looking for a few piranhas Willis?" laughed Simon. "When you're ready, we'll be off then!" Willis walked quickly to the car, looking a little flustered. "Late on parade, Willis? Unlike you, isn't it? Whatever next!"

"I wasn't late actually, sir. I was early and thought I would spend a few moments enjoying your garden – I hope you don't mind?"

"Not at all, Willis, not at all. So how are you today? Nice tie by the way – must be your birthday then?" enquired Simon.

"I'm very well, thank you," replied Willis, "and as far as your second question is concerned, it was an anniversary present from my wife. I'm glad you like it. Good morning to you both." Willis glanced in the rear-view mirror, looking for an opportunity to change the subject. "You're looking very brown, sir."

"Thank you, Willis. I'll be happy to share my holiday stories with you later but right now, I'd like to introduce you to Gerry Manning, Finance Director at Alderton's," said Simon, barely acknowledging Willis' remark.

"Good morning, sir, nice to meet you too. I'm Willis." He started the car and headed for the main road.

Gerry Manning leaned forward. "Hi – I'm Gerry. Sorry, what did you say your name was?"

Simon intercepted Gerry's question. "He prefers to be called Willis, Gerry. Don't ask him why."

"I'm cool with that, Willis," said Gerry Manning. "Very British… very upstairs and downstairs and all that traditional class stuff that you guys like."

"You'll like this too Gerry – he also prefers to call me 'sir'," said Simon, as they passed by a windswept postman in the lane.

"I think of it as a mark of respect," added Willis defensively.

"I'm cool with that too, Willis. You can call me sir, bring me my meals and polish my shoes any time you like," said Gerry, settling down on the back seat of the Bentley.

Willis scowled, clearly irritated by Gerry Manning's remark. Simon leaned forward to engage Willis' attention. "I assume you got my text message last week, Willis. Mr. Manning came down last night for a working supper to go through a few statistics with me. We need to take him back to the station before going up to Dudley."

"Very good, sir," said Willis. "Did you have a useful meeting last night discussing…your statistics?"

"Very," said Simon, nodding at Gerry for confirmation. "Do I sense a problem?"

"Well, you know what they say about statistics, don't you?" said Willis. "*Statistics are rather like a lamp post to a drunken man*, etc etc."

Gerry Manning was surprised by the comment and glanced at Simon for a reaction and guidance. Simon was unruffled. He was used to it. "Come on then, Willis? Give me the next instalment…"

"*Statistics are like a lamp post to a drunken man because they're more for leaning on than illumination!*" said Willis.

"Thank you for that, Willis… so early in the day too! I can't say that I've missed your strange sense of humour whilst I've been away," said Simon, slowly shaking his head as he looked out of the window.

Gerry felt uncomfortable with Willis and Simon's banter and attempted to move the conversation on. "Err…I think that statistics are very important, actually. I used to teach the subject in college, back home in Boston years ago," he said.

"There are only three reasons to be a teacher," said Willis.

Simon intercepted the remark. "I hope that this is going to be a clean and inoffensive remark, Willis."

"The three reasons to be a teacher are called Christmas, Easter and Summer," replied Willis.

"What does he mean by that?" said Gerry, quickly glancing in Simon's direction.

"Don't let it bother you, Gerry. He means holidays…vacations. It's just his rather strange way…isn't it, Willis?"

"If you say so, sir, if you say so."

"How long will it take me to get to Worcester on the train, Willis?" said Gerry, quickly changing the subject.

"About two hours, if you're lucky, sir," replied Willis

Simon leaned forward. "Willis, if time is on our side perhaps we could take a detour through some of our lovely English countryside.

Gerry isn't used to seeing all this green back in Boston."

"Except on St. Patrick's Day!" added Gerry, laughing loudly at his own joke.

The Bentley left the dual carriageway and toured the countryside en-route to the station. Simon looked relaxed but Gerry Manning still looked confused and restless.

"Hey, Willis, I've got a question for you," he said finally. "Why do many British people tend to drive their German cars to an English pub, then travel home via the Indian takeaway to sit on Swedish furniture watching American TV shows on their Japanese TV's?"

"Very amusing, sir," said Willis trying to summon a polite smile. "I'm happy to talk about other countries but whilst we're on the subject, is it true that war is God's way of teaching you Americans geography?"

There was total silence on the back seat. "Enough, Willis, where are your manners? Don't step on Gerry's shoes again – he's my guest!" protested Simon, his cheeks reddening once again.

"Oh, I never step on anyone's shoes, sir, as they might be connected to the arse that I have to lick tomorrow!"

"Shut up, Willis, please shut up. We've got some work to do in the back here – just drive the bloody car!"

Thirty minutes went by as Simon and Gerry chatted about the various production numbers and sales ratios that were the cause of major concern. Willis was the only one who actually noticed the "English countryside" that morning. They dropped Gerry at the station, then headed north once again. Simon tidied his papers, leaned back and stretched his legs.

"Thanks for being so welcoming to our American neighbour, Willis! Sometimes you're the perfect gentleman and, other times, you can be a bit of a mystery to me. What's the matter with you today, for goodness sake? You obviously think that my FD is an idiot otherwise you wouldn't have argued with him like that!"

Willis looked up. "He proves the theory that light travels faster than sound, doesn't he?"

"What do you mean?" said a puzzled Simon.

"Well…he appeared bright until I heard him speak! I'm sorry but I had enough of him testiculating on the back seat."

"What are you on about, Willis?" said Simon.

"Waving his arms about and talking bollocks!" added Willis. "And by the way, I never argue with idiots, sir, as they tend to drag you down to their level, then beat you with their experience!"

"Enough, Willis...you know damn well that you were completely out of order! Gerry brings a lot of value to the business."

"Is that when he leaves the room?" enquired Willis. There was complete silence on the back seat. Willis said nothing and looked a little sheepish for the next ten minutes.

Eventually, Simon breathed deeply and smiled. "So what sort of weekend did you have," he asked, trying to preserve his calm and happy mental state from Florida.

"Not bad, sir, not bad."

"Nothing good, then?"

"Oh yes, plenty! We had some guests staying for the weekend – some old neighbours from years ago. I like having people around for a day but a whole weekend is a bit too much at times. House guests are the sort of people who invade your house without paying and expect to be served meals at regular intervals! My old neighbour, Roger, is a bit of a yawn as well. He thinks he's a farmer but has never really mastered it since he left the bank years ago."

"You mean he's a bit of a hobby farmer?" enquired Simon.

"Let me just say that if a farm is an irregular patch of nettles containing a fool and his wife who didn't know enough to stay in the city, then Roger fits the bill perfectly! And yourself, sir...what about your holiday?"

"We had a great time on holiday, Willis, thank you. The Americans do it all so well, don't they? Customer service at its best! Anyway, enough of all that. You'll know from my text message that we're staying overnight at the Brierley Manor Hotel, partly because I suspected that we might have a late start this morning and partly because I want to spend more time sorting out the ongoing problems in Dudley tomorrow."

"No problem, sir, I've packed my toothbrush. If I need to stay away, that's OK with me. Whatever it takes," said Willis, keenly re-stating his commitment to the Alderton's cause.

"Good," said Simon, "and is your wife happy with you staying away tonight?"

"Oh yes," said Willis, "Anne is used to it. So what's on your agenda in Dudley, sir?"

"That question sounds familiar, Willis. I think that was one of the first questions you asked me a couple of months ago. I feel better equipped to answer that now. We're going to Dudley to try and find out why they're not responding to change in the same way as the Lightwater site. For whatever reason, the Light Side is still way out in front on all aspects of production performance. I think I'm going to show the management team at the Dark Side the league tables to shake them up a bit – to motivate some sort of reaction."

"Like them downing tools, presumably?" said Willis, glancing up at the mirror.

Simon winced at Willis's question but remained calm. He was beginning to understand how Willis thought and worked. "I don't see why they would down tools, Willis, just because I'm going to show them a few numbers."

"What sort of behaviour do you get from them now?" said Willis.

"Not good, I'm afraid – sickness is high, factory downtime is high, I'm sure that some of the alleged machinery problems are sabotage. They're a surly lot, actually."

Willis sighed. "Ah well, some might say that managers get the workforce *they* deserve," he said.

Simon leaned forward. "You mean that poor performance from the workforce is all Management's fault?"

"Perhaps it is, sir," said Willis. "Have you heard of Field Marshall Slim?"

"I never knew him personally," taunted Simon, "but I know who you mean. So what?"

"Well, he believed that there was no such thing as a bad regiment – just bad officers. He believed that good officers could turn a bad regiment around and drive it forward with renewed vigour and motivation."

"That was a long time ago, Willis, the world has moved on," argued Simon.

"Ah, but nothing has changed, sir," said Willis. "You might have your new technology and new systems today but the definition of leadership will never change. It's the same now as it was when Jesus was around and will be the same in another 2000 years' time."

"Really, Willis? And your definition is what, exactly?"

"You sound a little tired of my remarks, sir – perhaps I should just do the driving, as you once said."

"No, Willis, I *am* interested. Don't take your bat home just because I may have a different view from yours. Now, are you going to tell me or not?"

"Just a minute, sir." Willis slowed to join a queue of vehicles trying to avoid a car that had broken down in the outside lane. A young man stood looking at his crumpled bumper in shock and disbelief. With mobile phone in hand, he was guiding the emergency services in to help him.

"Right, where was I? Sorry about that, sir."

"You were just about to enlighten me on the definition of leadership…according to the Willis School of Leadership," said Simon.

"Ah yes," said Willis, choosing not to react to Simon's remark. "Well, when you think about it, there are some things in business that people have to comply with, like hours of work or health and safety procedures and that sort of thing. But the majority of things that really matter in business rely on people *wanting* to do them."

"Like what?" said Simon, sucking on the end of his replacement Cross pen as he casually looked out of the window.

"Things like creativity…and customer service…and cooperation with colleagues. These things rely on people *wanting* to do them."

"So, according to you, Willis, leadership is about inspiring action then?" asked Simon.

"No, I think leadership is about inspiring *willing action*," concluded Willis, slowly emphasising the words to make his point. "It's not about consent, it's about commitment. As the old Chinese proverb says: *'He who complies against his will is of his own opinion still!'* Any idiot can get their people to nod their consent, but to get their genuine commitment is a very different ball game."

"So what have I got in Dudley, then, Willis – a lack of leaders?" asked Simon.

"From the sound of it, sir…yes! You appear to have bosses in Dudley and not leaders," said Willis, in a calm but authoritative voice. He looked up again at the rear-view mirror and could see that Simon was looking interested but uncomfortable. He was shuffling from side to side as if he was suffering from a bad case of haemorrhoids. Willis continued. "Did I see you write something down, sir?" he asked.

"I hope not, Willis, you're supposed to be looking at the bloody road!" said Simon. "But you're right Willis…I did write a couple of notes down, if you really want to know." He sighed as he turned back the page of his leather-bound notebook. "I wrote down the words 'bosses not leaders'…with a question mark. Are you happy now, Willis?"

"I think you might be missing a few extra words, sir."

"Really? You don't say!" said Simon, whose face had now coloured to resemble a ripened plum. "Well go on then, Willis, finish off what you're saying. My pen is poised – I'm waiting for the piranhas to swim around again and bite me on my bits! Come on – let's get it over with. Add your extra words! *'I've got bosses not leaders because…'* What do you want me to write next?"

"…because…perhaps the Alderton's board also consists of bosses not leaders," added Willis. He paused and waited for the reaction. It came quickly.

"That's enough, Willis, I've had enough! Stop snapping around my sensitive parts and making my life so bloody uncomfortable. I'll concentrate on managing my business and while we're on the subject, just remember the business you're in – minding your fucking own! Now just drive the bloody car! In fact, no, don't drive the bloody car! Pull into that garden centre coming up on the left. There! There! Steady or you'll miss it. I know it's early in the day but I could do with a break and some fresh air. Pull over, Willis! Pull over now!"

Simon got out, slammed the car door, stormed off and disappeared through a green arch marked "Toilets and Tea Shop". A woman and her surprised young daughter were parted as Simon walked purposefully between them without saying a word. Willis remained in the Bentley, deep in thought. He entered the garden centre 20 minutes later to find Simon sipping his coffee. Simon, sensing Willis' presence, looked up, managed to avoid direct eye contact and pointed to the counter. Willis collected a tray and made his way to the fresh-faced lad behind a tower of cups and mugs. He ordered a coffee and, whilst the machine fizzed, steamed and spluttered, looked over towards Simon who was now writing on his pad.

Willis approached slowly. "I'd like to apologise, sir. It's not my place to say things like that. I'm very sorry."

Simon looked up slowly and beckoned Willis to sit down. He leaned back and looked Willis in the eye. "Sorry for what, Willis?"

"Sorry for speaking out of turn, sir. It won't happen again," said Willis.

Simon rubbed his eyes, loosened his tie and said, "You don't need to apologise, Willis…not for being on the right track, anyway." Willis was completely surprised by the remark but chose to say nothing. Simon did not look angry. In fact he looked calm but vacant.

Willis blew across the top of his mug to cool the hot, brown liquid that claimed to be "exclusive" coffee. He sipped slowly, grimaced, but remained silent. Simon looked down at his pad, where one single sentence looked back at him, accusingly: *I have got bosses not leaders…because perhaps the Alderton's board also consists of bosses not leaders.* He managed a brief smile. "I'm going to staple this to your P45, Willis."

Willis glanced at Simon, sensed that he wasn't being serious, but went along with the remark anyway. "I understand, sir. When might that be?"

"Not until I've understood a little more," said Simon, "then I'm going to fire you!"

Willis smiled again. "As you wish, sir, as you wish."

Simon appeared relaxed as he slowly stirred his coffee. He looked thoughtful. "I suppose I should complete the paragraph, Willis, shouldn't I? You know…take the final step?"

Willis smiled again, acutely aware that they were approaching a critical point in their uneasy relationship. He paused and smiled, waiting for Simon to look him in the eye. "That would be for you to decide, sir, not me," he said.

"What you really mean, Willis, is that a true *leader* would decide to take the final step but a boss wouldn't. I'm happy to do it as I'm going to be a good leader, even if I've got a few shortcomings now." Willis was surprised by Simon's openness and consciously sipped his coffee to ensure that he did not say anything.

Simon smiled as he straightened the piece of paper. He took out his pen once again. "Here we go then. *I've got bosses not leaders…because my Board are also bosses not leaders….and that is because I, Simon Gray, the Chief Executive of Alderton's…am also a boss not a leader!*" He threw the pad on the table and startled a couple of pensioners enjoying their morning out at the garden centre.

Simon leaned forward and looked Willis in the eye. They were only 12 inches apart. "Happy now? Why is this important to you, Willis? I know we only meet every month but why are you in my face all the fucking time? And when you're not in my face you're always in piranha mode, causing me pain and grief. What is it with you?"

The pensioners moved tables, clearly unhappy with the general mood and bad language coming from the table to their left.

"Because we agreed that you didn't want to just look at the back of my head, sir," said Willis.

Simon smiled. "Yes, Willis, very good. I know that you're trying to help me in your rather strange way, but why? Why, for God's sake? Who the hell do you think you are? What's your agenda here?"

Willis leaned forward to take advantage of his opportunity. "As you know, I've worked for, and with, many CEOs, sir. They all needed a little nudge in the right direction from time to time to get the best out of them. I think you will also be a very good CEO but only once you realise that organisational change starts with the man in the mirror." Simon looked at Willis and slowly sipped his latte. Nothing was said for a further three minutes and they maintained their positions – only 12 inches apart.

"Right, Willis. Let's get to the bottom of this one, shall we? I'm going to phone Dudley to tell them that we're running late, but I won't tell them that we're having a cosy coffee somewhere near the arse-end of Kettering. You're going to buy yourself a decent coffee this time – the cafetière stuff, not that machine rubbish. Yes, I did see your face, Willis, when you were drinking it! I'm now going to the toilet and when I come back we're going to carry on talking until I've understood the implications of another monthly appraisal I've had this morning…from you…my bloody driver!"

Ten minutes later, the two men moved to a different, quieter corner of the palm-filled coffee shop at the Leaview Garden Centre, near Kettering. The manager found them "a quieter table" and, in the process, had dealt with the pensioners' complaint without making too much of a fuss. More pensioners arrived in the tea shop for their monthly outing and sat around talking about their distant pasts as

Simon Gray and George Willis embarked on a crucial conversation about their immediate future.

Willis fiddled nervously with his cafetière, but stopped when he noticed that Simon was ready to talk.

"Right then, Willis. Let's talk about this bosses and leaders thing. You start."

Willis was surprised by the instruction but leaned forward, slowly. He looked around to see if anyone was watching or listening, as he didn't want to embarrass Simon at such a critical moment. "Before I start, sir, I had a quick look at the greetings cards on the shelf over there and found this one for you. I didn't choose it – it chose me. Have a listen to these words." Willis held the card up so Simon could see the picture of clouds on the front:

"Success is failure turned inside out, the silver tint of the clouds of doubt

And you never know just how close you are, it may be near but seems so far

So stick to the fight when you are hardest hit

It's when things seem worse that you must not quit"

"And who wrote that, Willis?"

"The very famous Mr. Anon, apparently. He gets around, doesn't he?"

"Thanks for that, Willis. I won't dwell on the card but I take your point about hanging on in there. Now – let's get back to this leadership thing."

Willis leaned forward. "You, sir, can only lead Alderton's people if you have their consent. You've been appointed as CEO but you haven't been appointed as their leader – that's something that has to be earned. *They* will decide if you're a leader, not you!"

"Fair point, Willis. I can't argue with that."

Willis continued. "It doesn't matter how good your technical or financial skills are – you won't take the organisation to new heights unless you can work through others. Your business skills are obvious but Alderton's is going to need a lot more than your business skills if it's to survive. It needs your leadership." Willis fiddled with the dysfunctional cafetière again and noticed the two columns that Simon had drawn on his notepad. One was headed "bosses" and the other column was headed "leaders".

Willis put his coffee cup down, then waited for Simon to look up. He seized the moment. "In my lifetime, sir, I have worked for eight different CEOs and worked alongside many others. I have been on the receiving end of some brilliant leadership and on the receiving end of some appalling leadership. I have worked in centres of excellence and I have worked in prisons for the human soul. I have been in a leadership role myself on several occasions and although I wasn't in your league, I think I was a very good leader simply because, at times, I was also a very bad leader. I'm happy to give you my views on the subject sir, but they're not the right answer by any means."

"Yes, yes, Willis," said Simon impatiently. "Get on with it... preferably today!"

Willis remained calm and unruffled. He leaned back and waited for a clumsy young waiter to remove their cups before continuing. "OK, sir, let me give you my two-penny worth on bosses and leaders. Bosses like to lead the parade and do it all themselves with a small group of followers but leaders know that there is also a large group of people watching from a distance and an even larger one thinking 'what parade?' Good leaders know that they need to get *everyone* marching to the same tune if they are to succeed. Alderton's won't change if only one person wants it to – i.e. you!"

"But I'm not going to win over all 240 people, am I?" protested Simon.

"No, probably not, sir, but we're back to the heart-count theme here aren't we? You need a higher heart-count than you have now. You need a critical mass of 'heartbeat people'. From the sound of it, employee engagement should be your main priority."

"Fair comment, Willis. So, you were saying...?"

"Well, as I said, bosses create prisons for the human soul and leaders create laboratories for achieving human potential. Bosses see themselves at the top of the organisation but leaders see their customers at the top. Bosses like to get results from people – they wring every last drop out of them. Leaders like to get results *through* people, who then become re-energised and renewed.

"Bosses let their people know where they stand but leaders let their people know what they stand for – they have a set of values and beliefs that act as their personal compass. Their values are so strong that they become moral hills that they are prepared to die on. Working for a boss who has no values is sometimes like looking at the wrong side of a tapestry – you can see an image of some sort, but it's all blurry and indistinct. Bosses like power and authority but leaders prefer empowerment and prefer to win people over through respect. Bosses think that people need controlling tightly but leaders set their people free. Bosses see themselves as commanders but leaders see themselves as coaches.

"Bosses like to suppress difficult or radical people but leaders are clever enough to know that radicals are also capable of becoming loyal conservatives the day after the revolution! Bosses see challenge as resistance but leaders see it as legitimate concern – they see challenge as "destructive loyalty". Bosses make decisions autocratically which are then implemented democratically i.e. each department decides whether or not the decision applies to them and what it actually means. Leaders make decisions the other way. They *make decisions democratically*, with input from as many people as possible, then implement decisions autocratically with everyone sticking to the agreed plan. They are very firm about it – in fact, they take no prisoners. What the typical boss fails to realise is that decisions arising from debate are implemented quicker and more effectively because hopes, fears, concerns and expectations have already been aired. Because of democracy, people have had their say and will be 'up for it', even if the decision went against them.

"Bosses believe in confrontation but leaders prefer collaboration. Bosses like cornering people but leaders prefer getting people in their corner. Bosses like giving their people heat but good leaders prefer to give their people light! Bosses treat their staff harshly but leaders understand that the way you treat your staff is the way that they, in turn, will treat customers."

"New cups, gentlemen, more coffee is on the way." The two men hardly noticed the waiter's three attempts to attract their attention.

Willis continued. "Bosses see information as a source of power but leaders do not withhold, filter or retain information – they see information as enlightenment, they use information to remove pockets of dissatisfaction, bickering and political feuding.

"Bosses like to take centre stage but leaders see themselves as directors of a corporate play – they prefer to work in the wings, allowing others to take the applause, even including the encore. Bosses create a lot of busyness and spend their time progress-chasing the organisation into submission. Leaders concentrate on business and know that ten ideas are excellent but one or two actually put into practice are even better. Leaders get on with it – they know that a good plan actioned today is better than a perfect plan actioned next month.

"Leaders start with the end in mind and create powerful visions for their organisations. They have the ability to see the future whilst dealing with the realities of today. They understand that the art of leadership is getting something you want doing, done by someone who wants to do it. They hire good "attitude" and develop poor skills and fire poor attitude regardless of good skills. They also do what is right when no one is watching – that's always a great test isn't it?"

"Yes…I suppose it is, Willis."

Willis continued. "Bosses concentrate on knowledge, i.e. what there is, but leaders concentrate on imagination, i.e. what there will be! Bosses work in the business but good leaders take time out to work *on* the business. Bosses like to make decisions themselves but leaders delegate as much as they can. They try and ensure that all decisions are made as 'low' as possible within the organisation – by people who are on the ground looking at the real situation. Remember the Charge of the Light Brigade? It was ordered by an officer who wasn't actually looking at the territory!

"The poet Goethe said some interesting things that have implications for CEOs. He said that if you treat people as you find them, they then remain '*as you found them*'. But if, as a leader, you treat people as they can and should be, not surprisingly, they then become '*what they can and should be!*'

"Bosses often stop people coming through the ranks because they feel threatened by them, whereas leaders encourage the next generation not just to follow them, but to overtake. Bosses tend to cling on to their jobs for as long as they can, but leaders lead as far as they can, then move on before, as Anita Roddick once said, '*their ashes choke the fire that they themselves have lit*'. Good leaders know that they are right for a time and that they are fundamentally wrong for other times. Sadly, sir, one of my heroes, Margaret Thatcher, didn't understand this subtle key point.

"When bosses are in the room, things happen because they are there – rather like a Mexican wave – but when a leader is out of the room a wave still happens when they are *not there*. Bosses are builders and administrators – leaders are architects and innovators. Bosses concentrate on techniques but leaders concentrate on principles.

"Bosses step on people's toes with a heavy-handed style but leaders can step on shoes without even messing up the shine. Bosses concentrate on making life difficult for the organisation's 'weeds' but leaders spend most of their time cultivating the organisation's seeds. Good leaders give their people some drama because they know that, if they don't, the grapevine will create an alternative drama. Good leaders are great communicators – as commercial generals they know that speeches at the moment of battle do very little. The veteran in sales will scarcely listen and the new recruit in IT will forget the speech at the first shot. Good leaders know that their speeches are only useful *during* the battle – to keep morale alive as they fight in the trenches *alongside* their troops."

"I'm not sure that military analogies are really appropriate in this day and age, Willis," added Simon.

"They certainly are, sir. When businesses became sophisticated at the time of the industrial revolution, there were only two models for them to copy – the church and the army. Today, all businesses still use the same four strategies that armies throughout history have used – offence, defence, alliance and deterrence…and if you're looking for a good leadership case study, think of Vietnam. The victorious communist generals in the North knew what leadership was really about. There was nothing to distinguish them from their private soldiers apart from the stars they wore on their collar. Their uniform was the same, they had the same type of boots, their helmets were identical and the officers travelled on foot with their men. Together they lived on the rice they carried with them, the vegetables they pulled from the earth and on the fish they caught from the mountain streams that they camped by. There were no Bentleys, no secretaries and support staff, no director lunches and no corporate hospitality to lighten the load. They won the day through leadership with a capital L – they had victory! We can still learn from that today, surely?"

"OK…that's a fair point," conceded Simon.

"Oh, and another thing," continued Willis, "from what you've told me about Alderton's, you've got many good castles that you operate from, good technology and intelligence-gathering systems, some good people and many others with good potential; but maybe some of Alderton's guns are pointing in the wrong direction! Maybe some of your people are pointing their guns at each other rather than at the competitors. Friendly fire seems to be alive and well within your organisation, sir."

"I can't argue with that either," said Simon. "So staying with your military analogy then, I suppose that one of my challenges as a good commercial general is that I have to get my front line to care about my bottom line."

"Nicely put, sir…and remember that good leaders believe so much in their people that they will move them around to get the best out of them. One of my old CEOs, Sally O'Neill, used to say that there's no such thing as a bad employee – *just a person in the wrong job at the wrong time!* In the four years that I worked for her, she never fired anybody – she just moved people and found them their right place."

"Nice story," said Simon. "Is that it then…have we done bosses and leaders, Willis?"

"Not quite, but I'll summarise a couple more points if I may. Leaders are great communicators. In their businesses, if you asked anyone from the board to the lad on the shop floor what the business was trying to do, you would get the same answer! They make sure that everyone understands the strategic plan at a tabloid level. Good leaders know that if their people don't understand it and can't imagine it, they won't take part in it and won't be able to deliver it! Good leaders also recognise that, despite their excellent communication skills, many people will not give two hoots about the organisation's objectives…unless…by achieving them, it will help them achieve their *own* objectives! Good leaders are human gardeners – they provide 'beansticks' like structure, values and purpose that encourage people to grow quicker than they otherwise would have done."

Simon leaned back in his chair. "I'm impressed, Willis. For a driver, you're very passionate about this leadership stuff, aren't you? How did you come to all these conclusions that you've just shared with me?"

"As I said, I've worked for some good leaders and some bad ones," replied Willis.

"There's a lot more to you than meets the eye, Willis, but we won't dwell on that at the moment. So…bearing in mind that Alderton's is deep in the proverbial and there's clearly a shortage of leadership, how am I going to develop leaders quickly? More training? Or is it a genetic thing….you know, the good old nurture versus nature argument and all that?"

"Think of leaders, dead or alive, sir, that have made an impression on you. Who are they?"

"Do you mean the famous ones?" said Simon.

"Any of them, sir. They might be famous, they might not be."

"Well," said Simon, "my famous ones would include people like Martin Luther King, Ghandi…Churchill, of course. Then there have been a couple of people who have managed me over the years who were also great leaders – Geoff Campbell and Sarah Kingston, in particular. My famous business leaders would include Steve Jobs, the late Anita Roddick you mentioned a few moments ago and a few others, I suppose. Maybe some of the Dragon's Den crew."

"And do you remember these people for their ability to run a good meeting…or the way that they managed their time…or maybe the way that they delivered a sparkling presentation?"

"Certainly not," said Simon, looking a little puzzled.

"So why do you remember them – particularly the ones you've worked for?" said Willis.

"I remember them for their passion, their compassion, the fact that they dared to be different, their moral courage, risk-taking, their sense of fun and adventure, the belief they had in me, their integrity, their judgement, including when to use it and when to suspend it, their patience, resilience, trustworthiness, self-confidence, firmness, prudence, creativity and sensitivity…all sorts of things, really. Why?"

"Exactly!" said Willis.

"Exactly what?" said Simon, still looking puzzled.

"No, perhaps you should answer that question, sir…while I just go to the toilet. I'll be back in a minute. I'm going to let you think about it – enjoy the space."

Willis returned a few minutes later, catching the eye of the bemused waiter as he sat down once more. "Please allow me to get our waiter sorted, sir, and then I'll be all ears. Would you like another one of those frothy concoctions you had before?"

"You mean a latte, Willis."

"Whatever, sir…excuse me, young man, could we have the same

again please? Thank you. Right then, what conclusions have you come to about the leaders you've chosen?"

Simon leaned forward. "The conclusion I've come to, Willis, is a very simple one. I don't remember my list of influential leaders because of their leadership skills – I remember them because of their leadership *qualities*. I've never read about Churchill's interviewing or time management skills but I've certainly read about his ability to motivate and inspire…through his qualities and character."

"Exactly, sir, and there you have it in one!"

"So part of Alderton's longer term strategy needs to be the development of a team of people with the right *qualities*? It's obvious when you think about it – but that will take ages, Willis. I may not have the time."

"You have all the time there is, sir. You have the same amount of time as Marie Curie, Shakespeare, Bill Gates and John Lennon. It's what you do with it that matters! Saying you haven't got the time is as ridiculous as me saying that I haven't got the time to pull in for petrol because I'm too busy driving!"

"All right, all right, you've made your point, Willis. I can see that you're snapping around in the bidet again!" said Simon. "But what else will develop leadership qualities apart from the usual sort of training events?"

"It's not about training, sir. It's not about grafting on some knowledge and skills. It's about becoming what you're capable of becoming. It's about discovering yourself. Remember Ernest Shackleton and his famous exploits? He's often quoted as one of the best leaders in history, as I'm sure you know. Well, when he went to Dulwich College as a 13-year-old, he was seen as immature and inattentive. He was often asked to work with students who were a year younger than him and one teacher in particular reported that the young Shackleton '*needed waking up*'."

"Where is this going, Willis?"

"A schoolmaster who met Shackleton after he had become a famous and heroic explorer confessed, '*We never discovered you when you were here at Dulwich*'. Shackleton replied, '*No…but I had not, then, discovered myself!*'"

"Good story…but how does that affect us now, at Alderton's?" asked Simon.

"It means," replied Willis, "that your people need to go through development programmes that will allow them to discover themselves and what they are truly capable of. Cancel the skills training budget and replace it with 48-hour 'qualities' projects like working for charities. Encourage people to join volunteer organisations – volunteers don't respond to poor leadership – they just go home! It's a great challenge. It's a great place to develop the ability to…"

"…inspire willing action," said Simon, completing the sentence.

"Exactly," said Willis. "Get people doing secondments with other organisations, put them on outdoor exercises on Dartmoor, encourage them to work with prisoners at the weekend…or work with addicts… or with the Samaritans…anything that will develop their *qualities* as well as skills."

Simon stood up and beckoned Willis to do the same. "Stand up, Willis, please."

Willis stood up but was a little concerned as he was not sure if he was about to be on the receiving end of a left hook. Simon smiled and held out his right hand. Willis slowly responded. They shook hands for 20 seconds or so. Simon looked Willis in the eye once again. "That was good learning for me today, George, very good learning. Thank you – and I really do mean that. Things, for me, will never be quite the same again. I think the penny has finally dropped. Things will change with effect from today."

"Thank you, Simon, I'm glad my comments have not offended you," replied Willis.

"No they haven't," said Simon, "and when I say that things are about to change, I mean that *I* am about to change. This has been an important day for me, in so many ways." The two men shook hands again and returned to the car.

As they approached the Bentley, Simon thought about Willis and his Vietnam story: "No secretaries, no Bentleys, no corporate hospitality…but victory!"

They proceeded to Dudley and Simon spent the rest of the day in meetings with his managers. Willis spent a lot of time reading in the corner of the canteen although he enjoyed a team briefing led by Sharon Oliver, the manager of the Customer Services Department, who, recognising him as Simon's driver, had invited him to stay.

At 6.45pm the two men met up once again and headed for their hotel. They quickly checked in and agreed to meet later in the bar. Simon scanned the restaurant menu that was on display in reception and suggested that they should eat there later. Willis nodded his agreement and disappeared down a corridor leading to the Garden Room. Simon took his three bags and his laptop into the lift and headed up to the Galaxy Suite.

They met again at 8pm. "So, how is your Garden Room, Willis?"

"Very nice, actually," said Willis. "There's a great view of the garden, not surprisingly, and it has some beautiful wisteria growing outside. It comes right on to my balcony and gives it a stunning appearance. It frames it beautifully. It looks exactly like the sort of picture you would see in a posh calendar. Very nice. Thank you for booking it."

"A pleasure. My room has plenty of glass, including the ceiling," replied Simon. "There's a button you can press which opens a small ceiling panel – presumably so that guests can see the stars, although I won't be doing that tonight. Have you seen the weather, Willis? It's bloody awful. Now, what are you drinking?"

As the barman poured their drinks, Willis scanned the bar to observe the other residents and guests. Most of the place was occupied by a noisy group of fun-loving sales and account managers from a cosmetics company. They were taking part in a conference and the Sales Director, who was surrounded by a group of his loyal, obedient followers, was in full flow. By the time Simon handed him his pint of Guinness, Willis had been able to establish that the conference agenda that day had featured a new product launch and a presentation from *"those idiots in Marketing"* and the following day there was a going to be a review of goals for the future and a training session led by *"some smart-arsed outside consultant"*.

"Look at that lot," said a disapproving Willis. "Do you know what the difference is between a bar full of sales managers and a hedgehog?"

"No, Willis…can't say that I do."

"Well," continued Willis, "with the hedgehog, the pricks are on the outside!"

"Leave them alone, Willis. At least they're enjoying their meeting or conference."

"I was never a great fan of conferences," said Willis. "They consist of a lot of sightseeing and eating, with a dull bit in the middle!"

"Oh, I don't know," said Simon, "I always get something out of them. They're great fun too – plenty of beer, plenty of banter, lots of laughter…"

"…and a good source of blackmail for the coming year!" said Willis. "I think that's where the phrase 'horizontal integration' comes from."

"What are you on about?"

"You know, sleeping with a colleague!" said Willis as he sipped his black, Irish brew.

"I've always preferred vertical integration," said Simon, "you know, sleeping with the boss! Much better career prospects, don't you think?"

The two men laughed loudly, now very relaxed in each other's company. Simon handed Willis the menu featuring a range of dishes from Dudley and far beyond. Simon scanned the choices on offer, then became very aware that Willis had said nothing for some time. "You're very quiet, Willis. Everything all right?"

Willis straightened his tie. "A closed mouth gathers no foot, sir!"

"Very funny, Willis. Now I don't want you going all quiet on me tonight – I've got plenty of things I want to talk about."

"Oh really?" said Willis, sounding a little tired.

"Oh yes. I'm ready for a long productive evening," said Simon, who could sense that Willis was not exhibiting the same round-the-clock commitment to the cause. "What do you think to this place then, Willis? It's very modern, isn't it? It was designed by a team of TV designers – you know, the people who come round and swap your house with your neighbours!"

"It's a little modern for my personal tastes, sir," sniffed Willis. "It looks as if it's been designed by a team of footballers' wives after an evening of champagne and chips."

"Willis, if I'm going to buy you dinner this evening, the least you can do is to lighten up a bit."

Willis forced a smile. He could see that Simon was enjoying himself.

"So, Willis, did you see the news tonight, in your hotel room? Daniel Crowther has been appointed as the new Home Secretary. I really admire him."

"Isn't the definition of admiration the recognition of another's resemblance to oneself?" said Willis.

"You're back, Willis! I knew you'd return to your old form after a beer." said Simon. "Clearly you're not interested in politics then?"

"Not really. If I was trapped in a room with a tiger, a grizzly bear and a politician, I would shoot the politician...twice!" The two men laughed together again.

Their goats' cheese salad and carrot soup starters arrived and they ate them with hardly a word being said. It had been a long day. Willis, in particular, benefited from the food and quickly felt rejuvenated. He re-focused on Simon's stated intention of talking business. "So tell me about the Dudley managers that you're having the problems with," he said.

"Which ones?" said Simon, with a smile on his face. "At the moment my job seems to be keeping the managers who don't like me away from those who are undecided!"

Willis smiled. "I'm talking about the team you mentioned earlier today."

"The Production team is the one I'm having the problems with," said Simon. "The rest of the site – the sales team and customer service team – seem to be responding well to the change programme."

"So what's happened? Why doesn't Production want to play ball?" asked Willis.

"They see change as a threat, Willis. They're resisting it at the moment – the other departments are embracing change and are showing early signs of support and commitment."

"Well," said Willis, "I often think that the problem with change is that it usually arrives before people are ready for it. People quickly move into a state of denial muttering *'It won't happen'* or *'I'll believe it when I see it'* or *'It doesn't apply to us – it's just for the other departments'*."

"No, I think we're through that phase," said Simon. "We've got a period of resistance now where even stronger emotions are building up. People are saying things like *'Which bloody idiot thought of this idea?* and *'It will never work!'* or *'Why can't we go back to how we used to do it before?'* I've certainly heard Tom Wrigley, the evening shift Production Manager, say things like that...and much worse," he finished grimly.

"You're lucky then," said Willis. "If you're unlucky you won't hear any feedback at all – it goes underground as people decide to fight a private, negative and subversive battle behind the scenes. They stop fighting against change and start walking away from it. Is there a route within Alderton's for people to channel their emotions? Change is not just about getting new ideas in – it's also about getting the old ideas out! The first step towards change is to get the emotion out before you can get acceptance in. I've worked for a couple of CEOs who tried to move people too quickly – they tried to herd them out of resistance too early. In your case, sir, Alderton's people won't see things your way until they're convinced that you can see things their way and also understand the strong emotions they're feeling."

"I can remember you saying something like that once before," said Simon. He picked up his glass of Barolo and surveyed its colour. "So far, cards have been openly laid on the table," he continued. "Production don't like some of the new processes and procedures we need to bring in – but these changes have to happen, Willis, they're essential. I'm always amazed at how people react to change – bearing in mind that during our time on this bloody planet there are only three things that are certain – life, death and change! It's a no-brainer. All I'm trying to do is get us to change internally before the external environment forces us to change. Remember that Peter Drucker quote? He said, 'Tomorrow is going to be different from today and the only certainty is that it is not going to be the difference people expected.' Within Aldertons, there will be no such thing as 'business as usual'. Things are moving so quickly these days – to paraphrase Drucker, the future isn't going to be what it used to be!"

"Yes, but people don't like change, do they, sir? I know that when my son Trevor introduced some changes at the British Embassy in Paris a few years ago, there was uproar."

The waiter arrived with their main courses. Simon had selected a fish dish garnished with watercress and white grapes and Willis had chosen his favourite – mixed grill. His plate contained a mountain of meat jostling for position. The pork and sage sausage proudly pointed northwards on a mashed potato summit. "Are you going to eat that, or climb it?" said Simon, smiling. "Where were we…?"

Willis sipped his Guinness and continued with his usual seam-less delivery. "After people have resisted change, they can often be persuaded to at least experiment with some new ideas and actions. Some will still sound reluctant and say things like: '*I'll give it a go but I'm not sure it's right*' or '*If you want me to do this I will need some training first*', but many will take their first tentative steps towards a new future. No one can persuade another person to change – each of us guards a gate of change that can only be opened from the inside. Bosses come along and kick the door down but leaders create the environment that encourages people to come out to play. Change management isn't something you do – it is something that others allow!

"This experimentation phase starts with small steps which then become slightly larger steps. At times it may seem painfully slow but at least some action will now be taking place. Bearing in mind that many people come from the 'seeing is believing' school of life, this is an important time for them. As results start to come in, they realise that the new change is not quite as difficult or frightening as they thought it was going to be. However, don't expect to see delight on their faces. If you're lucky they might offer comments like '*Looking back I can see why we had to do this*' or '*I still don't like it but I'll do it.*' That is as good as it will get.

"From the sound of it, your sales and service teams have reacted positively to your proposed changes and have moved quickly into supporting them with high levels of commitment. Production may have to go on a little journey through stages of denial, resistance and experimentation before they can offer the same support and commitment."

"Fair enough," said Simon, "but I need some good practical ideas to turn them around, Willis – there's no point just giving me a lecture on change management, is there?"

"Of course not. Would you like me to comment on that now or after your dessert?" said Willis. "What are you having?"

"The fruit salad, I think," said Simon. "How about you?"

"I'm going to have the treacle sponge with the custard…and the cream," said Willis, stroking his stomach with affection. "Mind you, I do try and stick to a balanced diet so I might have to have eat the bread and butter pudding with my other hand!"

"You're lucky," said Simon. "You're still in very good shape…"

"…you mean, for a man of my age?" said Willis, smiling.

"I couldn't possibly say, Willis." Simon smiled again.

"I've always looked after myself," said Willis. "I decided years ago that I wanted to die young, but as late as possible. But I still enjoy my food, as you can see. A friend of mine once gave up smoking, drinking, sex and rich food, all at the same time."

"Really? What happened to him?" enquired Simon.

"Oh, he was very healthy…right up to the moment when he killed himself!"

Simon laughed loudly. "Very good, Willis. I should have seen that coming."

"But while we're talking about health," added Willis with a more serious tone, "and bearing in mind that I *am* getting on a bit, I'm appalled by the amount of money that society is spending on breast implants and Viagra these days, rather than on Alzheimer's. It's a disgrace!"

Simon raised his glass and sipped his wine. He had a twinkle in his eye and was not taking Willis' point seriously. "You're right, Willis. But at least by 2030 we'll have a large, elderly population with perky boobs and huge erections but with absolutely no recollection of what to do with them!" They laughed together but their alcohol-assisted laughter was soon interrupted by the arrival of the waiter, who removed their plates and took their dessert orders.

The restaurant began to thin out and many guests headed for the bar before it closed. Simon leaned forward as he was ready for the final instalment in the change management storyline that had dominated their evening. "Seriously, Willis, how about some tips on the Production boys? One thing that I think I'm doing well at the moment is *selling* change. I'm trying to explain the benefits of change – to our customers, to our staff and to our shareholders."

"Yes, but don't forget to spin the coin over from time to time," said Willis.

"Meaning what?"

"Meaning that you might also need to stress the consequences of failing to make the changes work – the damage it will do to customers, staff and shareholders if things *don't* change. For example, when you go to your doctor, he or she might look you in the eye and sell you the benefits of a healthier lifestyle but, on another day, the doctor might look you in the eye and say, '*Mr. Gray, if you don't lose a couple of stones you'll have a heart attack!*' It's the same coin – just the other side of it. People will sit up and think. My son calls it the '*burning platform theory*'."

"Why does he call it that?" said Simon, as he poured another glass of wine.

"Remember the Piper Alpha oil rig disaster all those years ago, sir? A number of people survived by jumping into a flame-red sea. They did it because the *certain* danger of staying where they were outweighed the *probable* danger of leaping into the unknown. For Alderton's people, jumping in your direction will have its dangers too but at least it carries some chance of success!"

"That's a good point, Willis. I read somewhere the other day that over the last ten years, 46 per cent of the world's top companies have disappeared because they failed to make changes quickly enough ....to jump maybe, using your platform analogy."

The waiter reappeared with their desserts and silence followed for the following 15 minutes as they ate. Simon licked his lips and said, "Willis, would you like a coffee?"

"Do you happen to have Brazil's Best?" asked Willis, turning to a passing waiter.

The waiter looked thoughtful for a moment and then said, "Sorry, sir, not much call for that in Dudley! I can do you West Midlands' Best...it's called black or white."

Simon smiled and Willis frowned. "I think he means they do 'take it or leave it' coffee, Willis." They eventually ordered two black coffees which arrived a few minutes later.

Willis spotted the chocolates nestling on the edge of the plate. "After you, sir."

"No, I couldn't, Willis. I'm full."

Willis peeled the gold wrapper from the chocolate as slowly as he could, popped it into his mouth and gave a long smile of satisfaction.

"Willis, you look just like that stupid smug woman on the TV ad," said Simon.

They returned to the bar where they chatted for another hour and were entertained in the background by the amusing decline of the noisy sales team from the cosmetics company. Assisted by far too many beers, their humour had become braver and more penetrating.

At one point, a seasoned sales manager from Dartford was lecturing a young executive from head office about the lack of support in the field. The executive withdrew and headed for bed when she was told that the head office team was nothing more than "*a group of people who turned up after the war to bayonet the wounded*".

Simon suggested a final nightcap in the Monet Lounge, which was quieter and more conducive to late-night learning. "Willis, I've enjoyed this evening but, to put it simply, the gin and tonic, red wine and Grand Marnier have got the better of me. You'd better summarise this change management stuff again for me before I head for the stars. I got the significance of your denial > resistance > experimentation > implementation process. It made a lot of sense and yes, you're right, I haven't yet created a proper vehicle for channelling their emotions and getting their old feelings out. What else can you tell me?"

Willis sat up in response to Simon's question. "Well, first of all, when you don't know what to do in a time of important organisational change, get a clipboard, walk fast and look worried!"

"Very good, Willis," said Simon. "Very amusing but I'm knackered so please get on with it."

Willis sat up then leaned forward. "Change has some similarities with my job as your driver – a change in the road is not the end of the road unless I fail to make the turn! People are fearful of change but it's not the end of the road for them unless they fail to respond. Change can be positive – you never hear a caterpillar complaining about the prospect of changing into a butterfly, do you? There is a positive outcome for it to look forward to! My last CEO had it absolutely spot-on about change. He believed that change done *to* people was always unwelcome and that change done *by* people was a much better alternative. The trick is to get people to achieve your objectives, their way…then get out of the way while they do it. Err… are you still awake, sir?"

"Yes, I'm fine, Willis. Please carry on – this is good stuff."

"Do you ever watch any of those nature programmes on TV, sir? You know – the David Attenborough programmes?"

"Yes, I do actually. The girls love them too – we often watch them as a family."

"Have you noticed," continued Willis, "that it isn't the strongest species that survive, nor the most intelligent, but the ones that are most responsive to change. Darwin said that years ago, but companies could learn a lot from that today."

"But what do you do with people who can't change or, even worse, don't want to change?" said Simon.

"At the end of the day, if I could borrow someone else's one-liner, *'if you can't change your people you'll have to change your people'*!"

"Presumably you mean that my poor performers will have to go – in this case production people who are producing poor results and are out of step with the new culture?"

"Maybe others too," said Willis. "I've seen CEOs make the mistake of retaining people who produce good results but are out of step with the culture."

"What's your point here, Willis?" said Simon "You're not going to get rid of people producing good results, surely?"

"Let me put it this way – people who produce good results but in the wrong way i.e. the people who are culturally out of step are nothing more than hostage-takers. They hold a gun to the organisation's head but are still tolerated, of course, due to their good results and the short-term damage to the bottom line if they were removed."

"And do I assume that you're suggesting that they should be removed?" said Simon.

"Yes, you can assume that, sir. As the writer Jim Collins said, *'organisations need to get the right people on the bus and the wrong people off the bus'*. Hostage-takers need to be 'fixed', regardless of their impact on the bottom line. Other people in the organisation always know who the hostage-takers are. They know who isn't pulling their weight – and don't think that they will respect you for putting up with them. People are not stupid – if they see Management failing to take action with the hostage-takers, they'll become disillusioned and de-motivated. Some will even leave because they expect Management to live up to its previously stated and promoted core values and standards of behaviour."

"Fair point, Willis."

"And another thing, sir, is to remember that every person in Alderton's defines you – the CEO. The hostage-takers, in particular, will live on to become the definition of what *you* find acceptable in terms of organisational behaviour. You have to protect the organisation from these people – they have to go. It might sound brutal but it isn't.

They were right for the organisation at one time in its development but they can also be wrong for it at another time."

Simon looked exhausted, so Willis decided to wrap things up quickly. "If you retain the hostage-takers, remember that you aren't being kind, sensitive or generous – you're acting dangerously and putting the organisation at risk."

Simon Gray nodded. "This all makes perfect sense and it has been a great day for me, Willis – in every sense of the word. I've learned a lot about myself and a lot about leadership. As I said earlier today, my life will be different from now on. But one thing bothers me, Willis. How do you know all this stuff? *It* makes sense but, somehow, *you* don't. I can't put my finger on it, but there's more to you than I know. One day I'll get to the bottom of it but not now – I'm off to bed, if I can find it. Good night, Willis. I'm going to join the stars but I'll see you in the morning. We need to be back at the factory at 7.45am."

Simon stood up, finished his nightcap, steadied himself and firmly shook Willis' hand. He looked tired but he was calm, relaxed and happy. He looked at Willis and smiled once again. Then, leaning forward and swaying a little, he whispered in Willis' ear, "Good night, George…whoever you are!"

Wit and Wisdom
Chapter 3 Summary

1. There is no such thing as a bad regiment – just bad officers (Field Marshall Slim). At the end of the day, managers get the workforce they deserve.

2. Leadership is about inspiring willing action – it is about commitment not consent.

3. Develop leadership *qualities* as well as leadership skills.

4. Values are moral hills we should all be prepared to die on (Bob Williams).

5. Decisions should be made democratically and implemented autocratically.

6. Change is not something you do – it is what others allow. We can't persuade someone else to change – they guard the gates of change and the gates are locked from the inside. Change done "to" people does not work – try change "with" people for a better result.

7. The right cultural behaviour is just as important as the right results – don't tolerate "hostage-takers" as they will hold your organisation to ransom.

8. The pace of change inside the organisation must keep up with the pace of change outside the organisation.

9. At the end of the day, if you can't change the people you must change the people!

10. Remember that there is often a very positive outcome from change – you don't hear caterpillars complaining about the prospect of becoming a butterfly. Change is not the end of the world – it is just a new and different world.

Chapter 4
Billy Crystal Saved My Life!

It was 25 September. Willis sat in the drive once again but, unusually, there was no sign of Simon. He was late. However, there was plenty to interest Willis as he surveyed the Grays' garden through the Bentley's open window. The leaves in the orchard were turning deep shades of yellow and brown. The russets hung from the trees and their mottled skins were starting to acquire a deep red colour and Willis thought that they resembled ripe cricket balls. He scanned the local radio stations. One reported the death of an old famous village swan called Vesta, which then prompted a heated phone-in conversation between local residents and a defensive official from the local authority that was refusing to collect the bird. Willis tutted and shook his head in disbelief.

He turned to locate his newspaper on the back seat but was suddenly distracted by Stella Gray, walking towards the car with her briefcase in one hand and her large black handbag in the other. Passing her handbag to a surprised Willis through his open window, she turned and blew a kiss to the girls who were jostling in the front porch as they tried to knock each other off the top step. Stella waved enthusiastically and opened the passenger door. "Good morning, George," she said. "The handbag doesn't really suit you by the way – not your colour!"

"Err…good morning, Mrs. Gray…is there a problem? No Mr. Gray today, then?"

"No, sadly not, George. He's ill in bed, looking very sorry for himself. I think it's a severe case of boy-flu," she said, with a smile. "Thank you, I'll take that back now."

"Here you are," said Willis, passing over the handbag. "So is Mr. Gray OK?"

"Oh yes, he'll be fine," said Stella as she turned to place her briefcase on the rear seat of the Bentley. "He went to a doctor yesterday who prescribed a mixture of pills, potions, rest and plenty of TV and DVDs for a few days – the usual sort of thing."

"So I assume that I'm driving you somewhere today, am I, Mrs. Gray?" asked Willis, as he gripped the steering wheel, waiting for his new instructions.

"You certainly are, George. Oh, and by the way, I won't be calling you Willis, and you'll be calling me Stella."

"Fine, Mrs…err…Stella. That's fine by me. So where are we going today?"

"I would like you to take me to the Heath Conference Centre in Hampstead. Do you know where it is, George? I have some details for you, if not."

"I do know where it is, actually," said Willis. "I went to a product launch there years ago. It's a beautiful place – very plush."

"That's nice to know. Which company were you working for at the time, George?"

"An engineering company based in Blackpool. So…are you attending the conference in any particular capacity…err…Stella?"

"I'm doing more than that, George. I've been asked to deliver a keynote address to WibCon."

"Is that the Women in Business Conference?" said Willis. "I've seen it advertised. Come to think of it, I think my daughter went to it a couple of years ago. It's an annual event, isn't it?"

"It is indeed, George," said Stella as she applied her lipstick, courtesy of the illuminated vanity mirror. "Shall we go then?"

Willis had never met Stella before and had only seen her from a distance. He was struck by his new passenger's self-confidence and manner, although he was struggling with her insistence on calling him George.

He headed south to join the busy A1. The roads were clear and the traffic was moving freely.

"So this is the Bentley then, George. It's a very nice car, isn't it?"

"I'm glad you like it…Stella."

"It's very nice, George, very nice indeed. I've often admired it as you leave Mapleford with my husband. It glides, doesn't it? I like the beautiful woodwork and cream leather with the smoky grey piping. Very plush."

"Thank you. I'd like to say it's mine but that wouldn't be true," said Willis.

"I feel very important in it, George. Have you noticed the way that people look at us as we cruise past? They probably think that we're royalty."

"Princess Stella – that sounds very good, doesn't it?" said Willis. "Yes, I know what you mean about the looks that we get – it's a strange mixture of envy and deep loathing, isn't it?" said Willis, smiling."

A further ten miles passed with Stella and Willis exchanging their Bentley observations and stories.

"So what exactly do you do, Stella? I'm sure I've heard your husband refer to Market Research but I'm afraid I don't know much more than that."

"Neither does Simon!" said Stella, laughing loudly. She looked up again into the vanity mirror and played with her brunette fringe until she was happy with it. She fiddled with the top button of her yellow and lime jacket, flicked off her expensive shoes and wiggled her toes. Stella Gray was a very attractive woman and 'George' was being charmed by the minute. "My job, George, used to be in Market Research but I run a children's charity now." She wiggled her toes again and sat back in her seat. "I decided to put my money where my mouth is and put something back…as they say."

"Really?" said Willis, not sure why he sounded so surprised.

"Yes, really, George. It's very rewarding and I don't mean financially. We all need money in life, don't we, but I've always believed that money motivates neither the best people nor the best in people."

Willis smiled as he reflected on Stella's comment. "That's very true, Stella, very true."

The Bentley was facing an uphill battle with the volume of traffic and soon ground to an abrupt halt, although the inside lane appeared to know something and was busy escaping to an industrial estate near Stevenage. Willis looked at the chrome clock on the dashboard.

"Don't worry George – time is on our side," said Stella. "We've got plenty of time."

Willis eased back into his seat, preparing for a long delay. He looked uneasy and wasn't enjoying the early interruption to his schedule. He was determined to meet and exceed the expectations of his stylish new passenger. "It must be a great honour to be asked to deliver a keynote address," said Willis, politely changing the subject. "Are you nervous about it?"

"Not really," said Stella. "An audience of 50 people doesn't frighten me…but the other 350 do!"

She laughed out loud at her own joke and was quickly joined by Willis. "I often think that the human brain is a marvellous piece of equipment that works well from the moment we're born to the moment we stand up and speak in public!" said Willis, who then nervously awaited her reaction to one of his famous one-liners.

"They do indeed, George, they do indeed," said Stella. "By the way, I think that was one of Winston Churchill's comments, wasn't it"

"Err…I think it probably was," replied a slightly deflated Willis. Stella's toes tried to re-locate the shoes that had managed to lose themselves in a cavern under the seat. "So what are you going to talk about today?" continued Willis.

"Well, I've been asked to talk about my life, for some strange reason. Don't ask me why, George. I suppose I must have got myself noticed in recent years. The whole conference is built around life and work-life balance in particular." As the traffic started to clear, Stella reached inside her handbag to locate a gold fountain pen and a small black pad. She went through her notes thoughtfully and marked the occasional page with either a dramatic tick or a delicate asterisk.

"I'll let you concentrate, Stella," said Willis politely, as he re-focused on the remaining two-thirds of their journey.

"Thank you, George. That's very considerate of you. You're not going to give me the same 'piranha treatment' that you give my husband, then?"

"Does he tell you about our conversations?" said Willis, looking surprised as he quickly turned his head towards Stella.

"Oh yes, of course he does. They're more than conversations though, aren't they, George? Mind you, I'm sure your observations and comments are good for him! He's always complimentary when he talks about you, by the way. He needs your fishy piranha questions and your biting wit – but don't tell him I said that!" She laughed again and quickly returned to her notes.

The ticks and asterisks continued once again, until they were interrupted by the sound of a fire engine. Willis pulled over into the middle lane of the motorway to let it pass by. As he started to pull out again, he was startled by a red sports saloon that was determined to follow in the wake of the fire engine to pick up lost time. The driver shook his fist in an aggressive manner and tooted his horn as he passed.

"Problem, George?" enquired Stella, looking up from her notes.

"Not really. Just a dickhead and a machine in perfect harmony! Sorry – pardon my language."

"That's OK, George. I hear worse at home…and that's just from the girls!"

Apart from a broken water main near Mill Hill, the rest of the journey was uneventful and they arrived on time at the Heath Conference Centre. They walked together towards the entrance door with Willis carrying Stella's briefcase. He looked like a 14-year-old boy walking the girl next door home from school. They located the reception area and Stella chatted to one of the organisers about the agenda and timings for the day whilst Willis stood to attention. He was not sure what was expected of him.

"I'll be off for a while then," murmured Willis as Stella began to walk away. "Here's your briefcase, Stella – what time would you like me to collect you?"

"No, George, you're now booked in…you're sitting next to me, actually." She smiled, turned away and set off to powder her nose. A surprised Willis looked around for something to do. He had never seen so many women in one place before. The noise was deafening and, as he wondered what the collective noun was for dozens of happy, noisy women, he found a conference programme and a comfortable chair under a huge, green weeping fig palm and waited for Stella's return. She re-appeared holding two cups of steaming coffee. 'Brazil's Best', George – your favourite, I believe. By the way, you look as if you're wearing that enormous palm like a hat. You could be back in Manaus or the carnival in Rio!"

"Wow – where did you find the coffee?" said an overjoyed Willis, quickly getting to his feet. "Not from that coffee machine over there, surely?" Willis cradled the insulated coffee as if it was liquid gold.

"No, from the rather nice, up-market coffee shop just around the corner," said Stella. "Simon mentioned that you had a bit of a thing about this brand of coffee. My treat."

"What…for driving you here?" said Willis.

"No, no….for driving my husband round the bend but also for

driving him forward....into a new way of thinking" said Stella. She raised her coffee cup as if it was a glass of champagne. "So George, here's to you and piranhas in the bidet, then!"

"Err...yes...oh, the piranhas!" said Willis, trying not to spill his special brew. "And here's to a successful speech too!" he added, as the distinctive aroma of the coffee re- entered his world.

They sat sipping their drinks together although their thoughts were on different things. Stella was calmly reading her notes once again and Willis was back in the merchant navy with the Brazilian coast on the starboard bow. The public address system crackled out an inaudible message, which signalled to those in the know that the conference was about to start. Dozens of women, and the occasional man, quickly gathered their bags and papers and started to file through the doors of the main hall. There was a buzz of excitement and a Cher track with a pounding bass line played in the background, whilst two men in black trousers and shirts made the final adjustments to the microphones on the stage. Many of the women re-introduced themselves to familiar faces from previous years and exchanged old stories and recent experiences. Willis sat down on the front row, next to Stella. He felt very proud, nervous and also a little protective. As the din subsided, a well-dressed lady in her late sixties strutted across the stage, looking very self-important.

"That's Gloria," said Stella, turning to Willis. "Gloria Hemmings – the chairman."

"Don't you mean chairwoman?" asked Willis.

Stella smiled. "George, you're so sweet. These days it's OK for us girls to be called 'chairman', you know but, as you once said to Simon, women will always need to be twice as good as men...to go half as far!"

Willis smiled. He liked Stella a lot. The lights dimmed, apart from one spotlight that focused on Gloria Hemmings and her expensively styled grey hair. Willis thought that she looked as if she had fallen into a candyfloss machine but he quickly returned to the moment as the buzz of excitement became an expectant whisper. Gloria coughed politely to signal that she was ready to open the conference.

"Ladies and gentlemen – welcome to this year's Women in Business conference. We're running slightly late so I am going to briskly wish you a happy and successful conference and, of course, I'm looking forward to catching up with some old faces and some new friends at lunchtime. In my capacity as Chair – for the fifth time, incidentally – it gives me great pleasure today to introduce five excellent speakers." Stella's heart started to race and she felt sick with nowhere to go. Gloria caught her eye and smiled. "As you will see from your programmes, we have two sessions before lunch and three shorter workshops this afternoon. So it gives me great pleasure to introduce our first keynote speaker today, Stella Gray, particularly as it is only a week since she received her MBE!" Gloria waved her hand in Stella's direction and the audience clapped enthusiastically, including a surprised Willis, who was annoyed with himself for being unaware of Stella's great achievement.

As Gloria slowly raised her hand, the audience responded and became silent once again. They knew how to behave in her presence – particularly the loyal "old faces".

Gloria returned to her notes. "Ladies, Stella Gray's achievements in the charity sector are impressive to say the least and the way that she has adapted to her new life, following a successful business career, is a model to us all. In her spare moments she is a mother of two and wife of a successful businessman. But, of course, it's not just her career that we will be hearing about today. In keeping with the 'My Life' theme of this year's conference, Stella will be talking about her own life, some of the things that she has achieved, some of the things that she values and some of the things she is planning in the future. She is well known for telling it how it is, so be prepared for an open and honest insight to her world. So please welcome to the stage our very special first guest…Mrs. Stella Gray MBE!"

Gloria Hemmings stepped to one side and led the applause. Stella left her seat and focused on the dozen daunting steps that led up to the stage. Fortunately it was a short walk. Stella's heart was pounding and she clutched her notes so tightly that it took her ten seconds to straighten them on the lectern in front of her. She could feel her left leg shaking violently so pushed it firmly against the lectern so that it would not betray her nerves in front of so many people. The applause continued until Gloria finally left the stage and sat down in the front row. Stella looked up in an attempt to acknowledge her audience of 400 women, a handful of men and a well-dressed chauffeur dressed in blue. The lights were so bright that she could only see the faces in the front three rows. Her throat felt dry, so she picked up a glass of water but quickly put it down as she could feel her hand trembling. She breathed deeply, spotted Willis's reassuring, friendly face in the front row and waited for two late arrivals to sit down at the back of the hall. The gift of an extra few seconds was both calming and invaluable.

"Good morning, ladies and gentlemen. First things first. I would like to thank WibCon, and in particular Gloria, for the very kind invitation to talk to you today about some of the things that have shaped and guided my life in recent years." There was complete silence. Willis watched nervously with his fingers crossed. He would later tell his wife that Stella got off to a safe but nervous start. "As you know, the theme throughout the conference today is 'My Life', but there is one thing I need to say straight away. I am certainly not qualified to tell you about the secrets to your happy life – all I can do is share with you the secrets to my *own* happy life. Hopefully, some things I say might ring a bell for you and help you to shape and build a happier future for yourself."

She sipped the water and successfully managed to hide the tremble. She looked up again and, this time, could now see ten rows of attentive delegates. "My story, in a sense, started eight years ago. By the way, I'm going to be very open with you today – as Gloria said, that's how I like to do things. I was an unhappy woman at that time, in an unhappy relationship, struggling along in my own little unhappy world. Family and neighbours would have observed little of this, although my close girlfriends – my real friends – knew that all was not well."

Stella looked up and engaged the front row. "That's an interesting point in itself, I think. Don't you think that real friends are the sort of people who walk in when the rest of the world walks out? Most friends will find time for you on their calendars but real friends won't even consult their calendars – they'll be there for you when you need them most." Rows of friendly faces nodded their agreement, as Stella paused for a moment.

"At that time in my life, I would finish each day exhausted and emotionally drained but, somehow, I would always feel that I had achieved nothing. I would often pour myself a drink, after another late supper with the TV, and say to myself: 'Is this it, Stella?' I longed for the day when I would be able to say 'Stella, this is it!' Although I was running a very successful market research agency, and had taken

114

it into a different league with some great results, I wasn't proud of who I was or what I was doing with my life. I had no meaningful goals and that also troubled me. I was also full of negative thoughts and, as we all know, over time our thoughts become words, our words become actions, our actions then become habits, our habits become our character and then our character becomes our destiny. I knew that I had to find a way of thinking differently or 'Is this it, Stella?' would become my reality and, therefore, my destiny.

"On the work front, I think I was struggling to be myself. To be honest, I was a bit of a 'karaoke leader', singing a verse from Tom Peters, followed by a verse from Maslow, followed by a chorus from Jack Welch, followed by a guitar solo from Anita Roddick. I was copying every good leader I could think of. Then I decided that I wanted to be a first-rate version of Stella and not a second-rate version of somebody else! I realised that I didn't need to be better than others – I just needed to be superior to my former self. Interestingly, my life changed dramatically when a number of wake-up calls happened – all at the same time.

"By the way, have you noticed that if you try and force the issue, to sit down and try and make rational decisions in your life, the whole thing can sometimes become more difficult?" The audience smiled. A woman in a pink suit nodded her agreement and nudged her neighbour to whisper a short summary of her own story. Stella continued. "There's an old Buddhist maxim that says that our 'teachers' in life appear only when we, the students, are ready to learn. That would certainly be true in my case.

"Let me tell you about the three wake-up calls that taught me a few things in the short space of 48 hours – two days when I was clearly ready to learn from life's teacher. One weekend, when my first husband was on a rugby tour with his workmates, I visited my sister, Carol, in Chester. Her young son, dressed in his Cub's uniform, showed me his watch and said '*Auntie Stella, did you know that this is a compass?*'

"I said, 'What do you mean – a compass? It's your watch, Nathan.'

"He took it off and said '*No, Auntie Stella, it is a compass. Did you know that if you point the hour hand towards the sun, the half-way point between the hour hand and midday points due South. So, you see, this watch is not a watch at all – it is a compass!*'

"That was my first wake-up call of the day. It struck me that my life, at that time, was governed by my watch, not my compass – by time, not by *direction*. I was dashing around, trying to squeeze in an extra meeting here and an extra meeting there, focusing on fitting more in rather than focusing on doing the right things. I was always running out of time and, looking back now, I can also see that I was obsessed with work and spending little time thinking about my own social, health and spiritual needs.

"I remembered Stephen Covey's famous comment about ladders – you probably know it too. He said that in the 'busyness' of life it is easy to work harder and harder, climbing the ladder of success, then arrive at the top of it *only to realise that the ladder has been leaning against the wrong wall!* Through Nathan's lovely and timely intervention, I realised that I needed some 'compass thinking', not 'clock thinking' to point my life in the right direction. As Mr. Covey would say, I needed to lean my ladder against a new wall.

"My second wake up call, on the same day, funnily enough, was a TV play called 'The Sentry'. I watched it with my sister and her husband. The lead character, a sentry played by Timothy Spall, ended up in an Army mental hospital that he frequently referred to as 'the home for the terminally bewildered!' In the play, there was a moment in the trenches when Tim, the sentry, heard a rustle in the bushes nearby and concluded that someone was hiding there. With rifle at the ready, the sentry nervously called out four questions which, for me, were also very profound:

Question one – *Halt, who goes there?*
Question two – *Who are you?*
Question three – *What are you doing here?*
Question four – *Where are you going?*"

"I sat there, with a glass of wine in my hand and a bowl of crisps in my lap, thinking: 'Who goes there? Who are you, Stella? What are you doing here on this planet? Where are you going with your life?' I shall never forget that moment. Later that night, and into the early hours, I revisited the sentry's questions and tried to answer them… but I couldn't.

"During the drive home the following day, I confined the Eurythmics and Madonna to the glove compartment and tried to get in touch with the silence within myself. By the way, don't bother saving up your pennies for a Virgin journey with Richard Branson to outer space – try the journey to inner space instead. It's more rewarding! I've been on many pleasant journeys with other people but, on this occasion, I needed to go on a journey with myself. By the end of the journey, I must have asked myself well over 20 more questions about my life. Some questions were inspired by various authors and training courses that impressed me over the years, some came from my good friends and some just occurred to me as I was driving along.

"I can't remember all of the questions, of course, but I can remember some." Stella turned her head to quickly check that the questions were coming up for all to see. She flicked a small hand-held gadget that assisted their speedy progress on to the large white screen behind her. "These are some of the questions that started my new life and I would like to share them with you. Don't write them down – there's a handout for you later. Here they are, coming up on the screen now... as you can see:

If Hollywood made a film of your life to date, what would they call it?

When are you at your happiest – what makes your heart truly sing?

What three words would you use to describe your life today?

If your marriage was a colour, a picture or a drink what would it be?

How many marks out of ten would you give your life?

What has to happen to give you a ten-out-of-ten life?

What would you do if you had twice the confidence and half the fear?

What decisions do you need to make about your life?

What is holding you up?

If you had one year to live, how would you live it?

What do you want to do before you leave this planet?

Who do you still need to talk to before you leave the planet?

What do you need to tell them?"

Willis looked around and noticed that, despite Stella's comments about her handout, many people were enthusiastically taking notes. There was a buzz in the room as people chatted enthusiastically to each other. Stella continued her presentation, raising her voice to emphasise some of the subtleties within her questions:

"If you went to sleep tonight and a miracle occurred, and you woke up to find that it was real, what would have happened?

If you had to design a personal logo for the future, what would it look like?

If Hollywood was to make a film of your future *life, what would you want them to call it?"*

Again, there was a buzz of excitement in the room. Stella sipped her water once more. She was feeling relaxed and confident and could now see the fine detail on people's faces. She was no longer blinded by the bright spotlights, she could see right to the back of the hall and could sense her audience's enthusiasm and support. She waited for the buzz to subside a little before continuing.

"So having already had two wake-up calls that weekend, courtesy of my nephew Nathan and good old Timothy Spall, I settled down in front of the TV after my long journey home from Chester. My husband had to go to London, ready for a business meeting the following day (so he said), so I sat down with my good friend, Tikka Masala, and flicked the channels for some Sunday night inspiration. So my third wake-up call that weekend came courtesy of Billy Crystal…you probably remember him from the film of the day, 'City Slickers'. For those of you who've seen the film you will remember that it features the adventures of three city executives who are in the middle of their respective mid-life crises. They decide to go on a cattle drive in an attempt to *'find themselves'*."

A lady in the fifth row smiled and whispered to her friend, "I don't want my husband to find himself – I want him to lose himself!"

"There's a lovely moment in the film where the lead character, played by Billy Crystal, is having a conversation with a leathery old cowboy called Curly, played by Jack Palance. The old cowboy says *'You city folk make me sick – you're all the same, you come out here with your fancy cars and fancy lifestyles trying to find some meaning to your pathetic little lives!'* Billy Crystal then says, *'And have you found the meaning of your life, Curly?'* Curly says *'Sure have, boy – it's only about one thing.'* And Billy Crystal says, *'You mean that you know what the meaning of life is – and it's about one thing? What is it? What is it, Curly?'* Curly looks at him and says, *'Life is only about one thing, son – and that's for you to find out!'*

"Then and there, in front of the TV, I decided what my 'one thing' in life was – the true meaning of my life. It was about helping others and making a difference and I realised that the secret of my future happiness would be to direct all of my energy towards this goal. With the help of Billy and his City Slickers, I finally figured out my life's purpose and things quickly fell into place for me. With this new focus and personal vision, I realised that I would never have to 'work' another day in my life. I resigned from my job as Chief Executive of the market research company the very next day. On that same day, I took a small step forward to leave the world a better place. I wanted my future life to touch people. Even if only one life breathed easier as a result of my contribution, that would be enough – that would be my new definition of success. I wanted to stand up for an ideal or do something that would improve the lot of others or strike out against some injustice. I wanted to do something that would send a tiny ripple of hope! I wanted to lose myself in something that was bigger than myself and decided to trade in my rich lifestyle to help others create a richer life.

"I also realised that some of the earlier misery in my life was optional and made the decision to be a happy, fulfilled person in the future. As Abraham Lincoln once said '*People are as happy as they make up their minds to be!*'" On the screen, a picture of a sombre looking gentleman, wearing a tall, black hat filled the screen. "Or to put it another way, I decided to treat pain in life as inevitable but to treat misery as something I could choose to leave behind. I decided to stop feeling sorry for myself and promised that I would never again complain about things that I had permitted!"

Stella was gaining in confidence, the audience was still buzzing with excitement and Willis was feeling very proud of her.

"At a personal level, and as part of my new life, I also decided to let my first husband go. I won't bore you with the details but he had never really been mine, and never would be mine. As Kahlil Gibran once said: '*If you love somebody, let them go, for if they return they were always yours and if they don't, they never were.*' It was an unhappy time as I found it difficult to forgive my husband for a number of 'misdemeanours' but there again, men will be men!"

Willis shifted in his seat and felt a little uncomfortable as he wasn't sure what was to about to come.

"You've probably heard the story about the creation of the universe," continued Stella. "When God was just about done with creating it, he realised that he had two things left over in his bag, so decided to split them between Adam and Eve. He told them one of the things he had left was a thing that would allow the owner to pee whilst standing up. *'This is a very handy thing,'* said God, *'and I was wondering if one of you would like it?'* Adam jumped up and down and begged God to let him have it. *'It sounds fab – just the sort of thing a man should be able to do! Please, please, please give it to me!'* Eve smiled and told God that if Adam really wanted it, then he should have it.

"So God gave Adam the thing that allowed him to pee standing up. Adam was so excited that he peed on the bark of a nearby tree, over a wall and then wrote his name in the sand, laughing all the time with delight. God and Eve watched Adam for a moment and then God said to Eve *'Well, here's the other thing in my bag. I guess it's yours.'* *'What's it called?'* said Eve. *'Brains!'* said God."

The audience roared with laughter and Willis managed a nervous smile. Eventually the noise subsided and Stella leaned forward. "So, girls, let's just say that men have what they want but we have all the brains! I'll leave it there and say no more."

The audience laughed again. "Returning to the subject of my ex-husband, a friend of mine reminded me that forgiveness is a form of freedom and unless I could forgive him, I would always be shackled to him. So I let him go. As Gandhi once said: *'Anger is an acid that can often do more harm to the vessel in which it stands than to anything on which it is poured.'* With my first husband out of the picture, I decided to just concentrate on learning to love the woman in the mirror. The person whose verdict would count most in the future was the person staring back at me."

Stella stared at her notes and felt a moment of panic as she had lost her way. She quickly attempted to summarise the story so far. "So, as you can see, within 48 hours of my three wake-up calls, my life had changed completely. I decided to get on with it and achieve my full potential. In the words of one of my favourite songs, *'I spent many days stringing and re-stringing my guitar, while the song I came to sing remains unsung'*. So I moved forward and also decided to stop worrying about things that I couldn't influence or improve. I realised that there was only one corner of the universe that I could be certain of improving and that was my own corner. I realised that changing my life was an inside job. I decided to stop watching the TV weather broadcasts and decided to carry my own personal weather around with me."

Stella sipped her iced water, which felt good as it slipped down her warm throat. "So…rather than work for a charity, I decided to start one. With the help of a few close friends I started 'One Day'. As some of you will know, I chose the title as I was fed up with hearing people say, '*One day it will be different!*' The charity helps underprivileged and abused children find a new world, a new peace and a new happiness. When we started, I wanted to find 365 people who, for one day each year, would be prepared to devote their time and efforts to raise money for the charity. The target was £100 per person but in year one, we exceeded this and raised just over £38,000. The next part of the plan was to encourage one per cent of the 365 people to set up their own groups and raise £100 per person, in a similar way. So at the end of year two, we had 1860 people across the country that, between them, raised just under £200,000. We're now in year three and with one per cent of the 1860 going on to set up their own groups with 365 people raising £100 each, we're set to raise a further £839,000.

"By repeating this model, by the end of year five we will be raising £18,140,500 each year and by the end of year seven we hope to be up to £392m! And all of this through one person giving up one day each year and a business model that assumes that just one per cent of our volunteers will keep multiplying the organisation."

The audience applauded loudly and acknowledged Stella's fantastic achievements. Four ladies, who had travelled together from Halifax, stood up and cheered enthusiastically. Stella smiled and caught Willis' eye. He was applauding so enthusiastically that he looked like a clapping seal waiting for the fish that is thrown following a successful trick.

"I'm coming to the end now so could I just say another big thank-you to Gloria for inviting me here today. I've enjoyed myself immensely and hope that my ramblings may have been of some interest to you. I'll summarise my presentation and bring you up to date with my life today. I'm now happily remarried and have a great relationship. I can remember reading somewhere that relationships are like sand held in your hand. If you hold the sand loosely, with an open hand, it will stay on your hand. But if you close your hand tightly the sand trickles through your fingers – you can try and hang on to it but most of it will be spilled. Held loosely with respect and freedom for the other person, a relationship is likely to remain intact. But hold the relationship too tightly, too possessively, and it will slip away and be lost. I certainly have that with Simon. We're very happy together and have two lovely daughters. By the way, if you decide to remarry, make sure that you find a man who wears earrings – they make great husbands as they've already experienced pain and know how to buy jewellery!"

The audience laughed loudly and Stella felt relaxed and elated. "Let me leave you with another thought. When you next experience a bad time in your life, just remember that there are probably some good reasons for it. Rather than trying to forget the bad time, try and understand the lesson that life is trying to teach you at that time. What is the lesson that life wants you to learn?

"Thirdly, remember that in times of stress, you have three options. You can either avoid the thing that's causing you stress, you can adapt to the thing that's causing you stress or you can alter the thing that's causing you stress. There are no right answers, of course. The choice is yours…but I have learned that *altering* my life has brought more rewards than the other two options. I have learned that action may not always bring you happiness but there is no happiness, at home or at work, without action. You have to *make* things happen."

Stella clicked the hand-held device and a picture of three frogs appeared on the screen behind her. "Let me ask you this – if three frogs were sat on a lily pad and one decided to jump off, how many would be left?" The audience looked a little confused but Stella would not be rushed. She waited for a response and eventually two ladies in the fourth row shouted out, "Two, Stella!" They waited for public recognition and praise.

Stella smiled. "No, not two frogs….still three frogs! Remember that *deciding* to jump off is not the same as *actually* jumping off!" There was warm laughter and much nodding and applause in the audience. "So if I've said a few things that have rung a bell for you today, please don't decide to take action…jump and *actually* make things happen in your life!

"Finally, I've learned that there are five steps to happiness – or perhaps I should say five steps to my own happiness." Stella glanced at the screen once again and flicked the device. "As it now says on the screen:

Number One – know what you want in life.
Number Two – know where you are now.
Number Three – know what you have to do to get what you want.
Number Four – remove your limiting beliefs.

"Be brave as life shrinks or expands in proportion to one's courage. As Mark Twain said, '*Courage is the mastery of fear, not the absence of it!*' Remember that whatever you're afraid of is a clear indicator of the next thing you probably need to do! Fortunately there is often liberation in making a difficult decision – the fear of fear is often worse than the fear itself. Don't be afraid to take big steps – as David Lloyd George once said, '*You can't jump a chasm in two jumps!*' Stay focused on what you want – we only see obstacles when we take our mind off our goals! Remember that, in this area of limiting beliefs, the only thing that gets in the way of you and happiness is *you!*" Stella lowered her voice and slowed the pace of her delivery. "Far too many of us in this hall today are not living our dreams because we're too busy living our fears!"

A woman in the front row discreetly located a tissue and dabbed her eyes.

"And finally…*Number Five* – live *your dreams!* Go confidently in the direction of your dreams. Live the life you imagine, not your history. The future belongs to those who truly believe in the beauty of their dreams! It's never too late to become what we are capable of becoming! Enjoy your life in the future and, in the words of a famous song, please remember that '*life is not about the number breaths you take, but the number of times that life takes your breath away!*'

"I wish you all best wishes and success in the future as you enjoy Life with a capital 'L'. Thank you all so much for listening to me today. Thank you!"

Stella gathered her notes and headed for the front row to join Willis. The applause was deafening and everyone gave her a standing ovation. Three photographers jostled competitively to get the best angles. Gloria held Stella's arm and led her back to the stage once more to acknowledge the enthusiastic applause. Gloria then took three paces to the side to let Stella receive the audience's full appreciation. It was her moment and the audience cheered loudly.

After a short break, Stella and Willis stayed to listen to the second keynote address, then headed north back up the A1 as the conference gathering started to munch their way through a mountain of quiche and sandwiches. Stella looked exhausted and said little. Willis was keen to talk and had many questions lined up for her. However, he sensed that time was running out, as Stella was beginning to yawn.

"Stella, that was a fantastic presentation – absolutely brilliant! I really enjoyed it – as did everybody else, I'm sure." He glanced at Stella, who was sitting next to him with her shoes off. "I liked your Gandhi quote on the acid of anger, and if I could offer you a compliment based around some of his other words of wisdom, '*You are truly the change you want to see in the world*',"

"Thank you, George. Thank you. You're very kind." Stella yawned once again. "I'm just trying to change the world by changing *my* world and I'm also still learning a lot, George."

"Well, I suppose we all are, but what do you mean exactly, Stella?" said Willis.

"I learn all the time, particularly from my children. Don't you find that we often learn most from the people who have the greatest investment in the future?"

"Yes, we do," said Willis. "I seem to remember having a conversation with your husband along similar lines."

Stella turned towards Willis. "Let me give you an example of the learning I'm talking about, George. Last weekend the girls decided that they were going to dig the garden. I thought this was rather odd as they've never shown any interest in the garden before. Being a good parent, I said nothing apart from encouraging them out into the fresh air and invited Rory, our nutty dog, to keep an eye on them.

"Anyway, after an hour I went out and asked the girls what they were doing. Claire jumped up and told me that they were digging their way to see Father Christmas in Lapland to make sure he knew what presents they wanted for Christmas. I smiled, as you do, and told Claire that digging to Lapland was impossible but then she held up a jam jar full of worms and spiders and strange-looking insects. Lucy took off the lid, showed me their wonderful assortment of wildlife and emptied a few on to her hand. Then she said, '*Ah, but even if we don't manage to dig all the way to see Father Christmas, Mum…look what we've found along the way!*'

"I stood there with a tear in my eye. Although their goal was far too ambitious, of course, it caused them to dig. And maybe that's the whole point of any of our goals – to set us digging in the right direction."

"That's a lovely story, Stella. I'll tell my wife that later – Anne will love it." Willis checked the dashboard clock and settled down for the journey as Stella yawned again. "Don't worry – we'll be home before you know it, Stella. Your long journey today will soon be over and you'll be back in Mapleford with your family."

"Of course, George…but don't miss the point will you?"

"What point, Stella?"

"The Father Christmas point, George. As the well known saying goes, 'It's nice to have an end to the journey but, in life, it's joy in the journey that matters in the end!'"

She ran her fingers through her long hair, turned her collar up, leaned back into the cream leather upholstery, yawned again and quickly fell asleep. Willis smiled. He felt very proud of Stella and glanced occasionally to see if she was still asleep. He turned up the heat so she did not awaken with a chill and looked at her from time to time to make sure that all was well in her sleepy world.

"Thank you, Stella. You may still be learning from your children but I've learned a lot from you today. *Joy in the journey is what matters in the end.'* Yes, I'll always remember that. Thank you."

Wit and Wisdom
Chapter 4 Summary

1. Money motivates neither the best people nor the best in people.

2. Don't be a karaoke leader – it's better to be a first-rate version of yourself rather than a second-rate version of someone else.

3. Be governed by your compass, not your clock.

4. Find the time to listen to the silence inside yourself.

5. If the (City Slickers) meaning of life is about finding one thing and one thing only – what's the *one* thing you need to find?

6. Unless you can forgive someone, you will always be shackled to them.

7. Stop listening to weather forecasts and start carrying your own personal weather around with you.

8. We should never complain about things we permit (Sue Cheshire).

9. The only thing that gets in the way of you and happiness…is you!

10. When you next experience a bad time in your life ask yourself the question: *"What is the lesson that life is trying to teach me right now?"*

Chapter 5
The Journey Up The Trust Mountain

It was 1 November. Simon Gray strolled across the gravel and walked towards the Bentley's open rear door. He held his briefcase in one hand and his blue coat in the other. George Willis stood to attention and smiled – his protégé was back.

"Good morning, Willis! How are you? I've missed your snappy wit and wisdom, although don't let it go to your head!" Simon tossed his briefcase across the back seat, smiled and shook Willis' right hand vigorously.

Willis smiled again in return. "Good morning, sir. Thank you for your kind words. I assume that you're feeling much better now?"

"I certainly am Willis – like a dog with two dicks, actually. I had a nasty bout of flu and it knocked me out for a while. Perhaps it was my body's way of telling me something I needed to take on board – who knows?" Simon folded his coat and eased himself into the sumptuous cream leather once again. "I've missed this too, Willis. It's nice to be back in the land of luxury. Let's go then. 'A journey of a thousand miles starts with a single step...' as they say."

"Your journeys might start like that," said Willis, "but before I drove this Bentley my journeys often used to start with a broken fan belt or a flat tyre!"

"Fair enough, Willis. I see you haven't lost your sense of humour."

The Bentley crunched its way down the drive once more and headed for familiar business territory although it was a mile before Willis had to determine the route for the day. "Left, right or straight on, sir?" he said.

"Straight on, Willis. We're heading north but not to the Dark Side. We are going to a hotel for a teambuilding day."

"Sounds interesting – what prompted that?"

Simon leaned forward. "Although I was ill for a week or so, the break gave me a great opportunity to reflect on a few things and plan for the future. The teambuilding day is part of the 'new me', you might say."

"I'm pleased to hear it," said Willis, as he adjusted the electronic wing mirrors. "So are things any clearer for you? Last time we met we both had an interesting and emotional day…to say the least!"

"You can say that again, Willis. But yes, I've reflected on the emotions of that day. Although there were more lows than highs, I think it was one of the most important days in my life. I've taken on board many of the things we talked about last time and I think I've finally got my head around the bosses and leaders thing, you'll be pleased to hear. As you would say, 'if it is to be, it's up to me'!"

"Did I say that?" enquired Willis.

"No, Willis, you didn't, actually. I heard a well known businessman say it on the radio this morning – one of the Dragons, if you watch the TV programme. He referred to it as the ten most important two-letter words of all time. Mind you, it's the sort of smart-arsed comment that you would say, isn't it?" Simon smiled as he opened up his briefcase to locate his diary and mobile. Willis ignored Simon's remark and focused on the road works ahead.

"So how did you get on with my wife, Willis? I hope she kept you busy for the day?"

Willis blushed. "Err…we had a great day, actually. She's an inspiration, isn't she? I was very impressed with her conference presentation. It was stunning. She had everyone on their feet for ten minutes at the end. Did she tell you all about it?"

"Of course," said Simon. "I'm very proud of her. And you're right, Willis, she is an inspiration."

"She certainly has a fantastic grasp of the things that are important in her life, doesn't she? I think everyone went away with the intention of seriously reviewing the choices they're making and how their work-life balance is doing."

"I'm sure they did, Willis. Stella is a woman who knows how to motivate an audience – and she's a leader not a boss, isn't she?"

"I think she is, sir – no doubt about it. She knows how to inspire willing action, that's for sure."

"Except from our dog – that seems to be left to me! By the way, do you know where the Three Shires Hotel is, Willis?"

"I certainly do, sir. It's another very nice hotel – you seem to have the knack of selecting them. Mind you, I'm assuming that we're talking about the same hotel – the one near Lichfield."

"It is," said Simon. "As this teambuilding day is going to feature another round of sparring with the production team, I thought I would find a neutral venue!"

"I see," said Willis. "So what's the score so far and how many rounds have you got left?"

"I think I'm a couple of points adrift with three rounds to go," said Simon, continuing the boxing analogy. "What do you think to my teambuilding idea then, Willis? A bit of a turnaround for me, don't you think?"

Willis glanced up at the rear view mirror but didn't get a chance to answer as Simon was in full flow. "Yes, I can see the look of surprise on your face, Willis, but this session is something I want to do to as part of our re-launch for the future. I was going to bring in an outside consultant for the day but I've decided to run it myself."

"I don't blame you," said Willis. "Consultants are good on theory but they know nothing of the real world. They are the sort of people who know 125 different ways to make love…but don't have a partner!"

"Ha, ha, very funny, Willis. I like that – I thought I'd heard most of the gags about consultants, but I haven't heard that one."

"Would you like to hear another one?" said Willis, responding to the warm appreciation of his backseat audience.

Simon was keen not to deflate Willis' enthusiasm. "If you must, Willis, if you must."

"Well, sir…did you know that scientists have started to use management consultants instead of white rats in their experiments?"

"Really…and the reason for this, Willis, is what exactly…?"

"There are three reasons actually, sir. Firstly, there are more management consultants than white rats! Secondly, you can't become emotionally attached to a management consultant and, thirdly, there are some things that a white rat just won't do!"

"Very good, Willis!" Simon laughed again then said, "Actually, I've decided not to use consultants as I'm beginning to realise that the best consultants are probably the 240 people who work for me…the problem is that I've not motivated or mobilised them…yet!"

"Really?" said Willis, looking surprised for the second time in five miles. "That's very insightful. I'm pleased to hear it, sir. No – that sounded far too patronising. Let me try again. I am really delighted to hear you say something like that! That is really truly significant."

"Perhaps I should be ill more often!" Simon was enjoying the early morning banter with Willis and both men were smiling, relaxed and totally at ease with each other. The countryside sped past as the Bentley headed north-west to the hotel. Simon was deep in thought and the only sound was the occasional flick from the pages of his notebook. Willis obliged and listened to the radio, which was barely audible from the back seat. As the 7am news approached, Simon asked Willis to turn up the volume.

The Home Secretary stumbled through an interview with the Radio 4 presenter. His response to a series of challenging questions on a national security issue was far from convincing.

"Right, I've had enough of him. The man's an idiot! It sounds as if he's reading a spin doctor's script! Turn him down, Willis, if you don't mind."

"I think that—" began Willis

"This isn't another of your management consultant jokes, is it?" interrupted Simon.

"Certainly not, sir. I'm on to politics now. My father used to say that politicians and nappies should be changed often…and for exactly the same reason!"

Simon burst out laughing. "That's marvellous, Willis – very funny!"

They laughed and joked their way past Northampton then Simon settled down to his paperwork and phone calls. Selected members of the Alderton's management team were about to receive their early morning calls once again. Today, the finance team, led by Gerry Manning, appeared to be on Simon's list. Willis concentrated on the traffic, whilst taking in the views of middle England. The ruins of an old castle looked down on to an emerging new science park that was being built

130

on the outskirts of a small town that was once the shoe capital of the world. The castle moat was now completely dry although, ironically, there were now acres of flood waters that circled menacingly around the town. The recent floods had devastated many farms and outlying areas and had left their oily, stinking residue behind. Simon could sense that the car had slowed and looked up to see the surrounding countryside. "Bloody hell, that's an unbelievable sight, isn't it?"

"It certainly is, sir, it certainly is. What a mess…and think of the human misery!"

After an hour of silence, and with Coventry now on the horizon, Willis found himself thinking of Simon's challenge. "So how do you see your teambuilding session today then?" enquired Willis, glancing up at the rear-view mirror.

"I wondered how long it would take you today, Willis. One hour of silence but I suppose I should be thankful – at least it wasn't a piranha question designed to attack my sensitive parts! Well, by definition, this teambuilding session is going to feature a lot of discussion and group exercises. I've given it a lot of thought actually – today is going to be a turning point in the progress and fortunes of the Dark Side."

Willis smiled. He was impressed with Simon's new determination and passion. "And what do you hope to get out of this programme, sir? What are the main outcomes that you have in mind?"

Simon leaned forward. "One of the outcomes will be people working together to produce results that are greater than the sum of the individual parts – 'synergy', I think the textbooks call it. *None of us is as strong as all of us*, and all that. If I can get one plus one plus one plus one to equal five, then that 25 per cent improvement could mean 25 per cent more turnover, 25 per cent less costs, 25 per cent more profit or 25 per cent less staff turnover. However I measure it, I want it! Aldertons needs an extra 25 per cent of everything that's going!"

Simon flicked through his notes. "Another outcome would be improved communication. At the moment there's a lot of damage being caused by an inaccurate and mischievous grapevine – we need a better official communication process. Did you once tell me about John Harvey Jones' book? Apparently, he said that the ideal organisation, and the one with the best chance of success, is one where, if you asked anyone, from the chairman to the newest recruit on the shop floor, what the business was trying to achieve…you would get the same answer!"

"I think that's very true," said Willis. I'm a great believer in tabloid communication – and lots of it. It's still more common for people to suffer from a lack of communication rather than too much of it. In my career I've often heard people moan about the lack of information but I've never heard anyone in business complaining of being over-informed, have you?"

"Very true," replied Simon, flicking another page of his notes. "We need to get it sorted as communication and trust levels rise and fall together. I've got some more stuff on teambuilding outcomes in here somewhere…other outcomes I want from this programme are a move towards innovation and creativity, less conflict and more cooperation. I want a company culture where creative sparks fly and where we have lots of wacky ideas floating around. But as far as cooperation is concerned, I've got my work cut out there! At the moment, we have a situation where there's almost complete ignorance of what anyone else is doing. The world of my sales people is seen as being different from life in production, accounts or the warehouse. Suspicion is based on ignorance and my managers reinforce this sectarian view and run their departments as if they were separate kingdoms. They dig in and repel all boarders. They carry on as if the enemy were within the organisation! They…no, let me change my words…*we* need to change from 'us versus them' to 'all of us versus the common problems'. I want cooperation within and competition without. That's the only way it can be.

"You gave me a lecture once, Willis, on the value of military analogies in business…and, having thought about it, I think you were absolutely right. Alderton's has traditionally dominated the high ground and has built some strong castles in the right places, has some good equipment and well trained soldiers, but at the moment we're not pointing our guns at our enemies – we're pointing our guns at each other. We should be called Friendly Fire Ltd!"

Willis smiled again. He had never heard Simon talk with such clarity, focus and calm determination. He seemed noticeably different, but Willis was looking for more evidence of the sustainable actions that would actually deliver Simon's outcomes. "So, how are you going to run this teambuilding day then?" he enquired.

"Well, I've got a few handouts and things here in my briefcase, but I won't show them to you now, if that's all right with you, Willis. You keep your eyes on the road. I want to arrive in Lichfield in one piece."

"Fair enough, sir. I would love to have a look when we park up but, in the meantime, what sort of things are you talking about?"

"The main thing I've got to do today is to encourage the team to attack the problems, not each other."

"And who is in this team?" said Willis

"Well, there are quite a few of them. There's the Production Manager, Dave Wilmott, who I've probably mentioned before. He has made my life particularly difficult up until now, but I'm hoping to improve my relationship with him as a result of today."

"Sounds good to me," said Willis, offering enthusiastic support from the front seat. "I like your comment about improving your relationship with him as, for one awful moment, I thought you were going to say that you were hoping to sort him out today."

"There's no point thinking of revenge, Willis. '*Any man who opts for revenge should dig two graves*'," said Simon, smiling. "I didn't think of that, by the way – it's an old Chinese proverb."

"I thought I was the one who was supposed to deliver the one-liners!" joked Willis.

"Don't worry, Willis, your job's safe!"

Willis looked up at the rear-view mirror. "Are you a fan of Martin Luther King?" he said.

"Who isn't?" replied Simon. "He's one of the greatest leaders ever."

"Do you know the story of his battle with Bobby Kennedy in the early sixties?" continued Willis, beginning to sound like a celebrity historian.

"What battle, Willis? The Kennedy family supported Martin Luther King, if I remember correctly."

"You're right – they eventually became great friends and allies but in the early days, Bobby Kennedy was a pain in King's side and made life very difficult for him in the corridors of power in Washington. So King said to his aides, '*Go and find out some good things about Bobby Kennedy – we need to work on them.*' One of the aides said, '*There is nothing good about Bobby Kennedy!*' Apparently King persisted and asked his team to bring back some good news about Kennedy's character and personality but, again, the aides came back with nothing but bad news. One of the aides said, '*Forget Bobby Kennedy, he's not on-side and never will be!*'"

"So what did Martin Luther King do about it?" enquired Simon, who had abandoned his paperwork and was actively listening to Willis' story.

"He turned to his team and said, '*Gentlemen, go and find me one good thing about Bobby Kennedy – that will be the door that we drive this Movement through!*'"

"Good story…so let's have the action point, then," said Simon.

"Well, I suppose the action point is that although your Dave Wilmott has made life difficult for you, he probably has one small door, one good point, that you can work on and drive your change-management movement through."

"That's a good point, Willis…a very good point."

"Who else is in the team?" enquired Willis.

"Also in this teambuilding session today is Sarah Leeson, my Quality Manager, Rajesh Mureshi from the Warehouse, a young guy called Jaffa Carr from Dispatch, Linda Williams from R&D and Billy Wicklow – he is one of the Production Supervisors."

"Why is your Mr. Carr called Jaffa?" asked Willis.

Simon smiled. "Because he's got ginger hair – he's OK about the nickname though."

Willis continued: "And when you say that you want the team to attack the problems not each other, how are you going to get them to put their cards on the table and talk about these…problems?"

"I'm going to use a DotComm exercise, Willis."

"A what-comm?" enquired Willis

"A DotComm, Willis. Don't tell me I've come across something you know nothing about?"

Willis looked a little deflated. "Sorry…can't remember that one."

"Don't worry, Willis, you haven't heard of it because I only invented it on my sick bed!" Simon laughed loudly and was clearly enjoying being in the driving seat for once. Willis, who actually was sitting in the driving seat, and was feeling a little perplexed and out of it, was happy in the knowledge that Simon was clearly making some progress and was responding to the hundreds of miles of provocative remarks and uncomfortable piranha questions from their earlier trips.

"My Dot Comm exercise actually means 'dotted line communication', Willis. I'm going to give everyone a handout with a number of incomplete sentences on it. Each team member will have to complete the dotted lines, then read them out."

"Sounds a bit complicated to me," replied Willis. "What sort of sentences are you planning to give them?"

"It's not complicated at all, Willis." Simon leaned forward. "Here, listen to these:

The three words I would use to describe Aldertons are…
Communication works well when…
Communication works poorly when…
If I had to score our customer service I would score it…
I feel happiest when …
I get concerned when I think about…
Tension builds up when we…
We work particularly well when…
Things are getting…
Relationships within this team are…
If I could wave a magic wand over this team I would…
Three things we need to do more of are…
Three things we need to do less of are…
Three things we need to be better at are…
Our team motto for the future should be…

How does that lot sound on your ears, Willis?"

Willis smiled. "They sound very good on my ears actually, sir, and I also like the fact that your unfinished statements will uncover and encourage some strong *emotions* around the table."

"They certainly will," said Simon, with a content smile on his face.

"Also," continued Willis, "I've always believed that the best way to give feedback when emotions are running high is to describe yourself, not the other person. So they will describe how *they* feel rather than attacking a colleague or you, won't they?"

"They will, Willis. The exercise should help to get us up the trust mountain."

"What mountain is that, exactly?" enquired Willis, glancing at the rear-view mirror once again. "Is it near Lichfield?"

"Don't tell me that I've found something else you're not familiar with, Willis! However, I must come clean – it's something I read at the weekend in a business magazine. Apparently, when people meet for the first time, communication tends to be fairly superficial. They suss each other out, then, as the relationship develops, topics of conversation are quite broad but mostly factual. Then the conversation moves from *facts* to *opinions*. Finally, when people feel very safe and really know their colleagues, they'll be happy to move from facts and opinions to *feelings*. According to the article, feelings sit at the top of this trust mountain. There's no higher form of verbal communication than exchanging feelings, working through their implications and building an agreed way forward."

"Well, your unfinished DotComm statements sound like an excellent, fun way of encouraging people to get things out in the open. But what's the key log for you and the team today?"

"The what-log?" said Simon, looking confused.

Willis smiled as he looked up at the rear-view mirror to make eye contact with Simon. He felt that he was regaining some control and influence once again. "Surely you've come across that one, sir. When trying to solve problems with your team, why not copy the Canadian logger's technique when clearing a logjam. He climbs a tall tree or stands on a prominent rock to identify the key log causing the logjam. He then places an explosive charge, blows it and lets the power of the river do the rest.

"An amateur would start at the edge of the logjam and move all the logs, eventually getting to the key log. Both approaches work, of course, but finding the key log first saves both time and effort. All problems have a key log – you just need to find it. So what's yours?"

"Hmmm," replied Simon, stroking his chin. Another five minutes went by without a word. "Pull into the Services please, Willis. I need to stretch my legs."

The Bentley slowed to negotiate the narrow entrance to the Services. The car park was full of activity. For some strange reason, well over 20 caravans were parked line-abreast on one side of the car park and, on the other side, dozens of OAPs were escaping from two coaches and were rapidly heading for the main entrance with the intention of locating the toilets.

"Look at that lot parked over there – what's the collective noun for two dozen caravans, Willis?"

"I think the phrase is 'an irritation of caravans'," muttered Willis, clearly sharing Simon's feelings towards the caravanning community. He eventually found a parking space and Simon then headed for the entrance. By pretending to be on his mobile, he narrowly escaped an ambush from two competing roadside breakdown sales agents. He returned, telephone still attached to his ear, clutching a brown bag containing a bottle of water and a bottle of orange juice. He flopped back into the car.

"Take your pick, Willis."

"Thank you. I've just been listening to the local radio," said Willis. "There was a problem this morning further up the M6 but it has cleared now."

"So has my mind, Willis. I can now see the key log, as you called it. I know what has to happen in order for this team to un-jam itself and make progress."

Willis turned around, put the cap back on his bottled water and said "Really…and your key log is…?"

"Me!" said Simon, smiling. "*I* am the key log. I've been their problem. They don't trust me and they don't trust my motives. If I can get some open discussion on that issue we'll move forward and, as you said earlier, the 'power of the river' will do the rest. Let me use a different metaphor. Sadly, during recent months, armed with my size ten, heavy-duty hammer, I've hit a few nails into Production's 'fence' – you know, their territory – and, even if I take them out, one by one, I'll leave the holes and their fence will never be quite the same. I've said a few things in anger since I joined and I know that the holes in the fence will remain like scars. My aggressive verbal wounds have been just as damaging as aggressive physical ones."

Willis turned back and fiddled with the keys. "So how will you encourage them to give you feedback on their lack of trust and their views of your management style? That's not going to be easy," he said. "If you say 'talk to me about your lack of trust', it's going to be a very short and rather quiet meeting, isn't it?"

"Exactly. I'm happy to share my fence and nails story with them but I think I'll need to add some more DotComm statements to the list. I'll let you know in a minute what I come up with. Shall we go?"

The Bentley resumed its steady, northerly progress. Five minutes later, as Willis surveyed a bewildering array of blue motorway options displayed on overhead gantries, Simon leaned forward once again.

"Right, Willis, have a listen to these unfinished Dot Comm statements:

One thing I would like Simon to carry on doing is…
One thing I would like Simon to stop doing is…
One thing I would like Simon to start doing is…
In order for me to give Simon my total support I would like him to…"

"They're very good, sir. I think that you've got a great idea there. I think that your DotComm statements will encourage the team to give you the honest feedback you need to start again and move forward."

"But I'm still worried about one thing, Willis. Teams are more likely trust each other if they really know each other and I'm not sure that we do really *know* each other. I think we know each other's roles and responsibilities but we don't know each other as…*people*…we only know the masks that we all wear to work."

Willis turned his head slightly. "Well, why don't you first run an exercise that encourages the team to talk openly about themselves, their likes, dislikes, their families and so on. You could easily use your same Dot Comm format. For example, you could have a handout that has on it:

The happiest day of my life was when…
The greatest achievement in my life so far is…
If I won the National Lottery I would…
If you talked to my partner about me they would say…
A particularly difficult time in my life was when…"

"Isn't that last point a bit risky, Willis? It's a bit intrusive isn't it?"

"Ah, but when people share a bit of personal information it works like glue. Exposing a little vulnerability, in one's own words in one's own time, leads to a tighter bond and more mutual respect."

"OK. I can see your point," said Simon. "So how about some more statements like:

My greatest claim to fame is…
The person I most admire in life is…
At home I relax by…
Two things you don't know about me are…"

"They sound perfect, sir. And if you're looking for another team building exercise I can also recommend the Twelve Teams exercise."

"You'd better explain that, Willis. Hang on, I need to find my pen. It's disappeared down the back of the seat. Got it…right, fire away."

"My daughter, Debbie, came up with this one when she joined the construction company. Imagine that you have twelve teams written on a flip chart or on a handout, like the cast of a play, fire crew at an emergency, a gang of criminals, a human family, the staff of an operating theatre, a hockey team, the Cabinet…how many is that, sir?"

"Let me count them…that's seven, Willis."

"OK, so we need a few more. How about the members of a rock band, the crew of a yacht, soldiers on operational duties… I can't think of any more."

Simon leaned forward. "What about a group of dancers and the crew of a spacecraft? That would make a nice round dozen. What would I do now?"

"You would ask each team member to write down, without conferring, the team that they think most closely resembles the Production team today and then write down the team they would like the Production team to resemble in the future."

"So, presumably, they talk openly about team characteristics today, team characteristics that they would like to see in the future and the action the team needs to take to make it all happen? Is that how it works?" asked Simon.

"Exactly. There's no right answer, of course. All twelve teams of people are *teams* but, in the minds of each team member, some will be more of a team than others…"

"…and presumably, one team member could think that the Cabinet is a good example of an effective team and another team member could think that the Cabinet is a poor team?" said Simon.

"They certainly could," said Willis. "As I said earlier, there's no right answer on any of these issues – just perceptions. You will have a rich and lively discussion about life in Production by using an interesting and fun team exercise that runs parallel to it."

"I like that, Willis…or perhaps I should be thanking your daughter."

"I'll pass that on to Debbie, sir. I'm sure she'll be delighted."

"Well that's that then, Willis. I can see from the power station on the horizon that we must be approaching the Three Shires Hotel."

Willis parked the car close to reception and watched as Simon entered the building, joined by three members of the Production team who had travelled together. He gave the Bentley its customary once over and detected a minute scratch on the door panel. "Bloody caravans!" he muttered. He located his trusty chamois and spent the next 20 minutes applying tender love and care to the vehicle.

For the rest of the day, Willis busied himself in a local museum and a number of tea shops and cafes around Lichfield Cathedral. In the morning he joined a walking tour of the city and learned about life there during the Civil War. They visited the lodgings of famous Cavalier generals and studied the marks on the cathedral walls from shot fired by Roundhead muskets.

Willis thought that the tour guide resembled his old chemistry teacher, Mr. Newson, who always wore his glasses on the end of his nose. To Willis and his classmates, the specs had been a mystery. For the five years that Willis attended Rosemount Grammar, those glasses had defied gravity and remained glued in place with their owner's beady eyes constantly scanning the room for the prospect of any disruptive behaviour. The discovery of gambling, and the prospect of winning a handful of coins, had encouraged the boys to try and dislodge Mr. Newson's glasses. There were many attempts to nudge him, run into him or force him to turn quickly, but all had resulted in failure. The glasses always stayed in place and Mr. Newson's own place in school history was therefore assured. He would be discussed at school reunions for decades to come.

In the afternoon, Willis went to Cannock Chase for a walk along the tracks and hills. The views were stunning and, on the return journey, he visited a famous wartime cemetery and had a cup of tea in a nearby café. Willis collected Simon at 4.30pm and they headed south, once again staying just ahead of the rush-hour traffic. Willis waited for ten minutes to detect the mood on the back seat. Simon looked relaxed and had removed his tie.

"So how was your teambuilding session?" enquired Willis.

"It went exceptionally well, actually, Willis. All of the DotComms were well received and they loved your Twelve Teams thing."

"What was the general view?"

"The majority of the team felt that the Production team, including its relationship with me, of course, resembled a human family. We have our own rooms and respect for each other's position, but, just like all families, we have tiffs, sulks and rows that could be handled better. The team's dream team of the future, by the way, was the crew of a yacht where '*all team members pull in the same direction and take their turn at the wheel*.'"

"Nice language. And did the team identify the actions that are needed to become the dream yacht of the future?" asked Willis.

"We did, and I'll come on to those in a minute."

Willis slowed to negotiate a police convoy and a slow-moving vehicle with a huge earthmoving truck on its trailer. It took ten minutes to pass it, which prompted some frustration for Willis as he was keen to return to the business of the day. "And what about your trust issue – the key log – did you deal with that, sir?"

"Yes, Willis. I just decided to talk openly about my feelings, my regrets, my hopes and fears for the future and they warmed considerably. That discussion, along with the 'get to know me' DotComms, really did get us up the mountain where, not surprisingly, we could then clearly see what we needed to do in the future."

"So what exactly does the team need to do in the future?" enquired Willis.

Simon leaned forward. "The team have come up with a number of suggested action points and I'm also going to focus on a couple of personal development actions to ensure that I exceed their expectations. One of the things that came out of today is an interesting contrast. The Production team are basically happy with teamwork within their team but they're very unhappy about teamwork *between* the various Aldertons teams across our two sites. Within the Production team, words like *good, positive, supportive, friendly, united and focused* were used to describe life in the team but the words used to describe teamwork between Alderton's teams included *distant, cool, unhelpful, competitive, bastards, tribal and poor.*"

"I see," said Willis, nodding slowly, deep in thought.

"So we're going to implement a number of action points. Firstly, we're going to make Internal Service a core value."

"Hmmmh…" muttered Willis. "Is that wise? Sometimes when CEOs start to talk about core values it can signal to the workforce that fraud is nigh. I've known many CEO word-smiths in my time..."

"Rest assured, Willis. I'm not word-smithing here. This is serious. In the future, our internal meetings will start on time and finish on time – we won't keep each other waiting. All designated staff will attend meetings or, in the worst case scenario, send their number two. Internal Service will also mean that if a department or division is running behind on a project that affects another team, it will be proactive and inform them immediately. Emails will only be used for information, clarification and motivation – they will not be used for criticism. There will be no more aggressive emails copied to 15 others for effect. If someone has a criticism of A. N. Other, they'll go and sort it out face to face. There's more stuff on this Internal Service theme but I won't bore you with all the details."

"Not at all, not at all," protested Willis. "I'm interested…I'm happy to hear the lot."

"OK," said Simon, "I'll give you one more action then. We're going to introduce internal service audits. You know the exercise you encouraged me to do at Durkin and Timperley when I met Colin Durkin, their CEO?"

"I remember it well," replied Willis. "You mean the list of audit questions we built over tea and ginger biscuits at The Highwayman Hotel?"

"Exactly. I suggested to the Production team that we should introduce internal service audits across the business. So, once or twice a year, I will now be expecting my directors and senior managers to be pairing up with each other and asking a range of questions over coffee, or a lunch off-site somewhere."

"Questions like what?" asked Willis.

"Well, the team have already built them, Willis! Questions like:
Where is my department currently meeting your department's expectations?
Where is my department exceeding expectations?
Where is my department falling short of expectations?
What outstanding issues are there between our two departments?
What have been the high points and low points in recent months?
Who have been the star performers in my team?
Who could have done more in our team…and did you tell them?

How do you feel about the support you have had from me, the team's manager/director?"

"I like those, sir," said Willis. "Would you like a couple of additional audit questions built around the future?"

"How do you mean, Willis?"

"Well, I've always believed that inter-departmental strife is rarely caused by someone deliberately setting out to shaft someone else. Problems are often caused through a lack of understanding about someone else's problems, pressures and priorities."

Simon interrupted and was scribbling as he spoke. "So we need a few audit questions like:

What do we need to understand about your future problems, pressures and priorities?

How can we help your department achieve its future objectives?

What could our teams do that would improve the way that they work together?"

"They sound good to me, sir. Spot on!"

"Oh…and I've not finished yet, Willis. Another action point from the teambuilding day is to improve communication. Alderton's team briefings came in for some real stick and we need to find a better way of doing them. Any ideas?"

"Years ago," said Willis, "the Industrial Society came up with a very good model, based around the Five Ps."

"I've heard of the six Ps…preparation and planning prevent piss-poor performance!" said Simon, smiling. "The sergeant in the Cadets at school used to say it a lot."

Willis looked serious, as he often did when waiting to impart his words of wisdom. "You'll be pleased to hear that my five Ps bear no resemblance to your rather grubby military expression. When thinking of team briefings, the first P is Performance. You might like to start the team briefing by giving information on the team's performance, the company's performance, other teams in the business etc. This big picture 'results' stuff sets the scene nicely.

"The second P is Policy – maybe new policies that have been introduced, existing policies that have been amended or dropped and old policies that need to be revisited or re-emphasised in some way and—"

Simon interrupted. "Is the third P anything to do with People?"

143

"Exactly, sir. People who have joined, people who have left, promotions and births and so on. The usual stuff – hatchings, matchings and despatchings. The fourth P is Problems. Asking the team if they have any problems is obviously important, as is identifying any likely problems."

"Presumably, Willis, this part of the model also allows for brainstorming with the team to solve these problems?"

"Yes, it certainly does," replied Willis.

"And your last P?"

"That would be P for Plans," offered Willis. "Talking with fellow team members about plans for the future and the actions that the team, and nominated individuals, need to take. This P can also include the company's long-term plans, of course. Anything really that allows you to finish on a high. So that's the Five P's – Performance, Policy, People, Problems and Plans – it is a good model, isn't it?"

"It is actually – very good! Much better than 'Preparation and planning prevents piss…'"

"Poor performance? Typical Army – we would never say anything like that in the Merchant Navy, of course!"

"No, of course not Willis. Next time I must remember to bring my bullshit deflector with me!"

Willis smiled and continued. "What other communication issues were there, apart from this team briefing area?"

"Well, there was a lot of discussion about the lack of understanding of the company's objectives for the future. The team came up with a brilliant idea which Dave Wilmott, the Production Manager called 'Strategic Bridges'."

"This wouldn't be the very difficult, very unhelpful, awkward bastard Mr. Wilmott, would it?" said Willis, smiling.

"OK, Willis, no need to rub it in! He was very active and very helpful today, actually. We developed a one-page diagram which has on it 'where we are today', 'where we want to be in three years' time' and 'how we are going to get there'. It also shows the company's top three priorities. I'll show it to you when we stop. I was so impressed with it that I'm going to get our IT people to build the software version of it.

"By the end of next month I'm going to make sure that all of Alderton's people have it as a screensaver – I want everyone to understand where we're headed and the role they can play in getting us there."

"All of that sounds really great – is that it?"

"Certainly not, Willis. There's lots more. I want to get a better handle on how my people are feeling so we're going to implement a 'company medical' questionnaire that will be accessed on the web. This will ensure that it remains confidential and anonymous."

"Why have you decided to call it a company medical?" enquired Willis.

"I haven't decided to call it that – the idea came from the team. In fact it was the used-to-be very difficult Mr. Wilmott who came up with the good idea…again. He felt that we needed to get people to comment on Alderton's 'brain', i.e. its use of market intelligence and the formulation of the right policies, Alderton's 'eyes and ears', which is all about listening and our communication processes, and finally Alderton's spirit and soul', i.e. the levels of team spirit, morale and commitment."

"So have you decided what questions you're going to ask people in these three areas to audit the health of your company?" said Willis.

"We're going to ask people to tick or cross a number of statements depending if they think they're true or false," replied Simon.

"What sort of statements did the team come up with?"

"I knew you were going to ask me that, Willis. Hang on…I need to get these flip chart pages out." Simon proceeded to unfold and wave the pages about, trying to locate the key statements from earlier in the day.

Willis quickly intervened. "Sorry, sir, I can't see a thing out of the back window now – do you think you could keep the pages down a bit?"

"Yes, of course, Willis. Here are the first batch of statements on the health of our corporate 'brain'. Remember that people will either tick or cross these:

I understand our vision for the future
I understand Alderton's top three objectives for the future
I understand my team's top three objectives for the future
I understand my roles and responsibilities
The pace of change is about right for me
I trust the Directors' judgement."

"I like that one – do you feel comfortable with that?" said Willis.

"There's no such thing as bad feedback, Willis. All feedback is good feedback. I'm cool with it."

"Fair enough," said Willis, smiling. "Are there any more of your 'brain statements'?"

"There are, Willis. The team wanted ten statements in each area – a nice round number. How many have I covered?"

"Five or six, I think," said Willis.

"Right, let me find another four 'true or false' statements then. How about these?

We can challenge each other, including the Board
I get to hear what's going on in our marketplace
The reasons for change are always explained to me
I am trained before results are expected from me, not afterwards

Do you want to hear about our other corporate body parts?" enquired Simon.

"I'd love to," said Willis. "What did they come up with for your 'eyes and ears'?"

"Right…here they are. Can you still see out of the window?"

"Just about, but carry on, sir."

"OK. In this eyes and ears communication area we have things like:

Meetings are two-way and enjoyable
The quantity and quality of meetings are about right for me
I work for a good listener
I understand other teams' issues – that's the same as your earlier problems, pressures and priorities comment, Willis
My team goes out of its way to obtain feedback on its performance
I work for someone who has an open door and is accessible
My manager can normally detect if I am not happy."

"That's a good one," said Willis. "I like that."

"Then we have:

My performance is reviewed regularly
I feel that my contributions are seen and recognised

That's nine – I'm one short. I'll have to give that some more thought," said Simon.

Willis looked up to the rear-view mirror. "What about: *Our working environment lends itself to good communication?*"

"I like that," said Simon, "but I'll have to pass that by the team to get their approval."

"Fair enough," said Willis, who was impressed with Simon's new collaborative style. "What did they come up with in the 'spirit and soul' area?"

"I've got plenty in this area," said Simon. "We won't have any trouble finding ten statements on these flip charts:
I enjoy working for Alderton's
New people are welcomed and valued
We trust each other
We do not have any 'us and thems' in the organisation. To be honest, Willis, I shoe-horned that one in, based on one of your previous comments
I have a good relationship with my manager/director
Work does not have a negative effect on my home life
Friction is dealt with openly and effectively in our team
We smile, have fun and laugh a lot
In Alderton's, there is a strong sense of belonging
I look forward to coming to work as I don't see it as 'work'.
You'll remember that last one as well, Willis."

"I do remember that remark of mine, sir, but I particularly liked the statements about smiling and laughing and the effect of work on home life. Sometimes we forget the importance of support and interest coming from the other side of the dinner table."

"Exactly. So this company medical will be carried out in January and we'll run with actions and improvements starting in February."

"Well, that will certainly get your new year off to a good start, won't it?"

"It certainly will, Willis. Shall we stop for a cuppa? I've got a dry throat – too much talking, I guess."

Willis turned off the M1 and found a quirky country pub called The Pheasant Plucker that was just opening up. Simon ordered a glass of Merlot and Willis settled for Earl Grey tea, having established that "Brazil's Best" was unheard of in this part of the county.

"We look like a couple of alcoholics, don't we, Willis? Two people who couldn't wait to get the beers in. Talking of beers…how's your tea?"

"Very nice," said Willis, as he savoured the smell of the bergamot.

He surveyed the pub to see if they were still alone. "So what about the action points that you said were part of your personal development?" said Willis.

"Yes, sorry, I did say that I would come back to them, didn't I?" said Simon. "One of the things that I'm going to do is to spend more time building a motivational environment. I have realised today that my Production people are delivering mediocre work because I'm driving them but they could deliver excellent work in the future if they drive themselves. I've probably spent too much time trying to motivate them with bonuses."

"Well, money will buy you a good dog but it certainly won't buy you the wag of its tail," said Willis. "I suppose you've heard your wife's saying about money?"

"Which one, Willis?"

"She used it at the conference – she said '*Money motivates neither the best people nor the best in people*'."

"Yes, I have heard her say that before, Willis, but I suppose it has taken me a little time to catch up with her wise head and wise ways. As I was saying, this motivational area is one of the keys to our future success. I'm going to find a reason to praise at least three people every day – some face to face, some by email, phone calls and so on. Praising people doesn't feature that often in my daily life and I'm going to change that."

"Well," said Willis, with a mouth full of ginger biscuit, "they say that 'thanks' is the most underused word in the English language. What many CEOs don't realise is the real value of praise and recognition. Although a pat on the back is only a few inches above a kick in the arse, it is a lot more effective, don't you think?"

Simon smiled as he sipped his wine. "Yes, you could say that, Willis. Another thing that I'm going to do is develop my coaching skills. I'm a bit of a tennis player in the summer and, last Sunday, when I was clearing out some piles of articles from old tennis magazines in my home office I came across something that Pete Sampras said. A journalist had reminded Sampras that his game had been transformed following the appointment of Tim Gullickson as his coach. When asked to comment on Gullickson's approach, Sampras said that he only ever talked about his strengths and reminded him how good he was and how good he could be. Sampras added that, in Gullickson's view, there was '*no such thing as constructive criticism*', as the only thing it constructed was '*nagging self-doubt and resentment that often produced high levels of match-losing mediocrity*'.

"So, back at Aldertons, I'm not going to focus on fixing weaknesses. I'm going to focus on drawing out *strengths* that are already there. I'm not going to ask people to do their best – I am going to ask them to do what they're best *at*. I'm going to water the seeds not the weeds... as you once said. I'm also going to develop a different culture, Willis. I know that we talked about this some months ago, but the penny has dropped now. Nobody will clock in, we'll all work the same hours, we'll never miss a delivery date (which also means that we won't accept an impossible delivery date), we'll treat people like adults and expect them to behave like adults. Continuous learning will become a way of life, people will not have to fight us for a pay rise because we'll pay higher than average wages for a higher than average performance. We will empower people to fix problems not pass them on, walk past them or ignore them and there'll be nothing in a manager's desk that isn't displayed on a wall for all to see and understand. I'm going to make sure that managers attend each other's meetings, offer more prizes for the removal of red tape and create a monthly award scheme where Alderton's people nominate a colleague for 'Hero of the month'."

"Or heroine, presumably?" added Willis.

"No, there'll be no drugs offered as incentives as long as I'm the Chief Executive, Willis!"

The two men laughed loudly together, totally at ease with each other. Simon leaned forward once more. "...and I'm going to make sure that each member of staff has a MAP for the month or quarter, depending on their role."

"A MAP...meaning what?...some guidelines on how to achieve their objectives?" enquired Willis.

"It's more than that, Willis. The 'M' stands for Measurables – clear objectives so they know exactly what they're expected to achieve and by when. The 'A' stands for Actions – i.e. what they're going to do to achieve the objectives and the 'P' stands for Personal Support – the training, coaching and resources needed to carry out the actions. Each MAP will be on one page – no more."

As they left the pub and returned to the car, Simon was still talking in an animated way about his plans for the future. However, the remaining journey home was spent mostly in silence. Simon's successful but demanding day, the red wine and the soft cream leather were all too much for him. As always, Willis enjoyed the countryside but occasionally checked the rear-view mirror to keep a discreet eye on his passenger. Willis smiled and looked very happy – with Simon and with himself.

All at once there was a cough from the back seat. "Sorry about that, Willis. I must have nodded off but I can see that we've made good progress. We must nearly be home. So what have you got lined up tonight, then?"

"It's my birthday today, sir. Mrs. Willis is treating me to a nice meal in."

"Good grief, Willis, you should have told me it was your birthday. We should never have stopped at the pub! Happy Birthday! Are we on time? Your wife will be furious with me!"

"Don't worry, sir, we're fine. We always eat quite late – I suppose it dates back to the days when we used to eat together after the children were tucked up in bed."

"And will Anne be baking you a birthday cake, Willis…with lots of candles?"

"No, sir, certainly not! I want a birthday meal, not a torchlight procession!"

"Ha ha! And how old are you today, Willis, if you don't mind me asking?"

"I'm 58 years old, sir…plus VAT!"

"Very good, Willis. I hear what you're saying."

"I'm so old now that when I go out with Mrs. Willis and order a nice pasta, the waiter asks for my money up front!" Simon laughed again and Willis continued, but with a more serious tone. "Come to think of it, we're due to go and have pasta soon at our favourite restaurant to discuss our plans for the future."

"Really…what sort of plans?" enquired Simon.

"You know…work, life, retirement, kids, grand-kids…the usual sort of stuff."

"Are you thinking of retiring then, Willis? I hope not as I was going to talk to you later about some more of these trips in the New Year. You may be surprised by what I'm about to say but I've enjoyed them all and, although I may not like to admit it, I probably still need them."

"Thank you, sir, but I think it's time that Anne and I talked about our future," confirmed Willis. "There are a quite a few things still on our 'to do' list."

"I am going to avoid retirement if I can, Willis. I think that retirement is when you move from '*Who's Who?*' to '*Who the fuck's he?*'"

Willis smiled. "I like that – I might use that if I have a family retirement do."

"Well, clean it up a bit please, if you do. I don't want your family thinking that I've been a bad influence on you!" Simon leaned forward. "So stop me if I'm on sensitive ground here, but what has prompted your thoughts about retirement…if you don't mind me asking?"

"No, I don't mind you asking at all," said Willis. "There are lots of things we want to do, I'm ready to slow down a bit now and I don't want to keep driving 40,000 miles each year…and I was also unwell at the start of the year."

"Really?" said Simon. "You didn't say anything."

"My job is to keep asking the piranha questions, remember, not to talk about me."

"Hmmh. I won't push you any further, Willis, but I hope that your retirement sees you happy and in good health. But I'll miss our trips together and I'll miss you. You've been a good adversary, a wise coach and a good friend. You're indispensable."

"Oh no, sir. You won't miss me and, by the way, there's no such thing as an indispensable man. Do you know the poem, by the way? My father used to recite it when he thought my brothers and I needed to hear it. Let me see if I can remember it:

Some time when you're feeling important,
Some time when your ego's in bloom,
Some time when you take it for granted
You're the best qualified man in the room,
Some time when you feel that your going
Would leave an un-fillable hole,
Just follow these simple instructions
And see how it humbles your soul.

Take a bucket and fill it with water,
Dip your hand in it up to your wrist,

Pull it out and the hole that's remaining
Will show how much you'll be missed.
You may splash all you like when you enter,
You may stir up the water galore,
But stop and you'll find in a moment
That it looks just the same as before!

The moral of this quaint example
Is to do just the best that you can.
Be proud of yourself and remember…
There's no indispensable man!"

"Very true, Willis…" said Simon. "…except in your case!"

The Bentley pulled up outside the Gray's house and, once again, Willis could hear the friendly mixture of laughing and barking.

"You need to get moving, Willis. Enjoy your evening….and Happy Birthday again!"

"I'll be off in a minute, Simon, but first I want to give you this."

"Give me what, exactly…? And I'm very happy with you calling me Simon, by the way. It's taken you long enough."

Willis opened the glove compartment, took out his leather-bound map and turned around. "You mentioned your MAP idea earlier, so here's is my map for you."

"Err, thank you…George…is it significant in any way?"

"It is, Simon. My father used to give me a road map every year – for my Christmas present. As he handed the map over he used to say, '*This is for you son, your best journeys are still to come!*' I kept all of them over the years and they are very precious to me. So I would like you to have my current map. You've put up with a lot of provocative questions from me and have bounced back with some great ideas and plans for the future. Although you once likened my questions to piranhas in the bidet, we've enjoyed our trips together and learned to respect each other in the process. We're both better men for the experience, I think, aren't we?"

"That would be very true, George…very true."

"And I think that you're becoming a great Chief Executive, Simon," added Willis.

Simon smiled. "Maybe, George. At least I'm pointing in the right direction now and the business is beginning to turn around."

Willis continued. "And although it's my birthday today, remember to open your birthday presents tomorrow."

"What presents? What do you mean? It's not my birthday until next April!" said a surprised Simon.

Willis continued. "I can remember reading an article in a magazine about a man called Hafiz. I think that he was an Iranian poet who lived centuries ago. He said that *'we all have many gifts still unopened from our Birthdays'* …i.e. from our Birth Day – the day we were born. We all have talents and skills that we, ourselves, don't know are there. In recent weeks I think that you've probably been opening a few of your Birth Day presents, Simon. So, tomorrow, why not start the day by opening another one….and another one the day after that. I know that we have one more trip lined up, but whenever you think of the future I'd like you to think of this map. Here it is, Simon. It's for you, your family and all the good people at Alderton's…for all of you, your best journeys are still to come!"

Chapter 5
Summary of Wit and Wisdom

1. The best management consultants in business are the people already in the business – your people – they need to be "set free" and allowed to deliver.

2. Plenty of tabloid communication is important – people never complain about being "over informed". Build a one-page strategic plan and try the "five Ps team briefing model" (Performance, Policies, People, Problems and Plans) to improve communication within and between teams. Remember that communication and trust levels rise and fall together.

3. Get your people to the top of the "trust mountain" – take them on a journey from a base of facts, along the slopes of opinions, to a peak of shared feelings. The best way to give feedback when emotions are running high is to describe how <u>you feel</u> not how you feel about the other person.

4. When solving problems try and locate the key log – if you can dislodge it, the "power of the river" will do the rest.

5. Emails should only be used for information, clarification and motivation – not criticism or sniping.

6. People rarely set out to make life difficult for others – there is often a lack of understanding about a team or an individual's problems, pressures and priorities. Try "internal service audits" once or twice each year to clear the air.

7. People will deliver mediocre work if they are driven – they will deliver exceptional work if they drive themselves!

8. Don't ask people to do their best – ask them to do what they are best at (Lars Sjogren).

9. Try building "MAPs" for your people – a one page summary of their Measurables, the Actions they need to take and the Personal Support they need.

10. Maybe Tim Gullickson had a point – there is no such thing as "constructive criticism". Try working with peoples' strengths instead. Water the seeds, not the weeds!

Chapter 6
Getting From A-Z

It was 7.30am on 14 December and there was no sign of George Willis. Simon sat in the kitchen looking uncomfortable and restless. He loosened his collar and tried to relax. "Where the hell is he?" he muttered, glancing at his watch. "He's over an hour late!" Rory looked up, realised that the comments were not meant for him, woofed and grumbled his displeasure, then flopped down again in his basket. A few minutes later, Stella appeared in her dressing gown. She leaned over, gave Simon a kiss on the top of his head then set off to find the kettle for her first cup of the day.

"Do you want one, darling?"

"One what?"

"Not that, I can assure you!"

"Stella, my love, I haven't got a bloody clue what you're talking about!"

"Never mind, darling, where is the wonderful George today?"

"He's late…which is strange because Willis doesn't do late. I bet he's never been late in his life. He was probably born days before he was expected. He's always early. It's what he does…it's what he is!"

Stella turned the radio down and pulled up a chair, changing her mood to show a little more empathy. She was surprised by Simon's animated response and could see that he was genuinely concerned. She poured two cups of tea. "Should we be worried about him, darling?"

"I'm not sure, Stella," said Simon. "I've tried his mobile and there's no answer – in fact it's making that unobtainable noise."

"I didn't realise that you talked to him on his mobile," said Stella.

"I don't," said Simon. "Come to think of it, I've never phoned him but I've always had his mobile number in my diary. I've never had to phone him as he always phones me the day before we're due to meet – apart from yesterday."

"Perhaps you're dialling the wrong number," said Stella. Simon raised an eyebrow and slowly shook his head. "Well, how do you know?" protested Stella. "If you've never phoned him, then you won't know for sure will you, Simon?"

Simon leaned back, with his arms folded. "OK, fair point, darling," he said. "I'll phone the agency that he works for."

Thirty minutes of searching through papers and diaries went by before Simon realised that he didn't have the agency's telephone number either.

Stella intervened once again. "Why don't you phone your PA, darling, she'll have it, surely? She's the solution here, isn't she? I'm sure she won't mind you phoning her so early in the morning."

"Probably not," said Simon. "I'm sure that she must have talked to the agency at some point during the last six months."

"Well, there you are then. Problem solved! I'm going for a shower, then we can have a family breakfast for a change. It's just what we all need after the busy weekend we've just had."

"Great idea," said Simon. "I'll go and walk the dog, then get the breakfast ready."

Stella gave Simon a long, slow, loving hug, kissed him briefly on the nose then headed up the stairs with her fuchsia dressing gown flowing behind her.

"Rory! Rory!" Simon went in search of the dog and eventually found him pretending to be asleep in his basket. Clearly the family weekend in the Lake District, and the 20 miles of hillside tracks and paths had taken their toll. He needed his sleep and was clearly surprised by the impatient tap from Simon's shoe on the side of his basket. He lowered his head in a final attempt to avoid the inevitable. "Come on Rory, you idle hound. Move your backside! We're going for a walk."

They circled the garden a couple of times, with Simon still deep in thought as he attempted to get through to his PA on his mobile. He assumed that Rory was following on behind but the dog was occupied with a new rabbit burrow that he had found in the corner of the vegetable garden. The only person going for a walk that morning was Simon.

They returned to a lively house, now full of female laughter, shrieks and tears. Simon looked at Rory and Rory looked back at Simon. They shared a "boy moment". Sometimes a house full of women was just too much. They re-entered the house, cautiously, but their efforts to conceal themselves did not last long.

"Now why did you do that, Claire?" said Simon, spotting Lucy's bloody nose.

"I didn't, I didn't! She fell over! She did it herself. Ask her Dad, ask her!"

Simon's attempt to reconcile the girls' differences was short-lived. They ran off together and, a few minutes later, Simon found an opened packet called "Stage Blood". He went to the bottom of the stairs and put on his best "grumpy-Dad" voice. "Good joke girls, good joke – you had me there, you naughty rascals! I'm going to rip your arms off and hit you over the head with the soggy ends!"

"Urrrrgh that's disgusting!" shrieked the girls in unison, as they raced each other across the landing.

Ten minutes later the Gray family was enjoying breakfast together. Simon and Stella had toast and boiled eggs, the girls munched their way through some Frosties and Rory weaved his way through the chairs and table legs, nose to the ground, trying to locate and hoover-up the crumbs and lost flakes of cereal. Christmas was on the horizon and there was a happy end-of-term mood and atmosphere in the house. The first Christmas cards had arrived and the girls had already painted a number of promotional posters for their school nativity play. Simon was first to get up from the table, sweeping a range of packets, cups and plates into his arms. He headed for the kitchen with Rory following closely behind. Rory could always sense a potential food opportunity and, with Simon leaning back and unable to see over the mountain of cereal packets in front of him, there was a high probability that another morsel would fall, unnoticed, to the floor.

Simon left the house at 8.30am and his journey to work was un-eventful, although he couldn't resist pressing the redial button on his mobile phone several times. Willis remained unobtainable, in every sense of the word, and Simon's PA was still engaged.

He arrived at his office at 9.25am and went straight to the coffee machine. Belinda walked past, trying to avoid eye contact as she was struggling with three large parcels. She always enjoyed a quiet half-hour before Simon's workload hit her but today, it was not to be. She nearly managed to conceal herself in a colleague's office but, with four yards to go, Simon spotted her.

"Belinda! Belinda, have you got a minute please?" called Simon. He still had his coat on and was looking anxious. She knew that something was wrong.

"Is there a problem, Simon?" said Belinda.

"There might be. I've been trying to get hold of you. You know the chauffeur who has been driving me around for the last six months?"

"Don't you mean driving you around the bend?" said Belinda, a huge smile on her face.

"That's another story," said Simon, keen to return to his immediate problem.

"Sorry," said Belinda. "You obviously mean your Mr. Willis?" she added, with a more serious and appropriate tone to her voice.

"Yes, my Mr. Willis, as you call him – do you have his mobile number?"

"It's on the laminated sheet on my desk. Here it is."

Simon checked the number and confirmed that it was the same number that he had dialled earlier. He picked up the nearest phone, dialled the number again and was greeted with the same unobtainable tone. "Shit! Pardon my language – have you ever phoned him on this number, Belinda?"

"I don't think I have, Simon. He's always so proactive and, if he can't get hold of you, he phones me to check the arrangements for your next day out. What's the problem exactly?"

"He's gone AWOL," said Simon. "You know – absent without leave. I was expecting him this morning but he didn't show up – did he say anything at all? Has anybody heard from him?"

Belinda thought for a moment. "No, I don't think so – can't remember anything. Perhaps he's ill. I'll check my emails then I'll go and see Security and also check the overnight phone log."

"No, send Carl. I need you here. Willis might be ill but the whole thing just doesn't feel right...if you know what I mean. Does that make sense, Belinda?"

"Hmmm," she thought. "Have you tried his home number?"

"No, I don't have it. I always tried to avoid that. He's a great family man and I never wanted to intrude, probably because I didn't want to encounter an irate Mrs. Willis and have to explain why I was phoning her husband at ten in the evening! Do you have the agency's number?"

"What agency?"

"The agency that he works for – did you ever phone them?"

"No, never. Why would I need to?"

"But didn't you phone them when I first joined Alderton's? You know, as part of my induction?"

"No – I thought you had arranged for a chauffeur. We all thought you were very flash…in a nice way, of course. This is the first time that I've heard it referred to as part of your induction," said Belinda.

"Well it was a welcome present from the chairman, actually, but a very good one, as it turned out. I thought it was a nice touch," said Simon.

"Anyway, the chairman will have the agency's number, won't she? She arranged it as part of my induction and said it was a monthly treat to allow me to have some quality thinking time…you know, *'to help me drive the business forward'*."

"Would you like me to phone her PA then?" asked Belinda. "To see if she has Mr. Willis' number?"

"Yes please – would you? Thanks. I'll catch up with you later. I need to have a word with Clive and Cheryl from the quality improvement team in a minute but I'll be out at 11.30am…I'll be in Meeting Room 4 if you need me."

"Fine, Simon, leave it to me." Belinda turned away and walked purposefully in the direction of the Chairman's office. The meeting with the two managers concluded very much as Simon had expected and he emerged at 11.40am with a completed action plan featuring many of Clive and Cheryl's ideas for improving the response times during Alderton's sales and service processes. Simon headed for the overworked coffee machine once again. He returned, a cup in each hand, and hovered impatiently over Belinda as she finished her telephone call. She looked up and glared at him.

"Don't look at me like that, Belinda. Did you get it?"

"You mean Willis' phone number?"

"Yes."

"No."

"No – what do you mean, no? Didn't Jean Scrivenor's PA have the number? Carol, isn't it?"

"Caroline is her name, actually – she doesn't know anything about it, Simon. She thinks that the chairman, Mrs. Scrivenor, must have booked your chauffeur direct. There's nothing in the file and nothing on the system that we can detect. If it was a welcome present from the chairman perhaps she treated it as a private matter."

"Bloody hell!" said Simon. "We're going to have to get Poirot in at this rate – it's getting more intriguing by the minute! Where is the chairman today?"

"She's still abroad, apparently," said Belinda. "She gets back in a few days – flies into Stansted then she's getting the train to London for a meeting with Claire Fullerton and Denis Carter in Pall Mall on Friday. We're not expecting to see her in head office for days."

"Shit!" said Simon. "I really can't understand this! Sorry for my language this morning, Belinda…I'm going to contact her and see if we can track Willis down."

Simon slowly walked over to the water cooler and poured himself an iced drink. He sipped the water whilst keeping one eye on the internal sales team's work-rate and productivity across the open-plan office. They didn't pay any attention to him. Their results were good, conversion rates were improving, they were happy and they had plenty to do. Simon returned and caught Belinda's attention once more. She looked up, with another look that Simon recognised.

"Yes Simon…how can I help you?" She shut her eyes but forced a smile.

"Book a table for two at Segovia's for tomorrow – lunchtime."

"That sounds *very* important!" she said, looking down so Simon could not detect her annoyance. "Just the sort of task I ought to be getting on with at the moment. Right then – what time exactly?" she said, with pen poised.

"That's up to you, Belinda. You're the one having the lunch, not me. Take a girl friend, or that boyfriend of yours who phones you 20 times a day! I want to apologise for my behaviour today and for my language too. I'm having a bit of a bad day but that's no excuse. And make sure that you order a decent bottle of wine too!"

"Thank you, Simon. Thank you very much. Matt and I will enjoy that – that's very kind of you."

Simon smiled. "Thank you, Belinda. You deserve it…having to work for me!"

"Yes, that's also very true, Simon…but if you really want to know…"

"What?" said Simon.

"Well, if you really want to know, working for you is getting easier…I won't say enjoyable in case it goes to your head!" She blushed and laughed, nervously.

Simon smiled again. "Thank you, Belinda. That's nice to know!" The next two days were very busy. Simon managed to cram in five meetings, two visits to key accounts, two interviews to find Gerry Manning's replacement and an interview with the local newspaper that had started to pick up on the turnaround at Alderton's, including two recent, large export orders.

The following day, Simon decided to collect the chairman from Stansted Airport himself. He arrived in plenty of time and enjoyed a relaxed latte and croissant whilst waiting for her to emerge from the Arrivals corridor.

"Simon, how nice to see you!" beamed Jean. "What a nice surprise! I feel very honoured – why are you picking me up today? Is there a problem?"

Simon kissed her on the cheek. "No, not at all, Jean" said Simon, lifting her heavy suitcase. "I thought it was about time we had an update on a few things and I wanted to ask you a couple of questions on the journey. Where are you headed now – is it still London?"

"Yes, so if you can take me down the M11 that would be wonderful. I have an industry do tonight and will be staying in town as I have another meeting with a charity tomorrow. Will that put you out in any way?"

"No, that's fine, Jean. The M11 is easy enough," said Simon. "We shouldn't have too many problems with the traffic at this time of day."

Simon put Jean Scrivenor's suitcase in the boot of the Mercedes Estate, then opened the passenger door for her. She clambered in and put her safety belt on. Although she was in her late fifties, Jean Scrivenor was very fit and energetic due to her obsession with running and she was soon encouraging Simon to make speedy progress.

"Come on, Simon, come on. I need to be there in an hour. Drive like Lewis Hamilton – let's go!"

"Alright Jean, I'm with you!"

Simon navigated his way out of the Stansted Airport complex and was soon heading south on the M11. He leaned behind the passenger seat to locate a bundle of documents. "Here you are, Jean. Here's a short progress report on the state of the business. You'll be pleased to hear that all indicators are good and that the culture change programme is already producing some good results. We're winning – at last!"

"Well, Simon, I always knew that you were the right man for the job. I hear on the grapevine that you've also been more relaxed recently – you know – in yourself."

"Well, whoever told you that is absolutely right," replied Simon. "I don't mind telling you, Jean, that it's taken me a few months to get the hang of this job and it's taken a few months to learn some home truths about myself."

"Really?" said Jean, trying to sound a little surprised. "If you want to share some of that with me one day, Simon, I'm a good listener…"

"I would be delighted to share that with you in detail on another day, Jean. Why don't we have dinner after the exhibition in Copenhagen and I'll tell you everything that I've learned."

"That sounds like a splendid idea," she replied. "You choose the restaurant, I'll pay for it. My treat."

"Talking of treats," said Simon, "could we just re-visit the chauffeur thing for a few minutes?"

"Ah yes, I was wondering when you'd mention that. You've remembered my little promise then?" she said. "We need to get that sorted out now that we're approaching the end of your first six months."

Simon turned his head. "What do you mean, Jean?"

"Well now that you've been our CEO for six months, and now that things are starting to turn around, I'd be delighted to treat you to one chauffeur-driven trip every month for the next six months… as I said I would at your interview…you know, to let you indulge in some quality thinking time to drive the business forward."

"But I've had one monthly chauffeur-driven trip for the *last* six months! Well, it's been five trips to be more precise – it should have been six but he didn't show up the other day!"

"Who didn't show up?" said Jean.

"Your chauffeur didn't turn up, Jean…that's who!"

"He's not my chauffeur, Simon. I haven't got a clue what you're talking about! Are you telling me that you went ahead and hired a chauffeur yourself – ahead of my formal offer?"

"I haven't gone ahead with anything, Jean. He turned up in my first month – the second week, I think it was. He came to the house and picked me up every month thereafter. His name is Willis – a provocative sort of chap but he turned out to be an excellent travelling companion in more ways than one. To be honest, he's been as good as any coach I've ever had and he's also the person who's largely responsible for my change of approach and management style, if you really want to know."

"Well I do want to know! I certainly haven't hired him for you. My offer was for your second period of six months – not your first six months. Are you sure you didn't hire him, Simon?"

"Certainly not, Jean. I would never have hired a chauffeur myself during the first six months. It would have been inappropriate, to say the least. But when you and I sat down for my second interview at your club, I'm sure you said it was an induction treat'."

"No, I said it would be a treat if you came through your induction successfully. After all, we have had quite a few CEOs in recent times. We needed to make sure that you were on the right track, to put it bluntly, Simon."

During their conversation, Simon's speed had gradually dropped to below 50mph. He was confused and distracted and could not understand how Willis could have appeared as an 'unauthorised' chauffeur. Jean Scrivenor was also deep in thought. Initially she had been upset and angry but, as time went on, she realised that Simon was equally confused.

"What did you say his name was?" The chauffeur?"

Simon turned to look at her. "Willis, Jean….George Willis."

"George Willis – that's quite a coincidence. A Mr. George Willis founded the company over a hundred years ago. It wasn't called Alderton's then, mind you. Perhaps his ghost has come back to haunt us – as your chauffeur!" She chuckled for a few seconds as Simon's face steadily reddened.

"Don't be ridiculous, Jean!" Simon paused and breathed deeply for a few seconds. "Sorry, Jean. My apologies. My George Willis is no ghost, I can assure you. He's as real as you or me…except we can't seem to find him at the moment."

"No offence taken, Simon. It just tickled me!" replied Jean.

They left the M11 and continued to navigate a number of dual carriageways and flyovers through Docklands for another 15 minutes.

Simon was looking a little more reflective. "So what can you tell me about the founder…*your* Mr. Willis, Jean.? Are there any facts and figures about him?"

"Well, not a lot is known about him, actually," said Jean. "I think we only have one paragraph in 'Then and Now'."

"That's the Alderton's official company history, isn't it?" enquired Simon.

"It certainly is," replied Jean. "Did I give you a copy of it when you joined?"

"No, Jean, you didn't."

"Not to worry. I'm sure we can let you have one – I'll ask Caroline to send you a copy. The only thing I can remember about George Willis, the founder, is that he started his career in the merchant navy and spent a lot of time in both North and South America before returning to England to run the company. He used his contacts in Argentina, Chile and Brazil to provide a lot of cheap raw materials that allowed the company to get started in the early days." Simon flicked the indicator and pulled over. He put the hazard lights on and turned towards Jean. "For God's sake Simon, we're on a dual carriageway! What on earth do you think you are doing?"

Simon did not hear her protests. "Jean…so you're saying that *your* George Willis was in the navy and spent time in South America…? That's how *my* George Willis started his career and—" Simon's sentence was cut off by the sound of an emergency vehicle behind them, in the distance.

"Move, Simon, move! We don't want to hold them up, do we? In fact, turn left in 50 yards' time, Simon – I can see an underground sign. I'll get the tube for the rest of the journey – it's a lot safer!"

Simon reacted quickly and followed his new instructions. He parked outside the tube station with hazard lights on, once again. Jean was clearly a little perplexed and wanted to get on with things, in her normal impatient way. She made light work lifting the heavy suitcase out of the boot that Simon had struggled with earlier and was now ready to set off on the final leg of her journey. "Perhaps we should meet before Copenhagen, Simon, not after it! I think that I need to give you a bloody good listening to…the sooner the better!"

"Yes…er…thanks Jean. Yes, let's meet up a.s.a.p. We can have a good chat over a nice meal. I'll stay overnight somewhere if I need to."

"No don't do that, Simon. Your ghostly chauffeur will take you home, I'm sure!" With that, she was gone, leaving Simon on the pavement being observed by a keen young traffic warden who was beginning to reach for his notebook and hand-held terminal.

Simon arrived home a little earlier than expected and went to find Stella. He gave her a big hug and suggested that they have a cup of tea in the conservatory. "It's freezing out there, Simon! Put the heaters on and I'll be with you in a second."

Stella returned with two cups of tea and a large slice of Battenburg cake – comfort food for her troubled husband.

"This is lovely, Stella, thanks. Are you warm enough, by the way?"

Stella nodded. "I am, Simon. By the way, the school nativity play was truly wonderful. It's a shame you couldn't make it."

"Yes, I know, darling. It won't happen again …and yes, I am also going to spend some time with the girls in a minute. Before I do, can I just talk to you about Willis and the stuff I mentioned when we talked on the mobile?"

"Of course. By the way, there's nothing on Google about your company founder. *Our* George Willis is definitely real, Simon. We both know that, we both met him and we haven't dreamed it! Our man is no ghost. This whole thing is just a strange co-incidence so drink your tea and relax. Here's the newspaper and here's the post. There's a padded envelope in the pile, at the bottom. Do you want to open it?"

"Not at the moment, darling," said Simon.

"But it might be something from him," urged Stella. "I didn't recognise the writing on the envelope." Stella shuffled the post and located the padded envelope. "Here you are, Simon, and here's the paper knife."

Simon opened the envelope and pulled out a booklet titled 'The

A-Z Partnership Toolkit'. He opened it and flicked the pages. "This must be from Willis," said Simon, "although there's nothing on it, or in it, to confirm that."

"Perhaps he just wanted you to have it, Simon. Maybe it was written by one of his previous CEOs and he thinks you'd benefit from reading it."

Simon flicked a few more pages and selected a sample of pages. He read page five then page ten, then page 20. "No, this is very Willis, Stella – he must have written it. I recognise some of the quotes and comments."

"So the good news, then, is that we know that our man must have posted it. He is alive and well – somewhere!"

Simon smiled and held the booklet tightly. "Yes, I suppose he must be alive and well somewhere, Stella. But who arranged for him to come here as my driver? Jean Scrivenor knows nothing about it. How could it happen? Who booked him? Who the hell is he? *Where* is he? Why has he disappeared?"

"Well, perhaps we'll never know, Simon. What we do know is that you enjoyed his company, shared some good times together and benefited from his wit, his wisdom and his snappy piranha questions. I'm sure that there's a logical explanation for all of this and I know that he'll probably turn up again one day. One thing's certain though, Simon."

"What's that, darling?"

"We should raise a glass tonight and thank him for everything he's done and said, then move on. From what you've told me, Alderton's has changed because you've changed and you're beginning to see some great results now. I'm sure that Jean Scrivenor must be a happy woman too!"

Simon smiled. "You're right, Stella, of course. George Willis will turn up again one day, I'm sure. And yes, Jean is happy with the way that things are going…I think…although we're due to talk about the business in more detail again soon. Thank you, my love."

Simon stood up, put the booklet down and gave Stella a long hug before kissing her on the forehead. Rory wagged his tail against Simon's leg in an attempt to receive some of his attention. "Thanks, Stella, my darling – for everything! I love you so much." He kissed her again on the forehead but she cupped his face and slowly moved his lips to hers.

As they kissed, Rory barked loudly and ran around the conservatory. Two minutes passed and he was still barking.

"All right, Rory. We've finished now, you jealous old thing! But we're not yet a complete Gray family – let's all go upstairs and see if we can find the Virgin Mary and Shepherd Number Three!"

Epilogue

Three years later, Simon Gray entered the training room and introduced himself to 12 young new recruits who were about to experience "Day Two" of Alderton's six-week induction programme. "Good morning everybody!" he beamed, as he enthusiastically went around the room shaking hands with the next generation of the company. "Right then, shall we kick off?"

As Simon waited for everyone to sit down, he noticeably took his mobile out of his pocket and turned it off. Twelve people did likewise.

"We all had a chance to meet yesterday over lunch in the boardroom so we won't bother with lengthy introductions today," said Simon when everyone was settled. "I just want to say a few words before I leave you in the capable hands of Maria and her HR team and I thought I would start with a short story.

"A man stepped into the shower just as his wife was drying off after hers. The doorbell rang and they argued over who should go and answer it. The man gave up and quickly wrapped himself in a towel and ran downstairs. When he opened the door, he was confronted by Vicki, the next door neighbour. Before he could say a word, she said '*I'll give you £500 if you drop the towel you have on*'. After thinking about it for all of three seconds, the man dropped the towel and stood naked in front of the smiling woman for two minutes or so. Vicki took out £500 from her handbag and left quickly. Confused but excited about his sudden good fortune, the man ran back upstairs and when he got back to the bedroom his wife asked, '*Who was that, darling?*'

'*Oh…err…only Vicki from next door,*' replied the man as he headed once again for the shower. '*Great,*' said his wife, '*Did she bring the £500 from all the church raffle tickets she's been selling?*'"

The 12 young recruits laughed warmly in appreciation. "So the moral of the story is…?" continued Simon, waiting to see if anyone

169

was going to complete his sentence, but no-one did. "The moral of the story is that if you share critical information with key people, you may be able to prevent avoidable exposure!"

The 12 laughed again. Harry Leemans attempted to write down the punchline in case he could use it in his best man's speech, planned for the following month.

Simon sat on the end of a desk at the front of the room and continued. He was dressed in stone-coloured chinos, a light blue shirt and an expensive blazer. He looked very relaxed and confident and was enjoying the opportunity to talk to the group. "As you probably know, I've been here now for four years or so and would like to share some critical information with you and some of the things that are going to be important to us all as we drive the business forward during the years ahead. If, as the managers and leaders of the future, you understand and implement these things, we'll avoid 'exposing ourselves' and making the company weak and vulnerable.

"First of all I want to stress the importance of our customers. They are the most important people in this organisation. They're not dependant on us, but we're dependant on them. Our customers are not cold statistics – they are flesh and blood with feelings and emotions like our own. When they contact us they're not an interruption of our daily work, they're the purpose of it. They're not people to argue or match wits with – they deserve the most courteous and attentive treatment we can give them. They are insiders not outsiders, and are the life blood of this and every organisation.

"I am passionate about our customers and if ever we lose a customer, however small, I always ask the relevant people to attend our quarterly 'Lost Customer Review Day' and explain why they have lost the customer, what they've learned from the experience and what we have to do to win the customer back."

There was a lot of furious note-taking as 12 people took Simon's point on board.

"Let me make a few comments about leadership. Alderton's people have high expectations of their team leaders. As your careers progress, and you move up the Alderton's ladder, remember that people will want you to do four things. Firstly, they will want you to show them a future. They will want to understand Alderton's purpose and its vision.

They will want to hear about our exciting longer-term possibilities and projects, to see powerful mental images of a brighter tomorrow and to hear stories that inform, educate and inspire. They will want to be actively involved in building something meaningful and worthwhile that will last for years to come and they will expect you to put the organisation before yourself. To put it another way, leadership is the ability to paint strong, energising pictures of the cathedral whilst the workers are mixing the cement!

"Secondly, they will want you, as their leader, to turn ideas into action. They will expect you to put the right plans, processes and systems in place. They will expect you to remove any obstacles to progress and find new ways to solve old problems. As Ross Perot once said, '*If you see a snake just kill it – don't form a committee on snakes!*' Your people will also tolerate healthy impatience on your part if you're trying to keep the momentum going – they will understand your speed and restlessness. Why? Because they know and understand, deep down, that the pace of change inside Alderton's must be quicker than the pace of change outside it – otherwise we are dead! Your job will be to make things happen with a mixture of common sense, judgement, curiosity and a love of learning.

"Thirdly, as one of our leaders of the future, I want you to enthuse, grow and appreciate others. Value and enjoy working with people who have different strengths, have fun in the workplace, build effective relationships within and between teams and connect with people at an individual and emotional level. Trust others and delegate as much as you can. As Jim Collins, the writer, once said, '*a good leader takes a little more than his/her share of the blame and a little less than his/her share of the credit.*' Be open, accessible, humble and vulnerable. Be yourself – be a real person, not a '*karaoke version of someone else*'…as my wife once called it.

"And lastly, as one of our leaders, I want to encourage you to clarify our values. Articulate and practice the beliefs that shape our unique culture, reward the behaviour you want more of, treat others with dignity and respect and put principles before rules. Be inclusive, compassionate and human. Understand that our values are the glue that holds Alderton's together. It's a well known fact that companies that enjoy enduring success have core values that remain fixed, whilst their policies and strategies adapt to a constantly changing world.

Speak up when behaviour is out of alignment with our values and understand that our values are more than just words – they are moral hills we should all be prepared to die on!

"How are we doing by the way? Is everyone happy with all of this?" Simon sipped from a glass of orange juice and checked his watch. "OK, we need to move on but I've just got time to say that as your careers progress, I'm very keen to develop your leadership qualities, not just your leadership skills. Maria will cover this in a lot more detail in a minute but let me now give you the challenge that I want you to deliver in week six, as it is linked to this particular topic.

"I want you to build, over two days, a sensory garden for our local charity, having first raised £10,000 to purchase all of the materials – you can decide how you're going to raise the money. It can't be gifts from friends and it can't be your own money. I also want you to obtain some good PR for the company as a result of this challenge – you're to appear on a local TV news channel on day two of the challenge and, again, you must work out how you're going to achieve this."

Twelve people suddenly became six pairs as they chatted enthusiastically to each other about the scale of the challenge that Simon had laid down. As the noise rose, Simon caught Maria's eye and they both smiled. They had used this type of project to develop leadership qualities twice before, with great success each time.

"So finally, let me tell you a few things about your future with Alderton's," continued Simon, as he beckoned the group to listen once again. "You'll find that there are no organisation charts in this company – if I put you all into divisions you'll reward me with divided behaviour! The future will be about speed and flexibility and we need to be light on our feet and able to change formation quickly to help each other. Your business cards will not have job titles for similar reasons – we need to do what we need to do, and if I give you all job titles you'll stay in comfortable little pockets of complacency and self-interest.

"Nothing in Alderton's is confidential, so you needn't worry about things going on behind closed doors. All information, including results and salaries, is openly published – you only have to ask. Office space is non-territorial and you're free to sit in a different place each day. You're free to attend any meeting you like, including board meetings – there are always two places available that can be booked via my PA.

You'll find that you can negotiate your hours, up or down, and also have unpaid sabbaticals if you want them.

"In this company, Alderton's people are actively involved in selecting their new colleagues and in assessing their managers. We're a very democratic outfit. Isn't it odd that outside work we are, as a nation, prepared to go to war to fight for democracy but timidly accept, in the workplace, that no-one has the right to choose their manager? Oh… and by the way, don't go calling yourself a leader…your people will decide if you're a leader or not, not you!"

Simon thought about the first time that he had heard Willis say those words. He could see Willis' face and hear his voice. For a moment, he was back in the comfortable cream leather of the Bentley. He re-focused and continued. "I also want you to become skilful communicators and 'stick with it' until you get your message through. Let me tell you another quick story. Years ago, at a conference in Jersey, I sat down to breakfast with a colleague of mine from Scotland. When his egg and bacon arrived he asked a passing waiter for some salt.

"Surprisingly, the waiter ignored my colleague completely and he soon realised that he needed to do something to get himself noticed. He started to raise his voice, to the point where other guests became aware of him, but still the waiters ignored him. Spotting the restaurant manager, he raised his hand to catch his attention but the manager turned away and walked to another table. My Scottish colleague remained calm but not dejected. He stood on the table and then, in front of 100 fellow guests, shouted at the top of his voice, '*Can I have some bloody salt please!*' Within seconds, four or five waiters rushed over to him, along with the restaurant manager, who begged my colleague to sit down whilst the salt was located."

The 12 managers laughed again enthusiastically. "Can anyone spot the moral of this story?" said Simon, standing up at the front of the room.

"It's clearly got something to do with communication," said Alan Burns.

"The moral of the story is that responsibility in the communication process always lies with the sender, not the receiver. You can't blame the other person if they're not actively listening or don't want to listen. You just have to turn up the volume and try again, in a different way. But all the time…the sender has the responsibility to get the message through to the receiver. Within Alderton's, please don't blame others for not understanding you or not listening to you. In business and in life, you'll get the behaviour you deserve! It's your job to get the message through." Simon caught Maria's eye. She was smiling but clearly looking at her watch. Simon sensed that his time was up.

"So, to help you on your way in your new careers, I would like to give you this 'A-Z Partnership Toolkit', which will help you deal with some of the people challenges that you'll face every day. It has lots of stuff in it about our customers, our culture and how we want to work with each other, every single day. The full version is also available in an electronic format, by the way. Working in a spirit of partnership is very important to me. I want you to form effective partnerships with our customers, each other and yourself! The A-Z has some useful ideas and tips in it and also some killer questions. Just think of them as 'piranhas in the bidet'!"

The group smiled. Danny Williams caught Simon's attention. "Is that because they're designed to cause us pain?"

"Yes, in a way, Danny. They're designed to make life a little uncomfortable but not designed to inflict any lasting harm. They are hard hitting questions that are designed to provoke a better way...for our customers, for you and for your people.

"One final thought before I leave...Alderton's now has 378 people on board across the four sites and needs 378 hearts and minds emotionally aligned with what the business is trying to do. We need our heart-count to match our headcount!"

Naomi Shaw put her hand up. "No need for hands, Naomi, just shout out your question if you have one," smiled Simon, who was enjoying the interest and energy in the room.

Eric Smith leaned over to his right and whispered to John O'Neill. "How does he remember all of our names?"

"I don't know, but it's impressive though, isn't it?"

"Was there a question then, Naomi?" continued Simon.

"Err...yes...Simon...thank you. On the front of this A-Z it says it's written by yourself and 'George Willis'. I haven't heard his name mentioned before. What does he do within Alderton's?"

"George wrote the original version of this A-Z and did a fantastic job, as you'll see. I've just changed a few things here and there and brought the text into line with some of our future challenges and goals.

He deserves all of the credit for a great piece of work…and I want it to guide our behaviour for many years to come."

"And is he still with the company?" continued Naomi.

Simon Gray looked out of the training room window. He noticed that the leaves on the trees outside were beginning to turn deep shades of gold, red and brown. He remembered his trips with Willis to the Dark Side and the meeting with Colin Durkin of Durkin and Timperley. He could see the Highwayman Hotel and the garden centre where he finally *'got it'* and realised that he, the CEO, was an irritating boss rather than an inspirational leader.

Simon glanced at his briefcase on the table next to him. It contained six months of Willis memorabilia - the postage stamp that *"sticks to one thing until it gets there"*, the card that Willis bought in the garden centre that urged Simon *"not to quit"* and the map for *"the best journeys still to come"*.

He could hear Willis' voice and remembered his controlled but provocative manner and the early invitation to listen to what was in the front of his mind rather than look at the back of his head. He remembered crossing swords with him and he remembered laughing with him and sharing an overnight merlot or three. Simon remembered a good coach and a good friend. He had no idea who he was or where he was but missed Willis a lot.

"Err…Simon?" continued Naomi, "Is Mr. Willis still with the company? Will we meet him at some point? Will he feature in our future development?"

Simon slowly sat down on the edge of the table once again and surveyed the group for ten seconds before answering. He leaned forward to gain their full attention.

"Is he still around? Will you meet him? Will he feature in your future development?" He smiled. "Those are good questions…all very, very good questions!"

Partnership Toolkit

Written by

George Willis
and Simon Gray

**The full version of this A-Z can be downloaded from
www.piranhasinthebidet.com**

ADDING VALUE TO KEY ACCOUNTS: If our organisation was arrested and charged with *"adding value to customers"*, would there be enough evidence to convict it? A strange question, perhaps, but it does capture the essence of key account management. KAM is not just about "cuddling" customers. It is about adding value to the customer's business by helping to improve their profitability and performance. It is not about "fighting over a slice of the cake" - it is about helping the customer to create a bigger and better cake.

Alderton's will then be perceived as a value-creator and will be rewarded with additional business opportunities - and our competitors will not. So how many different ways are there to add value to our key accounts?

Here are just a few:-

1. Help them to increase their sales
2. Help them to reduce their costs
3. Help them to improve their market share
4. Help them to become more profitable
5. Find ways to help them stay in front of their competitors
6. Anticipate and solve their future problems
7. Introduce them to our networks
8. Give them an order
9. Give them a lead
10. Give extra advice for free
11. Make them a hero – let them take the credit for your ideas – they will be keen to work with you again
12. Influence other companies to switch business to them
13. Offer advice where they are low on know-how
14. Give them a free place on one of our courses
15. Sponsor their conference or one of their social events
16. Send them useful press cuttings and market intelligence

17. Help them develop their plans and objectives – why not join their "away-days"
18. Part-fund a project or event
19. Help your contact achieve a personal goal
20. "Be there" when they need you – at both business and personal levels

BUSINESS v BUSYNESS: As an effective Leader you need to spend as much time as possible working proactively and reactively on *tasks that will develop your business* rather than working proactively and reactively on routine tasks and fire-fighting.

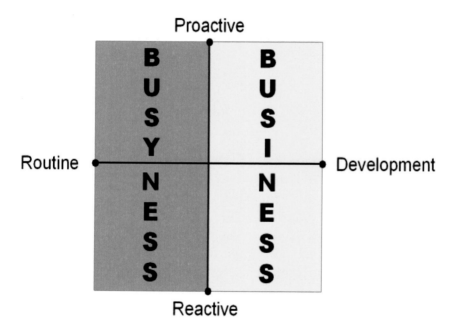

To put it another way, Alderton's managers should spend the majority of their day on the right side – i.e. on the business side, not busyness side! You can do nothing about yesterday, very little about today, a little about tomorrow but a lot about next week, next month and next year. Spend as much time as possible *proactively developing the future* as you are going to spend the rest of your life there!

CHANGE MANAGEMENT: Bearing in mind that there are few certainties on this planet apart from life, death and change, people often struggle coming to terms with change and its implications. Although the outcome of change is often uncertain the process, outlined below, is very predictable. Some Alderton's Managers and staff will react favourably to change, of course, and move swiftly to support a new idea or policy and take the necessary action to make it part of their everyday life. (The top three boxes and the horizontal arrows illustrate this process as people move quickly from Change to Support to Commitment.)

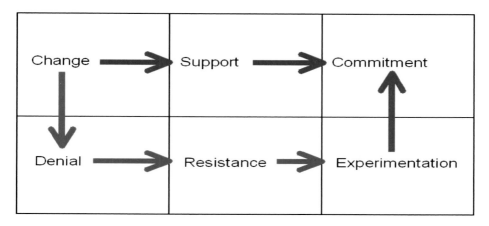

For others, change will be more menacing. The problem with change, for many, is that it usually arrives before they are ready for it. Typically, people head "south" into the Denial box muttering *"it won't happen"* or *"I'll believe it when I see it"* or *"it doesn't apply to us – it's just for other departments."* A period of Resistance soon follows as emotions start to build up. *"Which bloody idiot thought of this idea?"* and *"Why can't we go back to how we used to do it before"* and *"It will never work – it's impossible to achieve it!"* will be comments you will hear - if you are lucky! If you are unlucky you won't hear them - but these comments might still be gnawing away at the business if people decide to offer public support but fight a private, negative and subversive battle behind the scenes. Eventually, many people can be persuaded to at least Experiment with the required new ideas, actions and behaviour. Some will still sound reluctant and will say things like *"I'll give it a go but I'm not sure it's right!"* or *"You will have to give me some help if you want me to do this"* and *"Alderton's will only achieve this if we all pull together!"* This experimentation will start with small steps that will then become slightly larger steps. At times, it will seem painfully slow but at least some action is now taking place.

"A journey of a thousand miles starts with a single step!"

Old Chinese proverb

For many people, "seeing is believing" and when the results start to come in they realise that the new change is not quite as difficult or as frightening as they originally thought. However, don't expect to see delight on their faces – if you are lucky, people might offer comments like *"Looking back I can see why Steve wanted us to do this"* or *"I still don't like it, but I now accept it"* and *"I am more comfortable with it now and have learned a few things along the way!"*

As a leader, there are a number of things that you can do to help your people deal with the growing pains of change:-

1. Sell it, don't tell it. Explain where Alderton's is today on a particular issue, what is happening, why we can't carry on as we are, where we are going, how we intend to get there and the *benefits* of change to your customers, your staff and your business.

2. Don't be afraid to spin the coin over and also stress the consequences of *not* making the changes work – the damage it will do to customers, the company and the job security of your staff. This "loss language" will make people sit up and think. When the Piper Alpha oil rig exploded, a number of people survived by jumping 150 ft into a flame-red, stormy sea. They did it because the certain dangers of staying on the platform outweighed the probable dangers of leaping into the unknown. This "burning platform" story illustrates that change *has* to take place, however uncomfortable it may be. Trying to stay where you are is like trying to stay on a burning platform. For many people, jumping has dangers but carries with it the chance of success. Remember that during the eighties 46% of the top 500 companies disappeared because they failed to change quickly enough and "jump" when they needed to.

3. Emphasise that change management is crucial – it is about the business changing internally before the external trading environment forces it to change. Remember that if ever the rate of change outside our business is faster than the rate of change inside our business we will be heading for serious trouble.

4. Consider a well-timed leak of information – it often helps people get their heads around the issue (which is then not as bad as they thought it would be). Look at the way that successive Governments use this technique (i.e. a "leak") to condition us before a new piece of legislation becomes official.

5. Be genuinely open with your people – you need their trust.

6. Communicate regularly even if you say *"I've got nothing to report this week."*

7. Don't suppress people's emotions. Give them time to come to terms with their feelings and provide opportunities for them to express them.

8. Don't "herd" people out of Denial and Resistance too early. We can't make people change – each of us guards a "gate of change" that can only be opened from the inside. We cannot open the gate of another – don't kick it down either - they will open it when *they* are ready.

9. Offer coaching to help people come to terms with change – the problem is rarely getting new, innovative thoughts into someone's mind but how to get the old ones out.

10. Try and win over "Mr. Difficult" within your team. If you can get him (or her) on your side it could have a dramatic impact on others.

11. Managers and Directors suffer less stress than their people – this is because they have more *control* over their destiny. Try and give people as much control as possible during times of change. They may not be able to determine Alderton's policy destinations but they can certainly take part in determining the *route* to the destination.

"If people help plan the battle they won't battle the plan!"

Jim Clemmer

---

12. Avoid talking too much about the longer term – it will be too far away for people to see it. During a time of change go for short-term objectives – *"these are the three things we need to do today"* and enlist support for short trials – *"let's give this a go and review it on Friday"*.

13. Be positive and upbeat – people will want to see that you are up for it! Even if you disagree with the proposed change, don't let your feelings show. Remain loyal to the company. As Michael Heseltine once said, you have "Cabinet responsibility" once you are outside the meeting room. All eyes will be on you.

14. Provide any training and development <u>before</u> results are expected, not afterwards.
15. Maintain the new course – avoid frequent amendments or U-turns as they will breed uncertainty.
16. Remember the P.I.E. recipe for change – feed people lots of Participation, Information and Enthusiasm!

"Change is not what it used to be – we now live in a turbulent, constantly changing world. Expect the unexpected. There is no such thing as "business as usual".
There is no point waiting for the change storm to blow over – we all have to become much better at working in the rain!"
Sir John Harvey Jones

"It is not the largest or strongest species that survive, nor the most intelligent
  - *it is the ones most responsive to* **change!***"*
Charles Darwin

To summarise, in the future some of our people will love change, some will deny the need for it and some will resist it. There will be those who want to change but don't know how, those who can't change and, even worse, those who could change but don't want to.

The needs of our business and the pressures of a very competitive marketplace leave one very powerful conclusion. We have to change – constantly …and if we can't change our people then we must consider changing our people!

DEPARTMENTAL AUDITS: It is very rare to find a team that deliberately goes out of its way to make another team's life a misery. However, teams often cause each other a huge amount of grief by not understanding each other's problems, pressures and priorities. "Priority one" for one team is often priority 17 for another.

So when was the last time you banged on the door of an Alderton's colleague and asked for feedback on the support provided by you and your team?

Try these questions:-

1. *Where is my team meeting your expectations?*
2. *Where are we exceeding your expectations?*
3. *Where are we falling short of your expectations?*
4. *What have been the high points in recent months?*
5. *What have been the low points?*
6. *Who, in my team, deserves a "mention in despatches"?*
7. *Who could have done more?*
8. *How do you feel about my performance?*
9. *What unresolved issues are there?*
10. *What does my team need to understand about your team's future priorities?*
11. *How can we help you in the future?*
12. *Is there anything else I need to know?*

---

*"The quality of service we give the customer
is influenced by the quality of service we give each other"*

(Rosabeth Moss Kanter)

EXCEEDING EXPECTATIONS: Companies used to retain their customers by meeting their expectations. The world has moved on.

Performance	Score
Meets expectations	55%
Exceeds expectations	25%
Falls short of expectations	20%
Total	100%

Ten years ago, you could look at the numbers above (imagine them as the results of an independent piece of research), add together the top two numbers and say *"We have carried out some research and, to cut a long story short, 80% of our customers are happy with us, or thereabouts"*. Today, because of the way that customer loyalty has changed, adding the top two figures together would be commercial suicide.

What these statistics say, today, is that *"only 25% of customers are happy, with the other 75% "up for grabs""*. The safest key account is one where expectations are *exceeded* at each stage of the customer's experience with Alderton's. Try analysing each stage of the customer's experience and look for opportunities to turn a tragic piece of service into a magic piece of service.

Imagine that you run a hotel – here are the first two stages of the customer's experience – both tragic and magic. The right-hand side is a totally different experience. The good news here is that the additional cost of creating magic customer service is seconds and pennies. The additional value, however, is huge.

STAGE	TRAGIC	MAGIC
STAGE 1 TELEPHONE BOOKING	Polite staff take enquiry	Polite, friendly and helpful staff take enquiry and ask good quality questions to identify the reason for the enquiry, needs, special needs, if customer requires restaurant booking – they establish a personal connection
	They are friendly/ helpful	
	Confirmation letter sent by hotel secretary 2-3 days later	Map sent showing location of hotel along with "things to do in the area" sheet
		Manager personally signs confirmation letter which is sent on the same day.
		Voucher enclosed offering £3 off a bottle of wine from restaurant wine list
STAGE 2 CHECK-IN	Guest arrives, is greeted in friendly way and checks in	Guest arrives, porter carries luggage up to the room. Check-in is conducted speedily with personal connection re-established. Free cup of tea sent up to room. Duty manager phones guest 30 minutes later to check if all OK.

FOSBURY STRATEGY: Dick Fosbury was an American high jumper who "went as far as he could go" in his event, then changed the rules. At the 1968 Olympics in Mexico he jumped over the bar backwards (a technique that now bears his name and has become the "way to do it") and achieved a world record of 88.5 inches. We can all learn from this story. Within Alderton's there will be times when we need to think, long and hard....then jump over the bar backwards to set new records!

G.R.I.D. STYLES: Sometimes people are treated differently in companies for all the wrong reasons – sexism, racism, ageism, favouritism etc. The only two things that determine how Alderton's people *should* be treated differently are on the diagram i.e. their "competence" and "commitment".

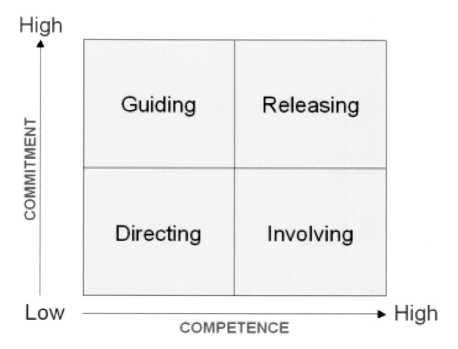

If someone is tackling a task and they have high commitment but low competence (top left) then a "GUIDING" style of leadership is needed e.g. *"This is what I suggest you do"*. The leader identifies the problem, involves the follower in discussing the options, makes the final decision having heard the ideas and offers advice and practical tips.

If they have high commitment and high competence (top right) then they should be set free and RELEASED e.g. *"You decide what to do and let me know the result on Thursday"*. Here, the leader defines the goals with the follower, occasionally monitors what's going on and the follower evaluates the results and reports back.

If someone has low commitment and high competence (bottom right) they need INVOLVEMENT e.g. *"What are your thoughts on this?"* The leader recognises that s/he can't direct the other person to become committed – they need to find out why the current level of commitment is low. The leader involves the follower by asking for ideas on the solution (because they do have the competence) and provides the necessary support.

If someone is tackling a task and they are offering low levels of competence and commitment (bottom left) then they need firm, clear DIRECTION e.g. *"These are the three things we need to do today Sid"*. The leader identifies the problem, sets the goals, builds the action plan, provides clear directions, supervises throughout and evaluates the result. There is no aggression and no heavy language, but there is clarity with no room for negotiation. Some points to remember about these GRID styles:-

1. No one single style is always right – leaders need different styles for different situations
2. Don't put the whole person in the box – put each <u>task</u> they do in the box. Ask yourself "How competent is s/he in this task? How committed is s/he?" You might have a review meeting to discuss a number of topics with someone where the styles you use are different.
3. Example below:-

Delivering a presentation for the first time **G**	Arranging the next meeting **R**
Paperwork **D**	Poor time management **I**

4. If you use the wrong style it will cause friction and de-motivation. For example, if someone deserves RELEAS-ING but receives DIRECTION s/he will feel "talked to" and restrained.
5. The other person may see your use of the GRID styles very differently to you. For example, you might think that you INVOLVE people but they might feel that you lecture them and tell them what to do all of the time.
6. One of the best ways to check out how they see things is to ask them to fill out the questionnaire below and then have a chat over a coffee and compare their thinking to yours after you have done the same exercise on yourself.

SITUATION	TICK
1. I feel recognised for the job that I do	
2. I am happy with the way work is delegated to me	
3. We discuss our disagreements and work them out	
4. Communication works well between us	
5. My manager is available when I need him/her.	
6. I have challenging and stimulating work assignments	
7. My manager is a good listener	
8. I receive honest feedback on my performance	
9. My manager involves me at all times	
10. I am coached well by my manager	

7. Alderton's managers who say *"I treat all of my people the same"* are poor managers. For example, at meetings there is no point praising the whole team if half are under-performing and there is no point giving the whole team a dressing down if only half are guilty. Don't "sheep dip" your people and treat them the same. Be selective, be tailored, and get *personal* with the GRID. Here's a relevant little tongue twister for you.......................

"There is nothing so unequal as the equal treatment of unequals!"

HYGIENE FACTORS: Some things in the workplace will de-motivate people. Poor work conditions, questionable company policy, ineffective processes and lack of a decent salary are good examples of "hygiene factors". Why the word "hygiene"? If these things are wrong people will moan and groan about them – just like an unhygienic toilet. When these things are right people will say nothing – nobody thanks us for having clean toilets because they expect them to be clean!

Removing hygiene factors will not increase motivation
- but it will reduce de-motivation!

So we need to keep an eye on hygiene factors like:-
1. Poor working conditions
2. Heating and lighting
3. Health and safety
4. Workspace hygiene
5. The quality and quantity of our communications
6. The visibility of senior managers and directors – when they are on the factory floor our people will say nothing but when they are not on the factory floor we will be accused of having "remote managers"

INDUCTION: In some companies people are inducted badly. They undergo a brief introduction to company processes and policies, shake the hands of 50 people they will forget by lunchtime and head for home with a weighty manual that explains what they are not allowed to do. If the company's leaders do show up it is often for cameo appearances only. In general, new people in these companies experience little emotion – except anxiety, boredom and regret. We need to be different. Spend time on promoting Alderton's values and beliefs – our way of doing things. Our induction programmes should also be conducted by our most experienced and talented people who see the job as an honour and challenge. Good induction programmes matter – not only to the new starter but also to his/her partner back at home watching the first weeks with interest and concern.

Good inductions help people "get off to a flying start", reduce staff turnover, help people unlearn old habits, ensure that the newcomer is quickly adopted by the peer group and improve our company's image as a caring, developmental employer.

However, a recent UK survey revealed eight common mistakes during inductions:-

1. Managers playing it by ear, not having a formal programme.
2. Not circulating details of newcomers to other staff who then greet them with the rather blunt and cold *"Who are you then?"* type of comment.

3. Managers not turning up on time as *"something more important has cropped up"*.
4. Putting newcomers with "old soldiers" who teach them bad practices, short-cuts and tricks-of-the-trade, many of which are outside company policy.
5. Little follow-up to review progress.
6. Expecting results too quickly including using "result" language rather than "activity" language.
7. Not having the right equipment, tools and clothing to do the job.
8. Not involving newcomers in the construction of the *next* induction programme – they will certainly be able to comment on the value they received and areas for improvement next time.

> *"Most people are known by the company they keep*
> *- Alderton's needs to be known by the people it keeps"*

JOINT ACTION PLANS: Imagine that an Alderton's account manager has just been involved in an important meeting with one of our key accounts. Rather than having his/her action plan, and the customer having theirs, we should produce a "joint action plan". This would be managed by the account manager but copied, by email, to all concerned. At the following meeting, the account manager would circulate hard copies of the joint action plan and chair the review. Imagine how frustrating this will be to our competitors – once again we will be the *partner* and they will be the supplier.

KASH PROFILE: Each job within Alderton's should have a KASH Profile - a very clear understanding of the *knowledge, attitudes, skills* and *habits* needed to achieve the objectives. Kash Profiles also explain why someone has been promoted (i.e. because they *met* the KASH requirement) and why someone has left the company (i.e. because they *failed* to meet the KASH requirement despite our attempts to train, help, coach, counsel and nurture the individual). Ideally, people should be able to see the KASH Profiles for any job within our organisation. If someone wants to work in sales in three years' time, they can start to develop themselves <u>now</u> to improve their chances of success.

The KASH Profile helps to allocate responsibilities during the interview process. Alderton's Managers interview and test for K and S (knowledge and skills) and psychometric tests, or references from previous employers, are used to check out the A and H (attitudes and habits) of the applicant. Also, if someone leaves our company then the KASH Profile becomes the profile for his/her replacement – it can help to shape the advert and help managers to build relevant interview questions.

A full-page version of a KASH profile can be seen in the electronic version of the A-Z.

LEADERS AND BOSSES: This is about inspiring *willing* action – it is not about ordering people to do things. The things that really matter (creativity, enthusiasm towards customers, willingness to innovate, high-quality work, helping a new colleague to find their feet, co-operation with others etc) rely on people *willingly* wanting to do them.

Things bosses say ✗	Things Leaders say ✓
I get results from my people	I get results through my people
My people always know where they stand	My people know what I stand for
My people have confidence in me	My people have confidence in themselves
I like authority	I like respect

My people are under-performing	I get the people I deserve
Power is important to me	Empowerment is more important
I move people	I motivate people
I believe in confrontation	I believe in collaboration
Go and fix it!	Let's go and fix it together
People need controlling tightly	People need to be set free
Tell me what you've done	Tell me what you are going to do
I push people along	I pull people along
I enjoy time in my office	What's an office?
Watch me – I will teach you	Discover it yourself and learn
I don't like risks	Risks take us into an exciting future
Leave your personal problems at home	You can talk things through with me
I like my reserved parking space	Customers should have reserved parking
I enjoying cornering people	I enjoy getting people in my corner
I look down to the bottom line	I also look up so I can see the horizon
I achieve 100% results	Together we can achieve 125% results
I keep an eye on my watch	I keep an eye on my "compass"
I like to work in the business	I also take time to work on the business

Things happen when I'm here	Things also happen when I'm not here
I work on my numbers	I work on our values
I run a closed team	I run a close team
I am a commander	I am a coach
I want you to follow me	I want you to overtake me
I imitate	I originate
I do things right	I do the right things
I'm at the top of the business	I am at the bottom of the business
People work for me	I work for my people
"Just do it my way"	"How can I help you?"
I give my people a lot of heat so they act	I give my people a lot of light so they see
I only celebrate results	I celebrate the behaviour I want more of
I review when things have gone wrong	I review before things go wrong

Leaders believe that:-

- they get the workforce *they* deserve – to quote Field Marshall Slim *"There is no such thing as a bad regiment, just bad officers!"*
- they will not advance far unless they can work through others.
- they should lead as far as they can, then move on and do something else, as *"their ashes might choke the fires they have just lit"*
- leadership is about emotional resources and management is about physical resources.
- you can be appointed as a manager but you can't be appointed as a leader – it has to be earned.

- a great person is someone who makes others feel great.
- a leader's key job is to get people from where they are to where they have never been - one of their main tasks is to show people a future and be a "dealer in hope".
- they are like directors of a play – never taking centre stage, working in the wings, allowing others to take the applause, including the encore.
- they are *"consultants in human potential"*.
- leadership is not a gene – it has *"more to do with nurture than nature"*.

MOTIVATING DIFFERENT TYPES OF CUSTOMERS:
Customers buy for a number of different reasons:-

- Fit for purpose - (the ability of our product/service to meet a particular need).
- The numbers – (the price, terms and ability to provide a return on investment).
- *Personal* – customers tend to have 1-2 strong personal motivators and these are outlined in this section of the A-Z. Some people are motivated by achievement in their lives, some by friendship, some by power and some by security. In each case, we need to understand the characteristics of the personal motivator and how to work with them.

  The golden rule here is to sell to customers in the way that *they want to buy*, not in the way that *we want to sell*.

MOTIVATOR	HOW TO WORK WITH THEM
Achievement – these people like to win, hit measurable goals and do better than others. They are often innovative and creative, like structure in their lives, plan for the longer term and anticipate likely barriers that will prevent them from achieving. On their desk or wall will be a number of certificates and trophies saying "Look at me!"	• Bite your lip and remember to tell them how wonderful they are. • Notice the trophies • Praise in writing • Emphasise things that allow them to beat their competitors • Always have an agenda • Build measurable goals into your proposals • Keep things clear and to the point • Show an interest in their longer-term personal goals • Don't waffle – get your meetings off to a good start
Friendship – they like warm working relationships with colleagues and suppliers. They don't like conflict and like to be part of a team. They come to work because of people and like to be liked. On their wall there will probably be a team photo – maybe their golf team, maybe their business team at a recent conference	• Make sure that social chat comes before business chat • Never refuse the offer of a cup of tea or coffee (even if you don't want one) • Don't be critical of others in front of them – they won't like the feeling of disloyalty • Have regular "pie and pint" business meetings where you can include a friendly social element • Help them sell your proposal to their boss (as they won't like the thought of falling out with their boss if the proposal falls short of his/her expectations)

Power – they need to influence and impress. They like to be forceful and threatening and often cause strong emotional reactions like anger and fear. They are often political and devious and are concerned with their reputation and how they are perceived in public. On their office wall they will have a photo of them shaking hands with a powerful figure like the Queen, Bill Gates, Tony Blair etc	• Be prepared to let them steal your good ideas and take them to their boss • Emphasise how your proposal will affect their status • Let them lead the discussions • Don't take the "hot air" too seriously – they like to flex their muscles in public • Talk to your friendly "allies" within the account to give you information on what is happening when you are not there
Security – they have a need to feel safe at work. They like to deal with secure, stable suppliers, don't like grey areas and avoid risk and uncertainty. They like evolution, not revolution, and need lots of support and reassurance. On their wall will be a reassuring photo of their family.	• Sell the benefits of change (as they won't like it) • Avoid grey areas – this type of person likes black and white • Make your proposal easy to buy e.g. 10 x £1000 chunks not £10000 all in the one go • Go for low volume, then add more over time • Offer testimonials and proof from other happy key accounts • Encourage phone calls to our happy accounts

Here is the tongue-twister of the day (already used in this A-Z). *"There is nothing so unequal as the equal treatment of unequals"*. People are different and should be treated differently. Look for the clues, then tailor your approach around these four personal motivators.

NEW RECRUITS: New people joining our organisation are VIPs. This acronym is a good way of remembering how our advertisements should be worded.

- V – visibility. Our adverts need to be highly visible and "fly off the page." Sometimes adverts look good when they are sketched out but often struggle for visibility and get lost on the page. We need to make good use of logos, colour, layout, type style and themes.

- I – identity. Adverts need to clearly identify who we are, what we do and what our business is famous for – being the industry leader, for example. We need to clearly identify what the job is and what the job isn't.

- P – promise. The advert should contain a promise and "what's in it for me" comments. This may be money, challenge, job satisfaction, responsibility, promotion prospects within Alderton's and so on.

- S – simplicity. We need to use everyday language that people will instantly understand. The advert should clearly explain what qualifications we are looking for and how the applicant should apply.

To summarise, make the job as easy as possible to apply for but as difficult as possible to win. Moving on to the next stages of the recruitment process here are a number of practical tips:

1. Try not to interview the CV – it is an easy mistake to make. Don't say to yourself *"I know why he probably left that job"*. Keep an open mind. When looking at CVs and application forms ask yourself, *"What are the good reasons why I should see this person?"*

2. Allow enough preparation time – including time between each interview to collect your thoughts.

3. Get the applicant to do most of the talking. Create the right environment. The main purpose of the interview is to establish if the applicant has what our company needs – this is difficult to achieve if you are doing most of the talking.

4. Avoid "gut feel interviews". Some managers say *"I know within 30 seconds if someone is right for us!"* Normally these managers then spend the next 30 months regretting their stomachs. Interviews should establish the applicant's performance abilities *before* looking at their personality. So how on earth could you assess someone's performance ability in the *"first 30 seconds"?*

5. Don't ask questions that can be interpreted quickly to produce the "interview answer". The examples below are all dreadful but, sadly, are real:-

    - *I see that your CV has been professionally produced – does this mean that you are putting yourself about on the job market?*
    - *Is this a spur of the moment decision for you?*
    - *Alderton's is looking for people that don't mind working during some weekends – how would that affect you?*

- *Would you say that you are an adaptable sort of person?*
- *Are you fit and healthy?*
- *Sometimes we have to handle irate customers – how good are you at doing that?*

6. Don't look for a mirror-image of yourself e.g. *"There is something about him that reminds me of me!"*
7. Don't take the best of a bad bunch – it will damage our business. Try not to compare applicants to each other – compare the applicant to the KASH Profile for the job – see earlier section.
8. Stay in control and don't get distracted or defensive if the applicant tries to gain control by using provocative questions like "Is your company financially stable?" or "I want to work for a people-organisation so could I just ask you what training would I receive?" Answer questions at the appropriate time – for you.
9. Be aware of personal prejudices. We all have them! What are yours? Do you believe that women will never succeed as Managers? Do you think that anyone over 55 is past it? Perhaps people with red hair are fiery? Maybe fat people are lazy? Or do you believe that all Celtic supporters are bad people?
10. Don't make assumptions – check out the references and ask to see the driving licence. Tie up all of the loose ends.

"Many things done at the time of firing should have been done at the time of hiring"

Here are some excellent open-ended interview questions.

Background to the interview

- *What has prompted you to look for a job?*
- *What appealed to you about our advertisement?*

- *How much do you know about Alderton's ?*
- *What is your understanding of the job advertised?*
- *What do you see as the main responsibilities of the job you've applied for?*

Present job/situation
- *What is a typical working month for you?*
- *What do you enjoy doing the most?*
- *What have been your greatest achievements?*
- *What don't you like doing?*
- *What experiences in your job wouldn't you repeat?*
- *How would your staff and your boss describe you?*

The job advertised
- *What strengths would you bring to us?*
- *What would your "weak spot" be?*
- *We are looking for someone who can do A, B and C... when was the last time that you actually did that?*
- *How would you approach your first three months?*
- *What training would you need to get started?*
- *How would I, as your Manager, get the best out of you?*
- *Who was your best Manager you worked for and why?*
- *Who was the worst and why?*
- *How should I measure you at the end of the first year?*
- *How would you like to see your career develop?*

The "real" person
- *What motivates you?*
- *What do you do outside work?*
- *What social issues move you?*
- *What's been your greatest mistake in life so far?*
- *Who do you admire in public life?*
- *What would you do if you won the Lottery?*
- *What else do I need to know about you?*
- *If I had to write down a sentence to remember you by what would you want me to write?*

O.P.E.R.A. PROJECT MANAGEMENT MODEL: This model is a useful five-stage checklist for any Alderton's task or project:-

OBJECTIVES
- What is the objective?
- Is it clearly understood by every team member?
- How do we know for sure?
- If we miss the main objective what is the secondary objective?
- Do people say if they don't understand the objective or do they keep quiet?

PLANNING
- What is the plan?
- Did we plan it "backwards" from the objective?
- Did everyone contribute?
- Do we have more than one plan?
- What are the benefits of achieving the plan?
- What are the consequences of failure?

EXECUTING
- Do people understand what to do?
- How do we know for sure?
- Who is leading each stage of the task?
- Have we delegated as much as we can or is the leader doing too much?
- Does everyone know what they are accountable for?
- Have we got the resources to execute the task?
- Do people need training first?

REVIEWING
- What is working well and why?
- What isn't and why?
- Do we review progress before we fail, or afterwards?
- What feedback should we give each other?
- What feedback does the team leader need?
- Are we on schedule or running out of time?
- Can we re-negotiate our deadlines?

AMENDING
- Do we need to change the way we are working?
- Do we need to amend the plan?
- Do we need to amend the original objectives?
- Does everyone understand this new situation?

PROBLEM SOLVING: Never whinge about problems because they are often the consequence of change, success and progress. So bring more problems to Alderton's table - and a few solutions as well, of course! Problems are often opportunities in disguise. However, when working with your team you may want to brainstorm the reasons for a problem and the range of possible solutions.

Record all contributions on a flip chart (however silly, crazy, or insignificant) and try not to evaluate them as they are called out. Later on, when you are trying to decide which solutions to run with, work out which ideas are the best – from a COST, TIME, HASSLE, FEASIBILITY and RETURN point of view.

In the example shown below, the first suggestion on the top line is unworkable because it is high-cost, high-time, high-hassle, low-feasibility and low-return. Suggestion two is better but suggestion three is the best because it offers the "dream solution" as it is low on cost, low-time, low-hassle, high-feasibility and high-return.

Suggestion	Cost	Time	Hassle	Feasibility	Return
Number 1.	H	H	H	L	L
Number 2	M	H	M	L	M
Number 3	**Low**	**Low**	**Low**	**High**	**High**

QUESTION TOOLKIT: Questions are one of a Leader's greatest tools. The best way to ask questions is to start with open questions, listen to the responses, follow-up with leading questions then finish with closed questions.

Open – *"How do you feel about this Sean?"*

Leading – *"What do you intend to do about it and what help do you need from me?"*

Closed – *"So if we agree to do those three things do you think it will solve the problem by the end of this month?"*

Not surprisingly, this is a "horses for courses" area. Some questions are particularly suited to specific situations:-

1. Reflective Questions (when you want someone to pick out the main points):
   "David – this problem occurred on Friday, it is now Tuesday, so what conclusions have you come to having had time to think about it?"

2. Hypothetical Questions (when you are trying to encourage creativity):
   "What would you do if we had £3000 available?"

3. Lifeline Questions (when you are trying to encourage openness and honesty):
   "In order for me to help you, Pat, I really need two more pieces of information…so could I just ask you…

4. Involving Questions (when you are trying to engage others):
   "OK, we've heard your views Alan…………what does everyone else think?"

5. Deflector Questions (when you don't want to get drawn in):
   "I could answer that Paul……… but I would like to hear Craig's thoughts first."

6. Magic Questions (when you want them to think positively about solutions):
   "If you had a magic wand and had three wishes to improve the motivation of your people what would they be?"

7. Challenging Questions (when you want to add a hint of pressure):
   "Where is your evidence for that comment Stella"

8. Missing Link Questions (when you want to stimulate analytical ability):
   "So what is missing from the process then?"

9. Devil's Advocate Questions (when you want to encourage lively debate):
   "Why don't we abandon this idea……… it is never going to work is it?"

10. Specific Questions (when you want to remove vagueness):
    "George, what specifically do you mean by that, exactly how much money will it cost and what is the date it will be completed by?"

11. Wrap-up Questions (when you are trying to bring things to a head):
    "So what are the action points then?" or *"Who would like to summarise the way forward?"* or *"What else would you like to say before I tell you the new Alderton's policy on this?"*

"I have six honest serving men – they taught me all I know. Their names are what, where and when, why, which and who"

Rudyard Kipling

REVIEWING PERFORMANCE: When sitting down with a team member to review his or her performance, remember that the main thing to do is to provide light not heat! Here are a number of guidelines:-

1. Find the right time and place to talk – create the right environment.
2. When notifying the other person about the meeting give them a "head start" so that they can prepare and come to terms with any difficult issues.
3. Explain what you want to talk about.
4. As a general rule, invite the other person to go first – *"How do you see the situation now Terry?"* and *"How would you describe your current performance Claire?"*
5. Use a range of good quality questions that encourage the other person to think so that "the penny drops in their own time".
6. Don't use "management speak". Keep your language at the same level as the other person's.
7. Listen to what is said and what is not said – often the latter is more revealing.
8. Don't generalise – *"my gut feeling tells me that this has probably happened before!"*
9. Encourage the other person to be open – *"Sue – I would prefer you to put your cards on the table and tell me how you see it please"*
10. Work together to find solutions.
11. Don't offer your CV as the solution – *"When I used to do your job I ...."* People will probably find this boring and, if it was some time ago, completely irrelevant to today's market conditions.
12. Avoid heated arguments by using the customer as "referee" e.g. *"When customers hear you say that, what impression do you think they have of Alderton's?"*
13. Don't make promises you can't keep.
14. Secure genuine commitment, not manipulated consent.
15. Use the right GRID style (see earlier section).
16. If you introduce new ways to measure and monitor the

situation try and position them as "tools" not systems.

17. You may like to invite the other person to summarise the meeting, including the action points that they, and you, now need to take.
18. Always finish the meeting on a high.
19. Agree follow-up dates and actions.
20. Be aware of the other person's emotions. A follow-up phone call or chat might be very useful. Let the other person empty their emotions through you.

I am not happy with you..........
.....................so I need to change....
before you can change....................
.........so I can then be happy with you!

Anon

If you are on the <u>receiving end</u> of feedback from an Alderton's colleague:

- Relax – you are not about to be attacked. Sit comfortably and show that you are "open for business".
- Thank the other person for their feedback – remember that there is no such thing as bad feedback. Any feedback is good feedback.
- Don't get defensive – *"But Steve, you don't understand, the reason why I did that was..."* Try and stay in question mode and ask *"What other options do you think I had Steve?"* or *"What would you have done then?"*
- Write the main points down so that you can refer to them later.

STRESS: There is a difference between people in trouble and troubled people – this section is about the latter. Stress takes place when there is an imbalance between the level of demand places upon us and our ability to cope with it. Although one person's stress is another person's stimulation, problems occur when a stressor is *too* *strong* or goes on for *too long*. Stress is often difficult to detect or see in ourselves but it will catch up with us eventually – it is rather like a screw given a quarter-turn every few days. People react differently to stress. For example, one person's work rate might increase, another's decrease. One person might become animated, the other quiet and withdrawn. Some people will lose weight and others will put weight on.

Watch for <u>changes</u> in health, habits and performance – they are the early clues. In any workplace the most common stressors are the speed and direction of change, politics and power struggles, working for an aggressive boss, poor working conditions, unrealistic deadlines, lack of training, workload, lack of recognition, threat of redundancy, being in the wrong job, angry customers and remote managers and directors. At home we have to deal with money problems, relationships, births, marriages and deaths, children, health problems, divorce and retirement.

At the end of the day there may come a time when you may have to do something about your work and personal stressors. Forget the complicated theories and hundreds of pages on the subject - there are only three options when dealing with a stressor:-

- AVOID IT
- ADAPT TO IT
- ALTER IT

The most frequent mistake that people make here is deciding to adapt to the stressor rather than altering it. "Adapting" tends to be a short-term fix whereas "altering" offers longer-term benefits.

TEAM BRIEFINGS: If you decide to run a short team briefing, the following five-part structure (originally developed by the Industrial Society) will accommodate everything you need to cover and ensure that nothing is left out.

- PERFORMANCE (results for Alderton's as a whole, the team's results, other corporate facts and figures, key performance indicators (KPI's), sales performance, customer feedback etc etc)

- POLICY (a new policy being introduced or maybe an existing policy that needs re-stating and reinforcing)

- PEOPLE (new people who have joined Alderton's , promotions, departures, retirements, happy events and people who deserve public praise)

- PROBLEMS (a discussion on something that is not going well, or simply an opportunity to ask people to share any current problems. Note that this "P" does not come at the end of the briefing where it would deflate the team.)

- PLANS (finish on an up-beat, optimistic note talking about exciting and important plans and actions for the future. You may also want to look at key dates for the month ahead or the agenda for the next session. Leave people on a "high".)

UPWARD MANAGEMENT: One of the key skills needed by our people is to "manage upwards". In key account management terms, managing upwards means making sure that your Director is available for activities with customers, attends and supports review meetings and operates as an integrated member of the team. For example, if a Director is going to a black-tie dinner where key decision-makers from one of our key accounts are going to be present, then s/he should be briefed by the account manager and given key pieces of missing intelligence to find.

VULNERABILITY TRAFFIC LIGHTS: We need to measure how stable (good news) or vulnerable (bad news) we are with each of our most important key accounts. To do this, we build a traffic light matrix for each account that has ten criteria on it....with a red-amber-green option depending upon the score. For example, if only 1-2 decision-makers have been seen within the account during the last year, then it shows up as a "red" on the matrix. Similarly, if there are no competitors operating within the account it shows up as a "green". The traffic light matrix example also provides an overall score out of ten. Reds score 0, ambers score ½ and greens score 1 full point. The traffic light matrix is just the piece of "intelligence", of course. We then sit down and work out what <u>objectives</u> should be set for the future and what <u>tactics</u> should be deployed to achieve these objectives i.e. who, within Alderton's is going to do what, by when? This piece of kit is also software-based and can be downloaded from the website.

WARFARE and WELFARE: Business (or perhaps we should call it commercial warfare) is built around the four key military strategies of defence, offence, deterrence and alliance. We have a lot to learn from the Military – for example, the ten principles of warfare shaped on the battlefield centuries ago still fit Alderton's business world today:-

1. Clear objectives	6. Concentration of force
2. Maintenance of morale	7. Economy of effort
3. The need for offensive action	8. Flexibility
4. Surprise	9. Co-operation with others
5. Security	10. Good admin and support

Good commercial "generals" also learn from their mistakes. Here are the ten reasons behind the hundred most famous military disasters. Again, you will see that our business world is affected by the same issues:-

1. Not learning from previous experiences	6. Poor reconnaissance
2. Underestimating the enemy	7. Suppressing feedback from the soldiers at the front
3. Overestimating own capabilities	8. Attacking the enemy's strongest point
4. Indecisiveness	9. Finding scapegoats after defeat
5. Rejecting sound intelligence which conflicts with own preconceptions	10. A belief in mystical forces like "fate" and "bad luck"

One of our objectives is to turn Alderton's into a formidable fighting force. To have all of our castles in the right places, to dominate the high ground, to have well-trained people led by effective leaders and to have the resources to equip our people with good quality weapons and ammunition. But next time you put your military hat on please make sure that your guns are pointing outside the organisation, not inside. Let's attack our competitors, not each other. Look after the troops and they will look after you. Here is a story from the Commanding Officer of a US Marine Corps unit.

"I will always remember my first posting – I was paired with a very experienced Sergeant Ian Smith, who had well over 20 years' experience. My learning process began on the first day of our partnership. My overly ambitious plan to issue gas masks and have the Marines clean their weapons in the same afternoon caused many men to miss their dinner. Morale suffered and the next day Sergeant Smith gave me his assessment of what had gone wrong. "Sir, your plan failed because you did not consult the experienced leaders in this unit – we have conducted these drills countless times before and know what to do." During out time together he also taught me a lot about the importance of developing others – he could always find time to share with others his views on the principles and values of the unit. He knew a lot about "welfare". Whenever a Marine faced a personal emergency Sergeant Smith focused his attention on it until it was resolved – he would often visit the Marine in the evening or phone from home.

If the men were transferred to another unit he would always put in three-four follow-up actions to ensure that their welfare needs were being met. My leadership approach today was fashioned and shaped by his genuine care and support for them, and me, then!"

J. A. Santamaria

EXIT INTERVIEW: If a key account decides to leave our care, they deserve an exit interview, in the same way that a member of staff would be interviewed to find out why they are leaving. Ideally, this exit interview should be carried out by the most senior person available (who has not been involved in the day-to-day management of the account). One thing is certain – the 30 minutes invested should produce many learning points for our company and, maybe, present a "last ditch" opportunity to retain the key account or, at least, set up a follow-up phone call in a few months' time.

YOU: You are the solution! If things are not happening and you are not getting the results or response you want <u>you</u> need to change what you are doing to get a different response. So if you are not getting the solution you want start with the person in the mirror! Success will never come to us – we have to go and find it. Remember the ten most important two-letter words of all time … "if it is to be it is up to me!!"

ZERO-DEGREE DEFECTS: Here is a four-stage guide to better, error-free, performance within Alderton's:-

1. Notice what is wrong – the first step in putting errors right is noticing that there is a problem in the first place. How you do it, of course, and the language you use, is important. *"I see you've screwed up again Ben!"* is not going to help Ben (although the release of emotion might make you feel better)
2. Understand *why* the error has occurred – again the right language is crucial. There is a world of difference from *"What went wrong again?"* to *"What happened?"*
3. Appreciate why it is important – don't tell, sell! Rather than say *"That's another customer you've lost Ben!"* try *"How do you think the customer feels now Ben?"* followed by *"What do you think the customer will do if that happens again?"* Make the team member *think*. Take them through a questioning process where they see things for <u>themselves</u> rather than you telling them how you see it.

4. Know how to prevent the error occurring in the future –
   rather than saying
   "Make sure that doesn't happen again or you're fired"
   maybe *"How can you make sure that doesn't happen
   again?"* will produce a much better result.

The full "A-Z Partnership Toolkit" can be downloaded free of charge from the website link www.piranhasinthebidet.com It contains 77 pages of useful tips, tools and techniques and the content is listed below. (Items in italics also appear in the "short version" of the A-Z featured in this book.) The website also features the award-winning "Strategic Bridges" software which will help you build a one-page, tabloid strategic plan to increase understanding and heart-count.

Activity management	Fallow periods	Planning
Adding value to key accounts	Favours log	Powell
Apologies	*Fosbury thinking*	Prioritising
Appraisals	Freedom	*Problem solving*
Assertiveness	Goose formation	Procrastination
Attitude	Getting it right first time	Quality thinking time
Backward planning	*GRID styles*	Quarterly review meetings
Big rock management	Health and wellness	*Question toolkit*
Business plans for account managers	Honesty	Rank means little
Business v busyness	*Hygiene factors*	Redgrave and Co.
Change management	*Induction*	*Reviewing performance*
Churchill	*Joint action plans*	Situational account leadership
Coaching	*KASH Profile*	*Stress*
Commitment	KAM applications	Surprise
Competitor analysis	Key customer personnel	Synergy
Conflict resolution	*Leaders and bosses*	*Team briefings*
Consultative selling	Learning styles	Teamwork
Contract management	Life	Team sport account management
Core values	Leading the customer campaign	Team relationships
Culture	Listening	Time management
Customer-driven structures	Lost customers	Tough love
Customer audits	Maslow	Upward management
Customer partnerships	Matrioshka dolls	VAT – not what you think
Customer retention	MAP thinking	Vision
Daughter to work day	Mind over matter	Visualisation
Decision makers	Motivation of people	Voice of the customer
Delegation	*Motivating different types of customers*	*Vulnerability traffic lights*
Departmental audits	*New recruits*	*Warfare and welfare*
Differences between salespeople and account managers	Objectives for key accounts	Woodward's strategy
Difficult people	*OPERA project model*	w.w.websites
Email policy	Openness	*Exit interviews*
Exceeding expectations	Paperwork	Year end
	Persuasion	*You!*
		Zero degree benefits

217